TH… YOUTH

Joseph C… odolia, one of the Ukra… istened Józef Teodor K… was three his father was… eft an orphan a few yea… up at Cracow by an uncle. In 1874 he travelled to Marseilles to become a sailor. After gaining some experience he joined three companions in using the vessel *Tremolina* for smuggling until she was deliberately wrecked; some of the adventures of this period are recounted in *The Mirror of the Sea* (1906) and *The Arrow of Gold* (1919). His first ship was the *Mavis* in which he visited England for the first time in 1878. Soon afterwards he sailed to Australia in a wool-clipper, and after passing the necessary examination he served as third mate in various ships in the Indian Ocean, which he made the scene of many of his best-known books such as *The Nigger of the Narcissus* (1897), *Lord Jim* (1900), *The Shadow-Line* (1917) and *The Rescue* (1920).

In 1886 he obtained his certificate as a master mariner and also became a naturalized British citizen. Four years later he fulfilled a childhood ambition by commanding a river steamer in the Belgian Congo, of which he told subsequently in *Heart of Darkness*. He was now writing his first book, *Almayer's Folly*, which appeared in 1895. His last ship was the *Torrens*, a famous sailing vessel, which he left in 1893. In 1896 he married Jessie George and settled down as a writer, but it was not until the publication in America of *Chance* (1913) that he became widely popular. For a time his reputation was second only to Hardy's among living authors, and he made his name as a stylist in English although he was unable to speak a word of the language before he was nineteen. Although he is usually thought of as a writer of sea stories, he also wrote a number of novels with other settings such as *Nostromo* (1904), *The Secret Agent* (1907) and *Under Western Eyes* (1911). His last two, *The Rover* (1923) and the unfinished *Suspense* (1925) tell of the Napoleonic period. Among his finest short stories are 'Youth' (1902) and 'Typhoon' (1903). *Some Reminiscences* (1912) is autobiographical. He died in England in 1924.

Also by Joseph Conrad in Pan Classics

Lord Jim
Victory
The Rover
The Secret Agent
Nostromo
Under Western Eyes
Heart of Darkness and *Typhoon*

A Pan Classic

THE NIGGER OF THE NARCISSUS and YOUTH

JOSEPH CONRAD

with a critical supplement

unabridged

Pan Books London and Sydney

The Nigger of the Narcissus first published 1897
'Youth' first published 1902
This edition published 1976 by Pan Books Ltd,
Cavaye Place, London SW10 9PG
ISBN 0 330 24818 9
Printed and bound in Great Britain by
Richard Clay (The Chaucer Press) Ltd, Bungay, Suffolk

CONTENTS

Preface to The Nigger of the *Narcissus*

A work that aspires, however humbly, to the condition of art should carry its justification in every line. And art itself may be defined as a single-minded attempt to render the highest kind of justice to the visible universe, by bringing to light the truth, manifold and one, underlying its every aspect. It is an attempt to find in its forms, in its colours, in its light, in its shadows, in the aspects of matter, and in the facts of life what of each is fundamental, what is enduring and essential – their one illuminating and convincing quality – the very truth of their existence. The artist, then, like the thinker or the scientist, seeks the truth and makes his appeal. Impressed by the aspect of the world the thinker plunges into ideas, the scientists into facts – whence, presently, emerging they make their appeal to those qualities of our being that fit us best for the hazardous enterprise of living. They speak authoritatively to our common sense, to our intelligence, to our desire of peace, or to our desire of unrest; not seldom to our prejudices, sometimes to our fears, often to our egoism – but always to our credulity. And their words are heard with reverence, for their concern is with weighty matters: with the cultivation of our minds and the proper care of our bodies, with the attainment of our ambitions, with the perfection of the means and the glorification of our precious aims.

It is otherwise with the artist.

Confronted by the same enigmatical spectacle the artist descends within himself, and in that lonely region of stress and strife, if he be deserving and fortunate, he finds the terms of his appeal. His appeal is made to our less obvious capacities: to that part of our nature which, because of the warlike conditions of existence, is necessarily kept out of sight within the more resisting and hard qualities – like the vulnerable body within a steel armour. His appeal is less loud, more profound, less distinct, more stirring – and sooner forgotten. Yet its effect endures for ever. The changing wisdom of successive generations discards ideas, questions facts, demolishes theories. But the artist appeals to that part of our being which is not dependent on wisdom; to that in us which is a gift and not an acquisition – and, therefore, more permanently enduring. He speaks to our capacity for delight and wonder, to the sense of mystery surrounding our lives; to our sense of pity, and beauty, and pain; to the latent feeling of fellowship with all creation – and to the subtle but invincible conviction of solidarity that knits together the loneliness of innumerable hearts, to the solidarity in dreams, in joy, in sorrow, in aspirations, in illusions, in hope, in fear, which binds men to each other, which binds together all humanity – the dead to the living and the living to the unborn.

It is only some such train of thought, or rather of feeling, that can in a measure explain the aim of the attempt, made in the tale which follows, to present an unrestful episode in the obscure lives of a few individuals out of all the disregarded multitude of the bewildered, the simple, and the voiceless. For, if any part of truth dwells in the belief confessed above, it becomes evident that there is not a place of splendour or a dark corner of the earth that does not deserve, if only a passing glance of wonder and pity. The motive then, may be held to justify the matter of the work; but this preface, which is simply an avowal of endeavour, cannot end here – for the avowal is not yet complete.

Fiction – if it at all aspires to be art – appeals to temperament. And in truth it must be, like painting, like music, like all art, the appeal of one temperament to all the other innumerable temperaments whose subtle and resistless power endows passing events with their true meaning, and creates the moral, the emotional atmosphere of the place and time. Such an appeal to be effective must be an impression conveyed through the senses; and, in fact, it cannot be made in any other way, because temperament, whether individual or collective, is not amenable to persuasion. All art, therefore, appeals primarily to the senses, and the artistic aim when expressing itself in written words must also make its appeal through the senses, if its high desire is to reach the secret spring of responsive emotions. It must strenuously aspire to the plasticity of sculpture, to the colour of painting, and to the magic suggestiveness of music – which is the art of arts. And it is only through complete, unswerving devotion to the perfect blending of form and substance; it is only through an unremitting never-discouraged care for the shape and ring of sentences that an approach can be made to plasticity, to colour, and that the light of magic suggestiveness may be brought to play for an evanescent instant over the commonplace surface of words: of the old, old words, worn thin, defaced by ages of careless usage.

The sincere endeavour to accomplish that creative task, to go as far on that road as his strength will carry him, to go undeterred by faltering, weariness, or reproach, is the only valid justification for the worker in prose. And if his conscience is clear, his answer to those who in the fulness of a wisdom which looks for immediate profit, demand specifically to be edified, consoled, amused; who demand to be promptly improved, or encouraged, or frightened, or shocked, or charmed, must run thus: My task which I am trying to achieve is, by the power of the written word to make you hear, to make you feel – it is, before all, to make you *see*. That – and no more, and it is everything. If I succeed, you shall find there according to your deserts: encouragement, consolation, fear, charm – all you demand – and, perhaps, also that glimpse of truth for which you have forgotten to ask.

To snatch in a moment of courage, from the remorseless rush of time, a passing phase of life, is only the beginning of the task. The task approached in tenderness and faith is to hold up unquestioningly, without choice and without fear, the rescued fragment before all eyes in the light of a sincere mood. It is to show its vibration, its colour, its form; and through its movement, its form, and its colour, reveal the substance of its truth – disclose its inspiring secret: the stress and passion within the core of each convincing moment. In a single-minded attempt of that kind, if one be deserving and fortunate, one may perchance attain to such clearness of sincerity that at last the presented vision of regret or pity, of terror or mirth, shall awaken in the hearts of the beholders that feeling of unavoidable solidarity; of the solidarity in mysterious origin, in toil, in joy, in hope, in uncertain fate, which binds men to each other and all mankind to the visible world.

It is evident that he who, rightly or wrongly, holds by the convictions expressed above cannot be faithful to any one of the temporary formulas of his craft. The enduring part of them – the truth which each only imperfectly veils – should abide with him as the most precious of his possessions, but they all: Realism, Romanticism, Naturalism, even the unofficial sentimentalism (which like the poor, is exceedingly difficult to get rid of), all these gods must, after a short period of fellowship, abandon him – even on the very threshold of the temple – to the stammerings of his conscience and to the outspoken consciousness of the difficulties of his work. In that uneasy solitude the supreme cry of Art for Art itself loses the exciting ring of its apparent immorality. It sounds far off. It has ceased to be a cry, and is heard only as a whisper, often incomprehensible, but at times faintly encouraging.

Sometimes, stretched at ease in the shade of a roadside tree, we watch the motions of a labourer in a distant field, and after a time, begin to wonder languidly as to what the fellow may be at. We watch the movements of his body, the waving of his arms, we see him bend down, stand up, hesitate, begin again. It may add to the charm of an idle hour to be told the purpose of his exertions. If we know he is trying to lift a stone, to dig a ditch, to uproot a stump, we look with a more real interest at his efforts; we are disposed to condone the jar of his agitation upon the restfulness of the landscape; and even, if in a brotherly frame of mind, we may bring ourselves to forgive his failure. We understood his object, and, after all, the fellow has tried, and perhaps he had not the strength – and perhaps he had not the knowledge. We forgive, go on our way – and forget.

And so it is with the workman of art. Art is long and life is short, and success is very far off. And thus, doubtful of strength to travel so far, we talk a little about the aim – the aim of art, which, like life itself, is inspiring, difficult – obscured by mists. It is not in the clear logic of a triumphant conclusion; it is not in the unveiling of one of those heartless secrets which are called the Laws of Nature. It is not less great, but only more difficult.

To arrest, for the space of a breath, the hands busy about the work of the earth, and compel men entranced by the sight of distant goals to glance for a moment at the surrounding vision of form and colour, of sunshine and shadows; to make them pause for a look, for a sigh, for a smile – such is the aim, difficult and evanescent, and reserved only for a very few to achieve. But sometimes, by the deserving and the fortunate, even that task is accomplished. And when it is accomplished – behold! – all the truth of life is there: a moment of vision, a sigh, a smile – and the return to an eternal rest.

1897
J.C.

The Nigger of the *Narcissus*

I

Mr Baker, chief mate of the ship *Narcissus*, stepped in one stride out of his lighted cabin into the darkness of the quarterdeck. Above his head, on the break of the poop, the nightwatchman rang a double stroke. It was nine o'clock. Mr Baker, speaking up to the man above him, asked. 'Are all the hands aboard, Knowles?'

The man limped down the ladder, then said reflectively:

'I think so, sir. All our old chaps are there, and a lot of new men has come.... They must be all there.'

'Tell the boatswain to send all hands aft,' went on Mr Baker; 'and tell one of the youngsters to bring a good lamp here. I want to muster our crowd.'

The main deck was dark aft, but half-way from forward, through the open doors of the forecastle, two streaks of brilliant light cut the shadow of the quiet night that lay upon the ship. A hum of voices was heard there, while port and starboard, in the illuminated doorways, silhouettes of moving men appeared for a moment, very black, without relief, like figures cut out of sheet tin. The ship was ready for sea. The carpenter had driven in the last wedge of the main-hatch battens, and, throwing down his maul, had wiped his face with great deliberation, just on the stroke of five. The decks had been swept, the windlass oiled and made ready to heave up the anchor; the big tow-rope lay in long bights along one side of the main deck, with one end carried up and hung over the bows, in readiness for the tug that would come paddling and hissing noisily, hot and smoky, in the limpid, cool quietness of the early morning. The captain was ashore, where he had been engaging some new hands to make up his full crew; and, the work of the day over, the ship's officers had kept out of the way, glad of a little breathing-time. Soon after dark the few liberty-men and the new hands began to arrive in shore-boats rowed by white-clad Asiatics, who clamoured fiercely for payment before coming alongside the gangway-ladder. The feverish and shrill babble of Eastern language struggled against the masterful tones of tipsy seamen, who argued against brazen claims and dishonest hopes by profane shouts. The resplendent and bestarred peace of the East was torn into squalid tatters by howls of rage and shrieks of lament raised over sums ranging from five annas to half a rupee; and every soul afloat in Bombay Harbour became aware that the new hands were joining the *Narcissus*.

Gradually the distracting noise had subsided. The boats came no longer in splashing clusters of three or four together, but dropped alongside singly, in a subdued buzz of expostulation cut short by a 'Not a pice more! You go to the devil!' from some man staggering up the accommodation-ladder – a dark figure, with a long bag poised on the shoulder. In the forecastle the newcomers, upright and swaying amongst corded boxes and bundles of bedding, made friends with the old hands, who sat one above another in the two tiers of bunks, gazing at their future shipmates with glances critical but friendly. The two forecastle lamps were turned up high, and shed an intense hard glare; shore-going round hats were pushed far on the backs of heads, or rolled about on the deck amongst the chain-cables; white collars, undone, stuck out on each side of red faces; big arms in white sleeves gesticulated; the growling voices hummed steady amongst bursts of laughter and hoarse calls. 'Here, sonny take that bunk!' – 'Don't you do it!' – 'What's your last ship?' – 'I know her' – 'Three years ago, in Puget Sound' – 'This berth leaks, I tell you!' – 'Come on; give us a chance to swing that chest!' – 'Did you bring a bottle, any of you shore toffs?' – 'Give us a bit of baccy' – 'I know her; her skipper drank himself to death' – 'He was a dandy boy!' – 'Liked his lotion inside, he did!' – No!' – 'Hold your row, you chaps!' – 'I tell you, you came on board a hooker, where they get their money's worth out of poor Jack, by—!'

A little fellow, called Craik and nicknamed Belfast, abused the ship violently, romancing on principle, just to give the new hands something to think over. Archie, sitting aslant on his sea-chest, kept his knees out of the way, and pushed the needle steadily through a white patch in a pair of blue trousers. Men in black jackets and stand-up collars, mixed with men barefooted, bare-armed, with coloured shirts open on hairy chests, pushed against one another in the middle of the forecastle. The group swayed, reeled, turning upon itself with the motion of a scrimmage, in a haze of tobacco smoke. All were speaking together, swearing at every second word. A Russian Finn, wearing a yellow shirt with pink stripes, stared upwards, dreamy-eyed, from under a mop of tumbled hair. Two young giants with smooth, baby faces – two Scandinavians – helped each other to spread their bedding, silent, and smiling placidly at the tempest of good-humoured and meaningless curses. Old Singleton, the oldest able seaman in the ship, sat apart on the deck right under the lamps, stripped to the waist, tattooed like a cannibal chief all over his powerful chest and enormous biceps. Between the blue and red patterns his white skin gleamed like satin; his bare back was propped against the heel of the bowsprit, and he held a book at arm's length before his big, sunburnt face. With his spectacles and a venerable white beard, he resembled a learned and savage patriarch, the incarnation of barbarian wisdom serene in the blasphemous turmoil of the world. He was intensely absorbed, and as he turned the pages an expression of grave surprise would pass over his rugged features. He was reading *Pelham*. The popularity of Bulwer Lytton in the forecastles of southern-going ships is a wonderful and bizarre phenomenon. What ideas do his polished and so curiously insincere sentences awaken in the simple minds of the big children who people those dark and wandering places of the earth? What meaning their rough, inexperienced souls can find in the elegant verbiage of his pages? What excitement? – what forgetfulness? – what appeasement? Mystery! Is it the fascination of the incomprehensible? – is it the charm of the impossible? Or are those beings who exist beyond the pale of life stirred by his tales as by an enigmatical disclosure of a resplendent world that exists within the frontier of infamy and filth, within that border of dirt and hunger, of misery and dissipation, that comes down on all sides to the water's edge of the incorruptible ocean, and is the only thing they know of life, the only thing they see of surrounding land – those life-long prisoners of the sea? Mystery!

Singleton, who had sailed to the southward since the age of twelve, who in the last forty-five years had lived (as we had calculated from his papers) no more than forty months ashore –

old Singleton, who boasted, with the mild composure of long years well spent, that generally from the day he was paid off from one ship till the day he shipped in another he seldom was in a condition to distinguish daylight – old Singleton sat unmoved in the clash of voices and cries, spelling through *Pelham* with slow labour, and lost in an absorption profound enough to resemble a trance. He breathed regularly. Every time he turned the book in his enormous and blackened hands the muscles of his big white arms rolled slightly under the smooth skin. Hidden by the white moustache, his lips, stained with tobacco-juice that trickled down the long beard, moved in inward whisper. His bleared eyes gazed fixedly from behind the glitter of black-rimmed glasses. Opposite to him, and on a level with his face, the ship's cat sat on the barrel of the windlass in the pose of a crouching chimera, blinking its green eyes at its old friend. It seemed to meditate a leap on to the old man's lap over the bent back of the ordinary seamen who sat at Singleton's feet. Young Charley was lean and long-necked. The ridge of his backbone made a chain of small hills under the old shirt. His face of a street-boy – a face precocious, sagacious, and ironic, with deep downward folds on each side of the thin, wide mouth – hung low over his bony knees. He was learning to make a lanyard knot with a bit of an old rope. Small drops of perspiration stood out on his bulging forehead; he sniffed strongly from time to time, glancing out of the corners of his restless eyes at the old seaman, who took no notice of the puzzled youngster muttering at his work.

The noise increased. Little Belfast seemed, in the heavy heat of the forecastle, to boil with facetious fury. His eyes danced; in the crimson of his face, comical as a mask, the mouth yawned black, with strange grimaces. Facing him, a half-undressed man held his sides, and, throwing his head back, laughed with wet eyelashes. Others stared with amazed eyes. Men sitting doubled up in the upper bunks smoked short pipes, swinging bare brown feet above the heads of those who, sprawling below on sea-chests, listened, smiling stupidly or scornfully. Over the white rims of berths stuck out heads with blinking eyes; but the bodies were lost in the gloom of those places, that resembled narrow niches for coffins in a whitewashed and lighted mortuary. Voices buzzed louder. Archie, with compressed lips, drew himself in, seemed to shrink into a smaller space, and sewed steadily, industrious and dumb. Belfast shrieked like an inspired Dervish: '... So I seez to him, boys, seez I, "Beggin' yer pardon, sorr," seez I to that second mate of that steamer – "beggin' your-r-r pardon, sorr, the Board of Trade must 'ave been drunk when they granted you your certificate!" "What do you say, you—!" seez he, comin' at me like a mad bull ... all in his white clothes; and I up with my tar-pot and capsizes it all over his blamed lovely face and his lovely jacket.... "Take that!" seez I. "I am a sailor, anyhow you nosing, skipper-licking, useless, sooperfloos bridge-stanchion you!" "That's the kind of man I am!" shouts I.... You should have seed him skip, boys! Drowned, blind with tar, he was! So ...'

'Don't 'ee believe him! He never upset no tar; I was there!' shouted somebody. The two Norwegians sat on a chest side by side, alike and placid, resembling a pair of love-birds on a perch, and with round eyes stared innocently; but the Russian Finn, in the racket of explosive shouts and rolling laughter, remained motionless, limp, and dull, like a deaf man without a backbone. Near him Archie smiled at his needle. A broad-chested, slow-eyed newcomer spoke deliberately to Belfast during an exhausted lull in the noise: 'I wonder any of the mates here are alive yet with such a chap as you on board! I concloode they ain't that bad now, if you had the taming of them, sonny.'

'Not bad! Not bad!' screamed Belfast. 'If it wasn't for us sticking together.... Not bad! They ain't never bad when they ain't got a chawnce, blast their black 'arts....' He foamed, whirling his arms, then suddenly grinned and, taking a tablet of black tobacco out of his pocket, bit a piece off with a funny show of ferocity. Another new hand – a man with shifty eyes and a yellow hatchet face, who had been listening open-mouthed in the shadow of the midship locker – observed in a squeaky voice: 'Well, it's a 'omeward trip, anyhow. Bad or good, I can do it on my 'ed – s'long as I get 'ome. And I can look after my rights! I will show 'em!' All the heads turned towards him. Only the ordinary seaman and the cat took no notice. He stood with arms akimbo, a little fellow with white eyelashes. He looked as if he had known all the degradations and all the furies. He looked as if he had been cuffed, kicked, rolled in the mud; he looked as if he had been scratched, spat upon, pelted with unmentionable filth ... and he smiled with a sense of security at the faces around. His ears were bending down under the weight of his battered felt hat. The torn tails of his black coat flapped in fringes about the calves of his legs. He unbuttoned the only two buttons that remained and everyone saw that he had no shirt under it. It was his deserved misfortune that those rags which nobody could possibly be supposed to own looked on him as if they had been stolen. His neck was long and thin; his eyelids were red; rare hairs hung about his jaws; his shoulders were peaked and drooped like the broken wings of a bird; all his left side was caked with mud which showed that he had lately slept in a wet ditch. He had saved his inefficient carcass from violent destruction by running away from an American ship where, in a moment of forgetful folly, he had dared to engage himself; and he had knocked about for a fortnight ashore in the native quarter, cadging for drinks, starving, sleeping on rubbish-heaps, wandering in sunshine: a startling visitor from a world of nightmares. He stood repulsive and smiling in the sudden silence. This clean white forecastle was his refuge; the place where he could be lazy; where he could wallow, and lie and eat – and curse the food he ate; where he could display his talents for shirking work, for cheating, for cadging; where he could find surely someone to wheedle and someone to bully – and where he would be paid for doing all this. They all knew him. Is there a spot on earth where such a man is unknown, an ominous survival testifying to the eternal fitness of lies and impudence? A taciturn long-armed shellback, with hooked fingers, who had been lying on his back smoking, turned in his bed to examine him dispassionately, then, over his head, sent a long jet of clear saliva towards the door. They all knew him! He was the man that cannot steer, that cannot splice, that dodges the work on dark nights; that, aloft, holds on frantically with both arms and legs, and swears at the wind, the sleet, the darkness; the man who curses the sea while others work. The man who is the last out and the first in when all hands are called. The man who can't do most things and won't do the rest. The pet of philanthropists and self-seeking landlubbers. The sympathetic and deserving creature that knows all about his rights, but knows nothing of courage, of endurance, and of the unexpressed faith, of the unspoken loyalty that knits together a ship's company. The independent offspring of the ignoble freedom of the slums full of disdain and hate for the austere servitude of the sea.

Someone cried at him: 'What's your name?' 'Donkin,' he said, looking round with cheerful effrontery. 'What are you?' asked another voice. 'Why, a sailor like you, old man,' he replied, in a tone that meant to be hearty but was impudent. 'Blamme if you don't look a blamed sight worse than a broken-down fireman,' was the comment in a convinced mutter. Charley lifted his head and piped in a cheeky voice: 'He is a man and a sailor' – then wiping his nose with the back of his hand, bent down industriously over his bit of rope. A few laughed. Others stared doubtfully. The ragged newcomer was indignant – 'That's a fine way to welcome a chap into a fo'c'sle,' he snarled. 'Are you men or a lot of 'artless cannybals?' 'Don't take your shirt off for a word, shipmate,' called out Belfast, jumping up in front, fiery, menacing, and friendly at the same time. 'Is that 'ere bloke blind?' asked the indomitable scarecrow, looking right and left with affected surprise. 'Can't 'ee see I 'aven't got no shirt?'

He held both his arms out crosswise and shook the rags that hung over his bones with dramatic effect.

''Cos why?' he continued very loud. 'The bloody Yankees been tryin' to jump my guts out 'cos I stood up for my rights like a good 'un. I am an Englishman, I am. They set upon me an' I 'ad to run. That's why. A'n't yer never seed a man 'ard up? Yah! What kind of blamed ship is this? I'm dead broke. I 'aven't got nothink. No bag, no bed, no blanket, no shirt – not a bloomin' rag but what I stand in. But I 'ad the 'art to stand up agin' them Yankees. 'As any of you 'art enough to spare a pair of old pants for a chum?'

He knew how to conquer the naïve instincts of that crowd. In a moment they gave him their compassion, jocularly, contemptuously, or surlily; and at first it took the shape of a blanket thrown at him as he stood there with the white skin of his limbs showing his human kinship through the black fantasy of his rags. Then a pair of old shoes fell at his muddy feet. With a cry: 'From under,' a rolled-up pair of canvas trousers, heavy with tar stains, struck him on the shoulder. The gust of their benevolence sent a wave of sentimental pity through their doubting hearts. They were touched by their own readiness to alleviate a shipmate's misery. Voices cried: 'We will fit you out, old man.' Murmurs: 'Never seed seech a hard case' – 'Poor beggar' – 'I've got an old singlet' – 'Will that be of any use to you?' – 'Take it, matey.' Those friendly murmurs filled the forecastle. He pawed around with his naked foot, gathering the things in a heap, and looked about for more. Unemotional Archie perfunctorily contributed to the pile an old cloth cap with the peak torn off. Old Singleton, lost in the serene regions of fiction, read on unheeding. Charley, pitiless with the wisdom of youth, squeaked: 'If you want brass buttons for your new unyforms I've got two for you.' The filthy object of universal charity shook his fist at the youngster. 'I'll make you keep this 'ere fo'c'sle clean, young feller,' he snarled viciously. 'Never you fear. I will learn you to be civil to an able seaman, you ignerant ass.' He glared harmfully, but saw Singleton shut his book, and his little beady eyes began to roam from berth to berth. 'Take that bunk by the door there – it's pretty fair,' suggested Belfast. So advised, he gathered the gifts at his feet, pressed them in a bundle against his breast, then looked cautiously at the Russian Finn, who stood on one side with an unconscious gaze, contemplating, perhaps, one of those weird visions that haunt the men of his race. 'Get out of my road, Dutchy,' said the victim of Yankee brutality. The Finn did not move – did not hear. 'Get out, blast ye,' shouted the other, shoving him aside with his elbow. 'Get out, you blanked deaf and dumb fool. Get out.' The man staggered, recovered himself, and gazed at the speaker in silence. 'Those damned furriners should be kept under,' opined the amiable Donkin to the forecastle. 'If you don't teach 'em their place they put on you like anythink.' He flung all his worldly possessions into the empty bed-place, gauged with another shrewd look the risks of the proceeding, then leaped up to the Finn, who stood pensive and dull. 'I'll teach you to swell around,' he yelled. 'I'll plug your eyes for you, you blooming square-head.' Most of the men were now in their bunks and the two had the forecastle clear to themselves. The development of the destitute Donkin aroused interest. He danced all in tatters before the amazed Finn, squaring from a distance at the heavy, unmoved face. One or two men cried encouragingly: 'Go it, Whitechapel!' settling themselves luxuriously in their beds to survey the fight. Others shouted: 'Shut yer row! ... Go an' put yer 'ed in a bag! ...' The hubbub was recommencing. Suddenly many heavy blows struck with a handspike on the deck above boomed like discharges of small cannon through the forecastle. Then the boatswain's voice rose outside the door with an authoritative note in its drawl: 'D'ye hear, below there? Lay aft! Lay aft to muster all hands!'

There was a moment of surprised stillness. Then the forecastle floor disappeared under men whose bare feet flopped on the planks as they sprang clear out of their berths. Caps were rooted for amongst tumbled blankets. Some, yawning, buttoned waistbands. Half-smoked pipes were knocked hurriedly against woodwork and stuffed under pillows. Voices growled: 'What's up? ... Is there no rest for us?' Donkin yelped: 'If that's the way of this ship, we'll 'ave to change all that. ... You leave me alone. ... I will soon ...' None of the crowd noticed him. They were lurching in twos and threes through the doors, after the manner of merchant Jacks who cannot go out of a door fairly, like mere landsmen. The votary of change followed them. Singleton, struggling into his jacket, came last, tall and fatherly, bearing high his head of a weatherbeaten sage on the body of an old athlete. Only Charley remained alone in the white glare of the empty place, sitting between the two rows of iron links that stretched into the narrow gloom forward. He pulled hard at the strands in a hurried endeavour to finish his knot. Suddenly he started up, flung the rope at the cat, and skipped after the black tom which went off leaping sedately over chain compressors, with its tail carried stiff and upright, like a small flagpole.

Outside the glare of the steaming forecastle the serene purity of the night enveloped the seamen with its soothing breath, with its tepid breath flowing under the stars that hung countless above the mastheads in a thin cloud of luminous dust. On the town side the blackness of the water was streaked with trails of light which undulated gently on slight ripples, similar to filaments that float rooted to the shore. Rows of other lights stood away in straight lines as if drawn up on parade between towering buildings; but on the other side of the harbour sombre hills arched high their black spines, on which, here and there, the point of a star resembled a spark fallen from the sky. Far off. Byculla way, the electric lamps at the dock gates shone on the end of lofty standards with a glow blinding and frigid like captive ghosts of some evil moons. Scattered all over the dark polish of the roadstead, the ships at anchor floated in perfect stillness under the feeble gleam of their riding-lights, looming up, opaque and bulky, like strange and monumental structures abandoned by men to an everlasting repose.

Before the cabin door Mr Baker was mustering the crew. As they stumbled and lurched along past the mainmast, they could see aft his round, broad face with a white paper before it, and beside his shoulder the sleepy head, with dropped eyelids, of the boy, who held, suspended at the end of his raised arm, the luminous globe of a lamp. Even before the shuffle of naked soles had ceased along the decks, the mate began to call over the names. He called distinctly in a serious tone befitting this roll-call to unquiet loneliness, to inglorious and obscure struggle, or to the more trying endurance of small privations and wearisome duties. As the chief mate read out a name, one of the men would answer: 'Yes, sir!' or 'Here!' and, detaching himself from the shadowy mob of heads visible above the blackness of starboard bulwarks, would step barefooted into the circle of light, and in two noiseless strides pass into the shadows on the port side of the quarter-deck. They answered in divers tones: in thick mutters, in clear, ringing voices; and some, as if the whole thing had been an outrage on their feelings, used an injured intonation: for discipline is not ceremonious in merchant ships, where the sense of hierarchy is weak, and where all feel themselves equal before the unconcerned immensity of the sea and the exacting appeal of the work.

Mr Baker read on steadily: 'Hansen – Campbell – Smith – Wamibo. Now, then, Wamibo. Why don't you answer? Always got to call your name twice.' The Finn emitted at last an uncouth grunt, and, stepping out, passed through the patch of light, weird and gaudy, with the face of a man marching through a dream. The mate went on faster: 'Craik – Singleton – Donkin.... O Lord!' he involuntarily ejaculated as the incredibly dilapidated figure appeared in the light. It stopped; it uncovered pale gums and long, upper teeth in a malevolent grin. 'Is there anything wrong with me, Mister Mate?' it asked, with a flavour of insolence in the forced simplicity of its tone. On both sides of the deck subdued titters were heard. 'That'll do. Go over,' growled Mr Baker, fixing the new hand with steady blue eyes. And Donkin vanished suddenly out of the light into the dark group of mustered men, to be slapped on the back and to hear flattering whispers: 'He ain't afeared, he'll give sport to 'em, see if he don't' – 'Reg'lar Punch and Judy show' – 'Did yer see the mate start at him?' – 'Well! Damme, if I ever!'

The last man had gone over, and there was a moment of silence while the mate peered at his list. 'Sixteen, seventeen,' he muttered. 'I am one hand short, bo'sen,' he said aloud. The big west-countryman at his elbow, swarthy and bearded like a gigantic Spaniard, said in a rumbling bass. 'There's no one left forward, sir. I had a look around. He ain't aboard, but he may turn up before daylight.' 'Ay. He may or he may not,' commented the mate, 'can't make out that last name. It's all a smudge.... That will do, men. Go below.'

The distinct and motionless group stirred, broke up, began to move forward.

'Wait!' cried a deep, ringing voice.

All stood still. Mr Baker, who had turned away yawning, spun round open-mouthed. At last, furious, he blurted out: 'What's this? Who said "Wait"? What...'

But he saw a tall figure standing on the rail. It came down and pushed through the crowd, marching with a heavy tread towards the light of the quarter-deck. Then again the sonorous voice said with insistence: 'Wait!' The lamplight lit up the man's body. He was tall. His head was away up in the shadows of lifeboats that stood on skids above the deck. The whites of his eyes and his teeth gleamed distinctly, but the face was indistinguishable. His hands were big and seemed gloved.

Mr Baker advanced intrepidly. 'Who are you? How dare you . . .?' he began.

The boy, amazed like the rest, raised the light to the man's face. It was black. A surprised hum – a faint hum that sounded like the suppressed mutter of the word 'Nigger' – ran along the deck and escaped out into the night. The nigger seemed not to hear. He balanced himself where he stood in a swagger that marked time. After a moment he said calmly: 'My name is Wait – James Wait.'

'Oh!' said Mr Baker. Then, after a few seconds of smouldering silence, his temper blazed out. 'Ah! Your name is Wait. What of that? What do you want? What do you mean, coming shouting here?'

The nigger was calm, cool, towering, superb. The men had approached and stood behind him in a body. He overtopped the tallest by half a head. He said: 'I belong to the ship.' He enunciated distinctly, with soft precision. The deep, rolling tones of his voice filled the deck without effort. He was naturally scornful, unaffectedly condescending, as if from his height of six foot three he had surveyed all the vastness of human folly and had made up his mind not to be too hard on it. He went on: 'The captain shipped me this morning. I couldn't get aboard sooner. I saw you all aft as I came up the ladder, and could see directly you were mustering the crew. Naturally I called out my name. I thought you had it on your list, and would understand. You misapprehended.' He stopped short. The folly around him was confounded. He was right as ever, and as ever ready to forgive. The disdainful tones had ceased, and breathing heavily, he stood still, surrounded by all these white men. He held his head up in the glare of the lamp – a head vigorously modelled into deep shadows and shining lights – a head powerful and misshapen with a tormented and flattened face – a face pathetic and brutal: the tragic, the mysterious, the repulsive mask of a nigger's soul.

Mr Baker, recovering his composure, looked at the paper close. 'Oh, yes; that's so. All right. Wait. Take your gear forward,' he said.

Suddenly the nigger's eyes rolled wildly, became all whites. He put his hand to his side and coughed twice, a cough metallic, hollow, and tremendously loud; it resounded like two explosions in a vault; the dome of the sky rang to it, and the iron plates of the ship's bulwarks seemed to vibrate in unison, then he marched forward with the others. The officers lingering by the cabin door could hear him say: 'Won't some of you chaps lend a hand with my dunnage? I've got a chest and a bag.' The words, spoken sonorously, with an even intonation, were heard all over the ship, and the question was put in a manner that made refusal impossible. The short, quick shuffle of men carrying something heavy went away forward, but the tall figure of the nigger lingered by the main hatch in a knot of smaller shapes. Again he was heard asking: 'Is your cook a coloured gentleman?' Then a disappointed and disapproving 'Ah! h'm?' was his comment upon the information that the cook happened to be a mere white man. Yet, as they went all together towards the forecastle, he condescended to put his head through the galley door and boom out inside a magnificent 'Good evening, doctor!' that made all the saucepans ring. In the dim light the cook dozed on the coal locker in front of the captain's supper. He jumped up as if he had been cut with a whip, and dashed wildly on deck to see the backs of several men going away laughing. Afterwards, when talking about that voyage, he used to say: 'The poor fellow had scared me. I thought I had seen the devil.' The cook had been seven years in the ship with the same captain. He was a serious-minded man with a wife and three children, whose society he enjoyed on an average one month out of twelve. When on shore he took his family to church twice every Sunday. At sea he went to sleep every evening with his lamp turned up full, a pipe in his mouth, and an open Bible in his hand. Some one had always to go during the night to put out the light, take the book from his hand, and the pipe from between his teeth. 'For' – Belfast used to say, irritated and complaining – 'some night, you stupid cookie, you'll swallow your ould clay, and we will have no cook.' 'Ah! sonny, I am ready for my Maker's call . . . wish you all were,' the other would answer with a benign serenity that was altogether imbecile and touching. Belfast outside the galley door danced with vexation. 'You holy fool! I don't want you to die,' he howled, looking up with furious, quivering face and tender eyes. 'What's the hurry? You blessed wooden-headed ould heretic, the divvle will have you soon enough. Think of Us ... of Us ... of Us!' And he would go away, stamping, spitting aside, disgusted, and worried; while the other, stepping out, saucepan in hand, hot, begrimed, and placid, watched with a superior, cock-sure smile the back of his 'queer little man' reeling in a rage. They were great friends.

Mr Baker, lounging over the after-hatch, sniffed the humid night in the company of the second mate. 'Those West India niggers run fine and large – some of them.... Ough! ... Don't they? A fine, big man, that, Mr Creighton. Feel him on a rope. Hey? Ough! I will take him into my watch, I think.' The second mate, a fair, gentlemanly young fellow, with a resolute face and a splendid physique, observed quietly that it was just about what he expected. There could be felt in his tone some slight bitterness which Mr Baker very kindly set himself to argue away. 'Come, come, young man,' he said, grunting between the words. 'Come! Don't be too greedy. You had that big Finn in your watch all the voyage. I will do what's fair. You may have those two young Scandinavians and I ... Ough! ... I get the nigger, and will take that ... Ough! that cheeky costermonger chap in a black frock-coat. I'll make him ... Ough! ... make him toe the mark, or my ... Ough! ... name isn't Baker. Ough! Ough! Ough!'

He grunted thrice – furiously. He had that trick of grunting so between his words and at the end of sentences. It was a fine, effective grunt that went well with his menacing utterance, with his heavy, bullnecked frame, his jerky, rolling gait; with his big, seamed face, his steady eyes, and sardonic mouth. But its effect had been long ago discounted by the men. They liked him; Belfast – who was a favourite, and knew it – mimicked him, not quite behind his back. Charley – but with greater caution – imitated his rolling gait. Some of his sayings became established, daily quotations in the forecastle. Popularity can go no farther! Besides, all hands were ready to admit that on a fitting occasion the mate could 'jump down a fellow's throat in a reg'lar Western Ocean style'.

Now he was giving his last orders. 'Ough! ... You, Knowles! Call all hands at four. I want ... Ough! to heave short before the tug comes. Look out for the captain. I am going to lie down in my clothes. . . . Ough! . . . Call me when you see the boat coming. Ough! Ough! . . . The old man is sure to have something to say when he gets aboard,' he remarked to Creighton. 'Well, good night. . . . Ough! A long day before us tomorrow. . . . Ough! . . . Better turn in now. Ough! Ough!'

Upon a dark deck a band of light flashed, then a door slammed, and Mr Baker was gone into his neat cabin. Young Creighton stood leaning over the rail, and looked dreamily into the night of the East. And he saw in it a long country lane, a lane of waving leaves and dancing sunshine. He saw stirring boughs of old trees outspread, and framing in their arch the tender, the caressing blueness of an English sky. And through the arch a girl in a light blue dress, smiling under a sunshade, seemed to be stepping out of the tender sky.

At the other end of the ship the forecastle, with only one lamp burning now, was going to sleep in a dim emptiness traversed by loud breathings, by sudden short sighs. The double rows of berths yawned black, like graves tenanted by uneasy corpses. Here and there a curtain of gaudy chintz, half drawn, marked the resting-place of a sybarite. A leg hung over the edge very white and lifeless. An arm stuck straight out with a dark palm turned up, and thick fingers half closed. Two light snores, that did not synchronize, quarrelled in funny dialogue. Singleton stripped again – the old man suffered much from prickly heat – stood cooling his back in the doorway, with his arms crossed on his bare and adorned chest. His head touched the beam of the deck above. The nigger, half undressed, was busy casting adrift the lashing of his box, and spreading his bedding in an upper berth. He moved about in his socks, tall and noiseless, with a pair of braces beating about his calves. Amongst the shadows of stanchions and bowsprit, Donkin munched a piece of hard ship's bread, sitting on the deck with upturned feet and restless eyes; he held the biscuit up before his mouth in the whole fist and snapped his jaws at it with a raging face. Crumbs fell between his outspread legs. Then he got up.

'Where's our water-cask?' he asked in a contained voice.

Singleton, without a word, pointed with a big hand that held a short smouldering pipe. Donkin bent over the cask, drank out of the tin, splashing the water, turned round, and noticed the nigger looking at him over the shoulder with calm loftiness. He moved up sideways.

'There's a blooming supper for a man,' he whispered bitterly. 'My dorg at 'ome wouldn't 'ave it. It's fit enouf for you an' me. 'Ere's a big ship's fo'c'sle! ... Not a blooming scrap of meat in the kids. I've looked in all the lockers....'

The nigger stared like a man addressed unexpectedly in a foreign language. Donkin changed his tone: 'Giv' us a bit of baccy, mate,' he breathed out confidentially, 'I 'aven't 'ad smoke or chew for the last month. I am rampin' mad for it. Come on, old man!'

'Don't be familiar,' said the nigger. Donkin started and sat down on a chest near by, out of sheer surprise. 'We haven't kept pigs together,' continued James Wait in a deep undertone. 'Here's your tobacco.' Then, after a pause, he inquired: 'What ship?' '*Golden State*,' muttered Donkin indistinctly, biting the tobacco. The nigger whistled low. 'Ran?' he said curtly. Donkin nodded: one of his cheeks bulged out. 'In course I ran,' he mumbled. 'They booted the life hout of one Dago chap on the passage 'ere, then started on me. I cleared hout 'ere.' 'Left your dunnage behind?' 'Yes, dunnage and money,' answered Donkin, raising his voice a little: 'I got nothink. No clothes, no bed. A bandy-legged little Hirish chap 'ere 'as give me a blanket.... Think I'll go an' sleep in the fore topmast staysail tonight.'

He went on deck trailing behind his back a corner of the blanket. Singleton, without a glance, moved slightly aside to let him pass. The nigger put away his shore togs and sat in clean working clothes on his box, one arm stretched over his knees. After staring at Singleton for some time he asked without emphasis: 'What kind of ship is this? Pretty fair? Eh?'

Singleton didn't stir. A long while after he said, with unmoved face: 'Ship! ... Ships are all right. It is the men in them!'

He went on smoking in the profound silence. The wisdom of half a century spent in listening to the thunder of the waves had spoken unconsciously through his old lips. The cat purred on the windlass. Then James Wait had a fit of roaring, rattling cough, that shook him, tossed him like a hurricane, and flung him panting with staring eyes headlong on his sea-chest. Several men woke up. One said sleepily out of his bunk: ''Struth!

what a blamed row!' 'I have a cold on my chest,' gasped Wait. 'Cold! you call it,' grumbled the man; 'should think 'twas something more. . . .' 'Oh! you think so,' said the nigger upright and loftily scornful again. He climbed into his berth and began coughing persistently while he put his head out to glare all round the forecastle. There was no further protest. He fell back on the pillow, and could be heard there wheezing regularly like a man oppressed in his sleep.

Singleton stood at the door with his face to the light and his back to the darkness. And alone in the dim emptiness of the sleeping forecastle he appeared bigger, colossal, very old; old as Father Time himself, who should have come there into this place as quiet as a sepulchre to contemplate with patient eyes the short victory of sleep, the consoler. Yet he was only a child of time, a lonely relic of a devoured and forgotten generation. He stood, still strong, as ever unthinking; a ready man with a vast empty past and with no future, with his childlike impulses and his man's passions already dead within his tattooed breast. The men who could understand his silence were gone – those men who knew how to exist beyond the pale of life and within sight of eternity. They had been strong, as those are strong who know neither doubts nor hopes. They had been impatient and enduring, turbulent and devoted, unruly and faithful. Well-meaning people had tried to represent those men as whining over every mouthful of their food; as going about their work in fear of their lives. But in truth they had been men who knew toil, privation, violence, debauchery – but knew not fear, and had no desire of spite in their hearts. Men hard to manage, but easy to inspire; voiceless men – but men enough to scorn in their hearts the sentimental voices that bewailed the hardness of their fate. It was a fate unique and their own; the capacity to bear it appeared to them the privilege of the chosen! Their generation lived inarticulate and indispensable, without knowing the sweetness of affections or the refuge of a home – and died free from the dark menace of a narrow grave. They were the everlasting children of the mysterious sea. Their successors are the grown-up children of a discontented earth. They are less naughty, but less innocent; less profane, but perhaps also less believing; and if they had learned how to speak they have also learned how to whine. But the others were strong and mute; they were effaced, bowed, and enduring, like stone caryatides that hold up in the night the lighted halls of a resplendent and glorious edifice. They are gone now – and it does not matter. The sea and the earth are unfaithful to their children: a truth, a faith, a generation of men goes – and is forgotten; and it does not matter! Except, perhaps, to the few of those who believed the truth, confessed the faith – or loved the men.

A breeze was coming. The ship that had been lying tide-rode swung to a heavier puff; and suddenly the slack of the chain cable between the windlass and the hawse-pipe clinked, slipped forward an inch, and rose gently off the deck with a startling suggestion as of unsuspected life that had been lurking stealthily in the iron. In the hawse-pipe the grinding links sent through the ship a sound like a low groan of a man sighing under a burden. The strain came on the windlass, the chain tautened like a string, vibrated – and the handle of the screwbrake moved in slight jerks. Singleton stepped forward.

Till then he had been standing meditative and unthinking, reposeful and hopeful, with a face grim and blank – a sixty-year-old child of the mysterious sea. The thoughts of all his lifetime could have been expressed in six words, but the stir of those things that were as much part of his existence as his beating heart called up a gleam of alert understanding upon the sternness of his aged face. The flame of the lamp swayed, and the old man, with knitted and bushy eyebrows, stood over the brake, watchful and motionless in the wild saraband of dancing shadows. Then the ship, obedient to the call of her anchor, forged ahead slightly and eased the strain. The cable relieved, hung down, and after swaying imperceptibly to and fro dropped with a loud tap on the hard wood planks. Singleton seized the high lever, and, by a violent throw forward of his body, wrung out another half-turn from the brake. He recovered himself, breathed largely, and remained for a while glaring down at the powerful and compact engine that squatted on the deck at his feet like some quiet monster – a creature amazing and tame.

'You . . . hold!' he growled at it masterfully, in the incult tangle of his white beard.

2

Next morning, at daylight, the *Narcissus* went to sea.

A slight haze blurred the horizon. Outside the harbour the measureless expanse of smooth water lay sparkling like a floor of jewels, and as empty as the sky. The short black tug gave a pluck to windward, in the usual way, then let go the rope, and hovered for a moment on the quarter with her engines stopped; while the slim, long hull of the ship moved ahead slowly under lower topsails. The loose upper canvas blew out in the breeze with soft round contours, resembling small white clouds snared in the maze of ropes. Then the sheets were hauled home, the yards hoisted, and the ship became a high and lonely pyramid, gliding, all shining and white, through the sunlit mist. The tug turned short round and went away towards the land. Twenty-six pairs of eyes watched her low broad stern crawling languidly over the smooth swell between the two paddle-wheels that turned fast, beating the water with fierce hurry. She resembled an enormous and aquatic black beetle, surprised by the light, overwhelmed by the sunshine, trying to escape with ineffectual effort into the distant gloom of the land. She left a lingering smudge of smoke on the sky, and two vanishing trails of foam on the water. On the place where she had stopped a round black patch of soot remained, undulating on the swell – an unclean mark of the creature's rest.

The *Narcissus* left alone, heading south, seemed to stand resplendent and still upon the restless sea, under the moving sun. Flakes of foam swept past her sides; the water struck her with flashing blows; the land glided away slowly fading; a few birds screamed on motionless wings over the swaying mast-heads. But soon the land disappeared, the birds went away; and to the west the pointed sail of an Arab dhow running for Bombay, rose triangular and upright above the sharp edge of the horizon, lingered and vanished like an illusion. Then the ship's wake, long and straight, stretched itself out through a day of immense solitude. The setting sun, burning on the level of the water, flamed crimson below the blackness of heavy rain clouds.

The sunset squall, coming up from behind, dissolved itself into the short deluge of a hissing shower. It left the ship glistening from trucks to waterline, and with darkened sails. She ran easily before a fair monsoon, with her decks cleared for the night, and, moving along with her, was heard the sustained and monotonous swishing of the waves, mingled with the low whispers of men mustered aft for the setting of watches; the short plaint of some block aloft; or, now and then, a loud sigh of wind.

Mr Baker, coming out of his cabin, called out the first name sharply before closing the door behind him. He was going to take charge of the deck. On the homeward trip, according to an old custom of the sea, the chief officer takes the first night-watch – from eight till midnight. So Mr Baker, after he had heard the last 'Yes, sir!' said moodily, 'Relieve the wheel and look-out'; and climbed with heavy feet the poop ladder to windward. Soon after Mr Creighton came down, whistling softly, and went into the cabin. On the doorstep the steward lounged, in slippers, meditative, and with his shirt-sleeves rolled up to the armpits. On the main deck the cook, locking up the galley doors, had an altercation with young Charley about a pair of socks. He could be heard saying impressively, in the darkness amidships: 'You don't deserve a kindness. I've been drying them for you, and now you complain about the holes – and you swear, too! Right in front of me! If I hadn't been a Christian – which you ain't, you young ruffian – I would give you a clout on the head.... Go away!' Men in couples or threes stood pensive or moved silently along the bulwarks in the waist. The first busy day of a homeward passage was sinking into the dull peace of resumed routine. Aft, on the high poop, Mr Baker walked shuffling and grunted to himself in the pauses of his thoughts. Forward, the look-out man, erect between the flukes of the two anchors, hummed an endless tune, keeping his eyes fixed dutifully ahead in a vacant stare. A multitude of stars coming out into the clear night peopled the emptiness of the sky. They glittered, as if alive above the sea; they surrounded the running ship on all sides; more intense than the eyes of a staring crowd, and as inscrutable as the souls of men.

The passage had begun, and the ship, a fragment detached

from the earth, went on lonely and swift like a small planet. Round her the abysses of sky and sea met in an unattainable frontier. A great circular solitude moved with her, ever changing and ever the same, always monotonous and always imposing. Now and then another wandering white speck, burdened with life, appeared far off – disappeared; intent on its own destiny. The sun looked upon her all day, and every morning rose with a burning, round stare of undying curiosity. She had her own future; she was alive with the lives of those beings who trod her decks; like that earth which had given her up to the sea, she had an intolerable load of regrets and hopes. On her lived timid truth and audacious lies; and, like the earth, she was unconscious, fair to see – and condemned by men to an ignoble fate. The august loneliness of her path lent dignity to the sordid inspiration of her pilgrimage. She drove foaming to the southward, as if guided by the courage of a high endeavour. The smiling greatness of the sea dwarfed the extent of time. The days raced after one another, brilliant and quick like the flashes of a lighthouse, and the nights, eventful and short, resembled fleeting dreams.

The men had shaken into their places, and the half-hourly voice of the bells ruled their life of unceasing care. Night and day the head and shoulders of a seaman could be seen aft by the wheel, outlined high against sunshine or starlight, very steady above the stir of revolving spokes. The faces changed, passing in rotation. Youthful faces, bearded faces, dark faces: faces serene, or faces moody, but all akin with the brotherhood of the sea; all with the same attentive expression of eyes, carefully watching the compass or the sails. Captain Allistoun, serious, and with an old red muffler round his throat, all day long pervaded the poop. At night, many times he rose out of the darkness of the companion, such as a phantom above a grave, and stood watchful and mute under the stars, his night-shirt fluttering like a flag – then, without a sound, sank down again. He was born on the shores of the Pentland Firth. In his youth he attained the rank of harpooner in Peterhead whalers. When he spoke of that time his restless grey eyes became still and cold, like the loom of ice. Afterwards he went into the East Indian trade for the sake of change. He had commanded the

Narcissus since she was built. He loved his ship, and drove her unmercifully; for his secret ambition was to make her accomplish some day a brilliantly quick passage which would be mentioned in nautical papers. He pronounced his owner's name with a sardonic smile, spoke but seldom to his officers, and reproved errors in a gentle voice, with words that cut to the quick. His hair was iron-grey, his face hard and of the colour of pump-leather. He shaved every morning of his life – at six – but once (being caught in a fierce hurricane eighty miles south-west of Mauritius) he had missed three consecutive days. He feared naught but an unforgiving God, and wished to end his days in a little house, with a plot of ground attached – far in the country – out of sight of the sea.

He, the ruler of that minute world, seldom descended from the Olympian heights of his poop. Below him – at his feet, so to speak – common mortals led their busy and insignificant lives. Along the main deck, Mr Baker grunted in a manner bloodthirsty and innocuous; and kept all our noses to the grindstone, being – as he once remarked – paid for doing that very thing. The men working about the deck were healthy and contented – as most seamen are, when once well out to sea. The true peace of God begins at any spot a thousand miles from the nearest land; and when He sends there the messengers of His might it is not in terrible wrath against crime, presumption, and folly, but paternally, to chasten simple hearts – ignorant hearts that know nothing of life, and beat undisturbed by envy or greed.

*

In the evening the cleared decks had a reposeful aspect, resembling the autumn of the earth. The sun was sinking to rest, wrapped in a mantle of warm clouds. Forward, on the end of the spare spars, the boatswain and the carpenter sat together with crossed arms; two men friendly, powerful, and deep-chested. Beside them the short, dumpy, sailmaker – who had been in the Navy – related, between the whiffs of his pipe, impossible stories about Admirals. Couples tramped backwards and forwards, keeping step and balance without effort, in a confined space. Pigs grunted in the big pigsty. Belfast, leaning thoughtfully on his elbow, above the bars, communed with them through the silence of his meditation. Fellows with shirts open wide on sunburnt breasts sat upon the mooring bits, and all up the steps of the forecastle ladders. By the foremast a few discussed in a circle the characteristics of a gentleman. One said: 'It's money as does it.' Another maintained: 'No, it's the way they speak.' Lame Knowles stumped up with an unwashed face (he had the distinction of being the dirty man of the forecastle), and showing a few yellow fangs in a shrewd smile, explained craftily that he 'had seen some of their pants'. The backsides of them – he had observed – were thinner than paper from constant sitting down in offices, yet otherwise they looked first-rate and would last for years. It was all appearance. 'It was,' he said, 'bloomin' easy to be a gentleman when you had a clean job for life.' They disputed endlessly, obstinate and childish; they repeated in shouts and with inflamed faces their amazing arguments; while the soft breeze, eddying down the enormous cavity of the foresail, distended above their bare heads, stirred the tumbled hair with a touch passing and light like an indulgent caress.

They were forgetting their toil, they were forgetting themselves. The cook approached to hear, and stood by, beaming with the inward consciousness of his faith, like a conceited saint unable to forget his glorious reward; Donkin, solitary and brooding over his wrongs on the forecastle-head, moved closer to catch the drift of the discussion below him; he turned his sallow face to the sea, and his thin nostrils moved, sniffing the breeze, as he lounged negligently by the rail. In the glow of sunset faces shone with interest, teeth flashed, eyes sparkled. The walking couples stood still suddenly, with broad grins; a man, bending over a washtub, sat up, entranced, with the soapsuds flecking his wet arms. Even the three petty officers listened leaning back, comfortably propped, and with superior smiles. Belfast left off scratching the ear of his favourite pig, and, open mouthed, tried with eager eyes to have his say. He lifted his arms, grimacing and baffled. From a distance Charley screamed at the ring: 'I know about gentlemen morn'n any of you. I've been intermit with 'em.... I've blacked their boots.' The cook, craning his neck to hear better, was scandalized. 'Keep your mouth shut when your elders speak, you impudent young heathen – you.' 'All right, old Hallelujah, I'm done,' answered Charley, soothingly. At some opinion of dirty Knowles, delivered with an air of supernatural cunning, a ripple of laughter ran along, rose like a wave, burst with a startling roar. They stamped with both feet; they turned their shouting faces to the sky; many, spluttering, slapped their thighs; while one or two, bent double, gasped, hugging themselves with both arms like men in pain. The carpenter and the boatswain, without changing their attitude, shook with laughter where they sat; the sailmaker, charged with an anecdote about a Commodore, looked sulky; the cook was wiping his eyes with a greasy rag; and lame Knowles, astonished at his own success, stood in their midst showing a slow smile.

Suddenly the face of Donkin leaning high-shouldered over the after-rail became grave. Something like a weak rattle was heard through the forecastle door. It became a murmur; it ended in a sighing groan. The washerman plunged both his arms into the tub abruptly; the cook became more crestfallen than an exposed backslider; the boatswain moved his shoulders uneasily; the carpenter got up with a spring and walked away – while the sailmaker seemed mentally to give his story up, and began to puff at his pipe with sombre determination. In the blackness of the doorway a pair of eyes glimmered white, and big, and staring. Then James Wait's head protruding, became visible, as if suspended between the two hands that grasped a doorpost on each side of the face. The tassel of his blue woollen nightcap, cocked forward, danced gaily over his left eyelid. He stepped out in a tottering stride. He looked powerful as ever, but showed a strange and affected unsteadiness in his gait; his face was perhaps a trifle thinner, and his eyes appeared rather startlingly prominent. He seemed to hasten the retreat of departing light by his very presence; the setting sun dipped sharply, as though fleeing before our nigger; a black mist emanated from him; a subtle and dismal influence; a something cold and gloomy that floated out and settled on all the faces like a mourning veil. The circle broke up. The joy of laughter died on stiffened lips. There was not a smile left among all the ship's company. Not a word was spoken. Many turned their backs, trying to look unconcerned; others, with averted heads, sent half-reluctant glances out of the corners of their eyes. They resembled criminals conscious of misdeeds more than honest men distracted by doubt; only two or three stared frankly, but stupidly, with lips slightly open. All expected James Wait to say something, and, at the same time, had the air of knowing beforehand what he would say. He leaned his back against the doorpost, and with heavy eyes swept over them a glance domineering and pained, like a sick tyrant overawing a crowd of abject but untrustworthy slaves.

No one went away. They waited in fascinated dread. He said ironically, with gasps between the words:

'Thank you ... chaps. You ... are nice .. and ... quiet ... you are! Yelling so ... before ... the door....'

He made a longer pause, during which he worked his ribs in an exaggerated labour of breathing. It was intolerable. Feet were shuffled. Belfast let out a groan; but Donkin above blinked his red eyelids with invisible eyelashes, and smiled bitterly over the nigger's head.

The nigger went on again with surprising ease. He gasped no more, and his voice rang, hollow and loud, as though he had been talking in an empty cavern. He was contemptuously angry.

'I tried to get a wink of sleep. You know I can't sleep o' nights. And you come jabbering near the door here like a blooming lot of old women.... You think yourselves good shipmates. Do you? ... Much you care for a dying man!'

Belfast spun away from the pigsty. 'Jimmy,' he cried tremulously, 'if you hadn't been sick I would—'

He stopped. The nigger waited awhile, then said, in a gloomy tone: 'You would ... what? Go an' fight another such one as yourself. Leave me alone. It won't be for long. I'll soon die.... It's coming right enough!'

Men stood around very still and with exasperated eyes. It was just what they had expected, and hated to hear, that idea of a stalking death, thrust at them many times a day like a boast and like a menace by this obnoxious nigger. He seemed to take a pride in that death which, so far, had attended only upon the ease of his life; he was overbearing about it, as if no one else in the world had ever been intimate with such a companion; he paraded it unceasingly before us with an affectionate persistence that made its presence indubitable, and at the same time incredible. No man could be suspected of such monstrous friendship! Was he a reality – or was he a sham – this ever-expected visitor of Jimmy's? We hesitated between pity and mistrust, while, on the slightest provocation, he shook before our eyes the bones of his bothersome and infamous skeleton. He was for ever trotting him out. He would talk of that coming death as though it had been already there, as if it had been walking the deck outside, as if it would presently come in to sleep in the only empty bunk; as if it had sat by his side at every meal. It interfered daily with our occupations, with our leisure, with our amusements. We had no songs and no music in the evening, because Jimmy (we all lovingly called him Jimmy, to conceal our hate of his accomplice) had managed, with that prospective decease of his, to disturb even Archie's mental balance. Archie was the owner of the concertina; but after a couple of stinging lectures from Jimmy he refused to play any more. He said: 'Yon's an uncanny joker. I dinna ken what's wrang wi' him, but there's something verra wrang, verra wrang. It's nae manner of use asking me. I won't play.' Our singers became mute because Jimmy was a dying man. For the same reason no chap – as Knowles remarked – could 'drive in a nail to hang his few poor rags upon', without being made aware of the enormity he committed in disturbing Jimmy's interminable last moments. At night, instead of the cheerful yell, 'One bell! Turn out! Do you hear there? Hey! hey! hey! Show leg!' the watches were called man by man, in whispers, so as not to interfere with Jimmy's, possibly, last slumber on earth. True, he was always awake, and managed, as we sneaked out on deck, to plant in our backs some cutting remark that, for the moment, made us feel as if we had been brutes, and afterwards made us suspect ourselves of being fools. We spoke in low tones within that fo'c'sle as though it had been a church. We ate our meals in silence and dread, for Jimmy was capricious with his food, and railed bitterly at the salt meat, at the biscuits, at the tea, as at articles unfit for human consumption – 'let alone for a dying man!' He would say: 'Can't you find a better slice of meat for a sick man who's trying to get home to be cured – or buried? But there! If I had a chance, you fellows would do away with it. You would poison me. Look at what you have given me!' We served him in his bed with rage and humility, as though we had been the base courtiers of a hated prince; and he rewarded us by his unconciliating criticism. He had found the secret of keeping for ever on the run the fundamental imbecility of mankind; he had the secret of life, that confounded dying man, and he made himself master of every moment of our existence. We grew desperate, and remained submissive. Emotional little Belfast was for ever on the verge of assault or on the verge of tears. One evening he confided to Archie: 'For a ha'penny I would knock his ugly black head off – the skulking dodger!' And the straightforward Archie pretended to be shocked! Such was the infernal spell which that casual St Kitt's nigger had cast upon our guileless manhood! But the same night Belfast stole from the galley the officers' Sunday fruit pie, to tempt the fastidious appetite of Jimmy. He endangered not only his long friendship with the cook but also – as it appeared – his eternal welfare. The cook was overwhelmed with grief; he did not know the culprit but he knew that wickedness flourished; he knew that Satan was abroad amongst those men, whom he looked upon as in some way under his spiritual care. Whenever he saw three or four of us standing together he would leave his stove, to run out and preach. We fled from him; and only Charley (who knew the thief) affronted the cook with a candid gaze which irritated the good man. 'It's you, I believe,' he groaned, sorrowful with a patch of soot on his chin. 'It's you. You are a brand for the burning! No more of YOUR socks in my galley.' Soon, unofficially, the information was spread about that, should there be another case of stealing, our marmalade (an extra allowance: half a pound per man) would be stopped. Mr Baker ceased to heap jocular abuse upon his favourites, and grunted suspiciously at all. The captain's cold eyes, high up on the poop, glittered mistrustful, as he surveyed us trooping in a small mob from halyards to braces for the usual evening pull at all the ropes. Such stealing in a merchant ship is difficult to check, and may be taken as a declaration by men of their dislike for their officers. It is a bad symptom. It may end in God knows what trouble. The *Narcissus* was still a peaceful ship, but mutual confidence was shaken. Donkin did not conceal his delight. We were dismayed.

Then illogical Belfast reproached our nigger with great fury. James Wait, with his elbow on the pillow, choked, gasped out: 'Did I ask you to bone the dratted thing? Blow your blamed pie. It has made me worse – you little Irish lunatic, you!' Belfast, with scarlet face and trembling lips, made a dash at him. Every man in the forecastle rose with a shout. There was a moment of wild tumult. Someone shrieked piercingly: 'Easy, Belfast! Easy! ...' We expected Belfast to strangle Wait without more ado. Dust flew. We heard through it the nigger's cough, metallic and explosive like a gong. Next moment we saw Belfast hanging over him. He was saying plaintively: 'Don't! Don't, Jimmy! Don't be like that. An angel couldn't put up with ye – sick as ye are.' He looked round at us from Jimmy's bedside, his comical mouth twitching, and through tearful eyes; then he tried to put straight the disarranged blankets. The unceasing whisper of the sea filled the forecastle. Was James Wait frightened, or touched, or repentant? He lay on his back with a hand to his side, and as motionless as if his expected visitor had come at last. Belfast fumbled about his feet, repeating with emotion: 'Yes. We know. Ye are bad, but ... Just say what ye want done, and ... We all know ye are bad – very bad....' No! Decidedly James Wait was not touched or repentant. Truth to say, he seemed rather startled. He sat up with incredible suddenness and ease. 'Ah! You think I am bad, do you?' he said gloomily, in his clearest baritone voice (to hear him speak sometimes you would never think there was anything wrong with that man). 'Do you? ... Well, act according! Some of you haven't sense enough to put a blanket shipshape over a sick man. There! Leave it alone! I can die anyhow!' Belfast turned away limply with a gesture of discouragement. In the silence of the forecastle, full of interested men, Donkin pronounced distinctly: 'Well, I'm blowed!' and sniggered. Wait looked at him. He looked at him in a quite friendly manner. Nobody could tell what would please our incomprehensible invalid: but for us the scorn of that snigger was hard to bear.

Donkin's position in the forecastle was distinguished but unsafe. He stood on the bad eminence of a general dislike. He was left alone; and in his isolation he could do nothing but think of the gales of the Cape of Good Hope and envy us the possession of warm clothing and waterproofs. Our sea-boots, our oilskin coats, our well-filled sea-chests, were to him so many causes for bitter meditation: he had none of these things, and he felt instinctively that no man, when the need arose, would offer to share them with him. He was impudently cringing to us and systematically insolent to the officers. He anticipated the best results, for himself, from such a line of conduct – and was mistaken. Such natures forget that under extreme provocation men will be just – whether they want to be so or not. Donkin's insolence to long-suffering Mr Baker became at last intolerable to us, and we rejoiced when the mate, one dark night, tamed him for good. It was done neatly, with great decency and decorum, and with little noise. We had been called – just before midnight – to trim the yards, and Donkin – as usual – made insulting remarks. We stood sleepily in a row with the fore-brace in our hands waiting for the next order, and heard in the darkness a scruffly trampling of feet, an exclamation of surprise, sounds of cuffs and slaps, suppressed, hissing whispers: 'Ah! Will you!' – 'Don't! . . . Don't!' – 'Then behave' – 'Oh! Oh! . . .' Afterwards there were soft thuds mixed with the rattle of iron things as if a man's body had been tumbling helplessly amongst the main-pump rods. Before we could realize the situation, Mr Baker's voice was heard very near and a little impatient: 'Haul away, men! Lay back on that rope!' And we did lay back on the rope with great alacrity. As if nothing had happened, the chief mate went on trimming the yards with his usual and exasperating fastidiousness. We didn't at the time see anything of Donkin, and did not care. Had the chief officer thrown him overboard, no man would have said as much as 'Hallo! he's gone;' But, in truth, no great harm was done – even if Donkin did lose one of his front teeth. We perceived this in the morning, and preserved a ceremonious silence: the etiquette of the forecastle commanded us to be blind and dumb in such a case, and we cherished the decencies of our life more than ordinary landsmen respect theirs. Charley, with unpardonable want of *savoir vivre,* yelled out. ''Ave you been to your dentyst? . . . Hurt ye, didn't it?' He got a box on the ear from one of his best friends. The boy was surprised, and remained plunged in grief for at least three hours. We were sorry for him, but youth requires more discipline than age. Donkin grinned venomously. From that day he became pitiless; told Jimmy that he was a 'black fraud'; hinted to us that we were an imbecile lot, daily taken in by a vulgar nigger. And Jimmy seemed to like the fellow!

Singleton lived untouched by human emotions. Taciturn and unsmiling, he breathed amongst us – in that alone resembling the rest of the crowd. We were trying to be decent chaps, and found it jolly difficult; we oscillated between the desire of virtue and the fear of ridicule; we wished to save ourselves from the pain of remorse, but did not want to be made the contemptible dupes of our sentiment. Jimmy's hateful accomplice seemed to have blown with his impure breath undreamt-of subtleties into our hearts. We were disturbed and cowardly. That we knew. Singleton seemed to know nothing, understand nothing. We had thought him till then as wise as he looked, but now we dared, at times, suspect him of being stupid – from old age. One day, however, at dinner, as we sat on our boxes round a tin dish that stood on the deck within the circle of our feet, Jimmy expressed his general disgust with men and things in words that were particularly disgusting. Singleton lifted his head. We became mute. The old man, addressing Jimmy, asked: 'Are you dying?' Thus interrogated, James Wait appeared horribly startled and confused. We all were startled. Mouths remained open; hearts thumped, eyes blinked; a dropped tin fork rattled in the dish; a man rose as if to go out, and stood still. In less than a minute Jimmy pulled himself together: 'Why? Can't you see I am?' he answered shakily. Singleton lifted a piece of soaked biscuit ('his teeth' – he declared – 'had no edge on them now') to his lips. 'Well, get on with your dying,' he said with venerable mildness; 'don't raise a blamed fuss with us over that job. We can't help you.' Jimmy fell back in his bunk, and for a long time lay very still wiping the perspiration off his chin. The dinner-tins were put away quickly. On deck we discussed the incident in whispers. Some showed a chuckling exultation. Many looked grave. Wamibo, after long periods of staring dreaminess, attempted abortive smiles; and one of the young Scandinavians, much tormented by doubt, ventured in the second dog-watch to approach Singleton (the old man did not encourage us much to speak to him) and ask sheepishly: 'You think he will die?' Singleton looked up. 'Why, of course he will die,' he said deliberately. This seemed decisive. It was promptly imparted to everyone by him who had consulted the oracle. Shy and eager, he would step up and with averted gaze recite his formula: 'Old Singleton says he will die.' It was a relief! At last we knew that our compassion would not be misplaced, and we could again smile without misgivings – but we reckoned without Donkin. Donkin 'didn't want to 'ave no truck with 'em dirty furriners'. When Nilsen came to him with the news: 'Singleton says he will die,' he answered him by a spiteful 'And so will you – you fat-headed Dutchman. Wish you Dutchmen were all dead – 'stead comin' takin' our money inter your starvin' country.' We were appalled. We perceived that after all Singleton's answer meant nothing. We began to hate him for making fun of us. All our certitudes were going; we were on doubtful terms with our officers; the cook had given us up for lost; we had overheard the boatswain's opinion that 'we were a crowd of softies'. We suspected Jimmy, one another, and even our very selves. We did not know what to do. At every insignificant turn of our humble life we met Jimmy overbearing and blocking the way, arm-in-arm with his awful and veiled familiar. It was a weird servitude.

It began a week after leaving Bombay and came on us stealthily like any other great misfortune. Everyone had remarked that Jimmy from the first was very slack at his work; but we thought it simply the outcome of his philosophy of life. Donkin said: 'You put no more weight on a rope than a bloody sparrer.' He disdained him. Belfast, ready for a fight, exclaimed provokingly: 'You don't kill yourself, old man!' 'Would YOU?' he retorted with extreme scorn – and Belfast retired. One morning, as we were washing decks, Mr Baker called to him: 'Bring your broom over here, Wait.' He strolled languidly. 'Move yourself! Ough!' grunted Mr Baker; 'what's the matter with your hind legs?' He stopped dead short. He gazed slowly with eyes that bulged out with an expression audacious and sad. 'It isn't my legs,' he said, 'it's my lungs.' Everybody listened.

'What's ... Ough! ... What's wrong with them?' inquired Mr Baker. All the watch stood around on the wet deck, grinning, and with brooms or buckets in their hands. He said mournfully: 'Going – or gone. Can't you see I'm a dying man? I know it!' Mr Baker was disgusted. 'Then why the devil did you ship aboard here?' 'I must live till I die – mustn't I?' he replied. The grins became audible. 'Go off the deck – get out of my sight,' said Mr Baker. He was nonplussed. It was an unique experience. James Wait, obedient, dropped his broom, and walked slowly forward. A burst of laughter followed him. It was too funny. All hands laughed.... They laughed! ... Alas!

He became the tormentor of all our moments; he was worse than a nightmare. You couldn't see that there was anything wrong with him: a nigger does not show. He was not very fat – certainly – but then he was no leaner than other niggers we had known. He coughed often, but the most prejudiced person could perceive that, mostly, he coughed when it suited his purpose. He wouldn't, or couldn't, do his work – and he wouldn't lie-up. One day he would skip aloft with the best of them, and next time we would be obliged to risk our lives to get his limp body down. He was reported, he was examined; he was remonstrated with, threatened, cajoled, lectured. He was called into the cabin to interview the captain. There were wild rumours. It was said he had cheeked the old man; it was said he had frightened him. Charley maintained that the 'skipper, weepin', 'as giv' 'im 'is blessin' an' a pot of jam'. Knowles had it from the steward that the unspeakable Jimmy had been reeling against the cabin furniture; that he had groaned; that he had complained of general brutality and disbelief; and had ended by coughing all over the old man's meteorological journals which were then spread on the table. At any rate, Wait returned forward supported by the steward, who, in a pained and shocked voice, entreated us: 'Here! Catch hold of him, one of you. He is to lie-up.' Jimmy drank a tin mugful of coffee, and, after bullying first one and then another, went to bed. He remained there most of the time, but when it suited him would come on deck and appear amongst us. He was scornful and brooding; he looked ahead upon the sea, and no one could tell what was the meaning of that black man sitting apart in meditative attitude and as motionless as a carving.

He refused steadily all medicine; he threw sago and cornflour overboard till the steward got tired of bringing it to him. He asked for paregoric. They sent him a big bottle; enough to poison a wilderness of babies. He kept it between his mattress and the deal lining of the ship's side; and nobody ever saw him take a dose. Donkin abused him to his face, jeered at him while he gasped; and the same day Wait would lend him a warm jersey. Once Donkin reviled him for half an hour; reproached him with the extra work his malingering gave to the watch; and ended by calling him 'a black-faced swine'. Under the spell of our accursed perversity we were horror-struck. But Jimmy positively seemed to revel in that abuse. It made him look cheerful – and Donkin had a pair of old sea boots thrown at him. 'Here, you East End trash,' boomed Wait, 'you may have that.'

At last Mr Baker had to tell the captain that James Wait was disturbing the peace of the ship. 'Knock discipline on the head – he will, Ough,' grunted Mr Baker. As a matter of fact, the starboard watch came as near as possible to refusing duty, when ordered one morning by the boatswain to wash out their forecastle. It appears Jimmy objected to a wet floor – and that morning we were in a compassionate mood. We thought the boatswain a brute, and, practically, told him so. Only Mr Baker's delicate tact prevented an all-fired row: he refused to take us seriously. He came bustling forward, and called us many unpolite names but in such a hearty and seamanlike manner that we began to feel ashamed of ourselves. In truth, we thought him much too good a sailor to annoy him willingly: and after all Jimmy might have been a fraud – probably was! The forecastle got a clean up that morning; but in the afternoon a sick-bay was fitted up in the deck-house. It was a nice little cabin opening on deck, and with two berths. Jimmy's belongings were transported there, and then – notwithstanding his protests – Jimmy himself. He said he couldn't walk. Four men carried him on a blanket. He complained that he would have to die there alone, like a dog. We grieved for him, and were delighted to have him removed from the forecastle. We attended him as before. The galley was next door, and the cook looked in many times a day. Wait became a little more cheerful. Knowles affirmed having heard him laugh to himself in peals one day. Others had seen him walking about on deck at night. His little place, with the door ajar on a long hook, was always full of tobacco smoke. We spoke through the crack cheerfully, sometimes abusively, as we passed by, intent on our work. He fascinated us. He would never let doubt die. He overshadowed the ship. Invulnerable in his promise of speedy corruption he trampled on our self-respect, he demonstrated to us daily our want of moral courage; he tainted our lives. Had we been a miserable gang of wretched immortals, unhallowed alike by hope and fear, he could not have lorded it over us with a more pitiless assertion of his sublime privilege.

3

Meantime the *Narcissus*, with square yards, ran out of the fair monsoon. She drifted slowly, swinging round and round the compass, through a few days of baffling light airs. Under the patter of short warm showers, grumbling men whirled the heavy yards from side to side; they caught hold of the soaked ropes with groans and sighs, while their officers, sulky and dripping with rain water, unceasingly ordered them about in wearied voices. During the short respites they looked with disgust into the smarting palms of their stiff hands, and asked one another bitterly: 'Who would be a sailor if he could be a farmer?' All the tempers were spoilt, and no man cared what he said. One black night, when the watch, panting in the heat and half-drowned with the rain, had been through four mortal hours hunted from brace to brace, Belfast declared that he would 'chuck the sea for ever and go in a steamer'. This was excessive, no doubt. Captain Allistoun, with great self-control, would mutter sadly to Mr Baker: 'It is not so bad – not so bad,' when he had managed to shove, and dodge, and manoeuvre his smart ship through sixty miles in twenty-four hours. From the doorstep of the little cabin, Jimmy, chin in hand, watched our distasteful labours with insolent and melancholy eyes. We spoke to him gently – and out of his sight exchanged sour smiles.

Then, again, with a fair wind and under a clear sky, the ship went on piling up the South Latitude. She passed outside Madagascar and Mauritius without a glimpse of the land. Extra lashings were put on the spare spars. Hatches were looked to. The steward in his leisure moments and with a worried air tried to fit washboards to the cabin doors. Stout canvas was bent with care. Anxious eyes looked to the westward, towards the cape of storms. The ship began to dip into a south-west swell, and the softly luminous sky of low latitudes took on a harder sheen from day to day above our heads: it arched high above the ship, vibrating and pale, like an immense dome of steel, resonant with the deep voice of freshening gales. The sunshine gleamed cold on the white curls of black waves. Before the strong breath of westerly squalls the ship, with reduced sail, lay slowly over, obstinate and yielding. She drove to and fro in the unceasing endeavour to fight her way through the invisible violence of the winds: she pitched headlong into dark smooth hollows; she struggled upwards over the snowy ridges of great running seas; she rolled, restless, from side to side, like a thing in pain. Enduring and valiant, she answered to the call of men; and her slim spars waving for ever in abrupt semi-circles, seemed to beckon in vain for help towards the stormy sky.

It was a bad winter off the Cape that year. The relieved helmsmen came off flapping their arms, or ran stamping hard and blowing into swollen, red fingers. The watch on deck dodged the sting of cold sprays, or, crouching in sheltered corners, watched dismally the high and merciless seas boarding the ship time after time in unappeasable fury. Water tumbled in cataracts over the forecastle doors. You had to dash through a waterfall to get into your damp bed. The men turned in wet and turned out stiff to face the redeeming and ruthless exactions of their glorious and obscure fate. Far aft, and peering watchfully to windward, the officers could be seen through the mist of squalls. They stood by the weather-rail, holding on grimly, straight and glistening in their long coats; and in the disordered plunges of the hard-driven ship, they appeared high up, attentive, tossing violently above the grey line of a clouded horizon in motionless attitudes.

They watched the weather and the ship as men on shore watch the momentous chances of fortune. Captain Allistoun never left the deck, as though he had been part of the ship's fittings. Now and then the steward, shivering, but always in shirt sleeves, would struggle towards him with some hot coffee, half of which the gale blew out of the cup before it reached the master's lips. He drank what was left gravely in one long gulp, while heavy sprays pattered loudly on his oilskin coat, the seas swishing broke about his high boots; and he never took his eyes off the ship. He kept his gaze riveted upon her as a loving man watches the unselfish toil of a delicate woman upon the slender thread of whose existence is hung the whole meaning and joy of the world. We all watched her. She was beautiful and had a weakness. We loved her no less for that. We admired her qualities aloud, we boasted of them to one another, as though they had been our own, and the consciousness of her only fault we kept buried in the silence of our profound affection. She was born in the thundering peal of hammers beating upon iron, in black eddies of smoke, under a grey sky, on the banks of the Clyde. The clamorous and sombre stream gives birth to things of beauty that float away into the sunshine of the world to be loved by men. The *Narcissus* was one of that perfect brood. Less perfect than many perhaps, but she was ours, and, consequently, incomparable. We were proud of her. In Bombay, ignorant landlubbers alluded to her as that 'pretty grey ship'. Pretty! A scurvy need of commendation! We knew she was the most magnificent sea-boat ever launched. We tried to forget that, like many good sea-boats, she was at times rather crank. She was exacting. She wanted care in loading and handling, and no one knew exactly how much care would be enough. Such are the imperfections of mere men! The ship knew, and sometimes would correct the presumptuous human ignorance by the wholesome discipline of fear. We had heard ominous stories about past voyages. The cook (technically a seaman, but in reality no sailor) – the cook, when unstrung by some misfortune, such as the rolling over of a saucepan, would mutter gloomily while he wiped the floor: 'There! Look at what she has done! Some voy'ge she will drown all hands! You'll see if she won't.' To which the steward, snatching in the galley a moment to draw breath in the hurry of his worried life, would remark philosophically: 'Those that see won't tell, anyhow. I don't want to see it.' We derided those fears. Our hearts went out to the old man when he pressed her hard so as to make her hold her own, hold to every inch gained to windward; when he made her, under reefed sails, leap obliquely at enormous waves. The men, knitted together aft into a ready group by the first sharp order of an officer coming to take charge of the deck in bad weather: 'Keep handy the watch', stood admiring her valiance. Their eyes blinked in the wind; their dark faces were wet with drops of water more salt and bitter than human tears; beards and moustaches, soaked, hung straight and dripping like fine seaweed. They were fantastically misshapen; in high boots, in hats like helmets, and swaying clumsily, stiff and bulky in glistening oilskins, they resembled men strangely equipped for some fabulous adventure. Whenever she rose easily to a towering green sea, elbows dug ribs, faces brightened, lips murmured: 'Didn't she do it cleverly,' and all the heads turning like one watched with sardonic grins the foiled wave go roaring to leeward, white with the foam of a monstrous rage. But when she had not been quick enough and, struck heavily, lay over trembling under the blow, we clutched at ropes, and looking up at the narrow bands of drenched and strained sails waving desperately aloft, we thought in our hearts: 'No wonder. Poor thing!'

The thirty-second day out of Bombay began inauspiciously. In the morning a sea smashed one of the galley doors. We dashed in through lots of steam and found the cook very wet and indignant with the ship: 'She's getting worse every day. She's trying to drown me in front of my own stove!' He was very angry. We pacified him, and the carpenter, though washed away twice from there, managed to repair the door. Through that accident our dinner was not ready till late, but it didn't matter in the end because Knowles, who went to fetch it, got knocked down by a sea and the dinner went over the side. Captain Allistoun, looking more hard and thin-lipped than ever, hung on to full topsails and foresail, and would not notice that the ship, asked to do too much, appeared to lose heart altogether for the first time since we knew her. She refused to rise, and bored her way sullenly through the seas. Twice running, as though she had been blind or weary of life, she put her nose deliberately into a big wave and swept the decks from end to end. As the boatswain observed with marked annoyance, while we were splashing about in a body to try and save a worthless wash-tub: 'Every blooming thing in the ship is going overboard this afternoon.' Venerable Singleton broke his habitual silence and said with a glance aloft: 'The old man's in a temper with the weather, but it's no good bein' angry with the winds of heaven.' Jimmy had shut his door, of course. We knew he was dry and comfortable within his little cabin, and in our absurd way were pleased one moment, exasperated the next, by that certitude. Donkin skulked shamelessly, uneasy and miserable. He grumbled: 'I'm perishin' with cold outside in bloomin' wet rags, an' that 'ere black sojer sits dry on a blamed chest full of bloomin' clothes; blank his black soul!' We took no notice of him; we hardly gave a thought to Jimmy and his bosom friend. There was no leisure for idle probing of hearts. Sails blew adrift. Things broke loose. Cold and wet, we were washed about the deck while trying to repair damages. The ship tossed about, shaken furiously, like a toy in the hand of a lunatic. Just at sunset there was a rush to shorten sail before the menace of a sombre hail cloud. The hard gust of wind came brutal like the blow of a fist. The ship relieved of her canvas in time received it pluckily: she yielded reluctantly to the violent onset; then, coming up with a stately and irresistible motion, brought her spars to windward in the teeth of the screeching squall. Out of the abysmal darkness of the black cloud overhead white hail streamed on her, rattled on the rigging, leaped in handfuls off the yards, rebounded on the deck – round and gleaming in the murky turmoil like a shower of pearls. It passed away. For a moment a livid sun shot horizontally the last rays of sinister light between the hills of steep, rolling waves. Then a wild night rushed in – stamped out in a great howl that dismal remnant of a stormy day.

There was no sleep on board that night. Most seamen remember in their life one or two such nights of a culminating gale. Nothing seems left of the whole universe but darkness, clamour, fury – and the ship. And like the last vestige of a shattered creation she drifts, bearing an anguished remnant of sinful mankind, through the distress, tumult, and pain of an avenging terror. No one slept in the forecastle. The tin oil-lamp suspended on a long string, smoking, described wide circles; wet clothing made dark heaps on the glistening floor; a thin layer of water rushed to and fro. In the bed-places men lay booted, resting on elbows and with open eyes. Hung-up suits of oilskin swung out and in, lively and disquieting like reckless ghosts of decapitated seamen dancing in a tempest. No one spoke and all listened. Outside the night moaned and sobbed to the accompaniment of a continuous loud tremor as of innumerable drums beating far off. Shrieks passed through the air. Tremendous dull blows made the ship tremble while she rolled under the weight of the seas toppling on her deck. At times she soared up swiftly as if to leave this earth for ever, then during interminable moments fell through a void with all the hearts on board of her standing still, till a frightful shock, expected and sudden, started them off again with a big thump. After every dislocating jerk of the ship, Wamibo, stretched full length, his face on the pillow, groaned slightly with the pain of his tormented universe. Now and then, for the fraction of an intolerable second, the ship, in the fiercer burst of a terrible uproar, remained on her side, vibrating and still, with a stillness more appalling than the wildest motion. Then upon all those prone bodies a stir would pass, a shiver of suspense. A man would protrude his anxious head and a pair of eyes glistened in the sway of light glaring wildly. Some moved their legs a little as if making ready to jump out. But several, motionless on their backs and with one hand gripping hard the edge of the bunk, smoked nervously with quick puffs, staring upwards; immobilized in a great craving for peace.

At midnight, orders were given to furl the fore and mizen topsails. With immense efforts men crawled aloft through a merciless buffeting, saved the canvas and crawled down almost exhausted, to bear in panting silence the cruel battering of the seas. Perhaps for the first time in the history of the merchant service the watch, told to go below, did not leave the deck, as if compelled to remain there by the fascination of a venomous violence. At every heavy gust men, huddled together, whispered to one another: 'It can blow no harder' – and presently the gale would give them the lie with a piercing shriek, and drive their breath back into their throats. A fierce squall seemed to burst asunder the thick mass of sooty vapours; and above the wrack of torn clouds glimpses could be caught of the high moon rushing backwards with frightful speed over the sky, right into the wind's eye. Many hung their heads, muttering that it 'turned their inwards out' to look at it. Soon the clouds closed up and the world again became a raging, blind darkness that howled, flinging at the lonely ship salt sprays and sleet.

About half past seven the pitchy obscurity round us turned a ghostly grey, and we knew that the sun had risen. This unnatural and threatening daylight, in which we could see one another's wild eyes and drawn faces, was only an added tax on our endurance. The horizon seemed to have come on all sides within arm's length of the ship. Into that narrowed circle furious seas leaped in, struck, and leaped out. A rain of salt, heavy drops flew aslant like mist. The main-topsail had to be goose-winged, and with stolid resignation every one prepared to go aloft once more; but the officers yelled, pushed back, and at last we understood that no more men would be allowed to go on the yard than were absolutely necessary for the work. As at any moment the masts were likely to be jumped out or blown overboard, we concluded that the captain didn't want to see all his crowd go over the side at once. That was reasonable. The watch then on duty, led by Mr Creighton, began to struggle up the rigging. The wind flattened them against the ratlines; then, easing a little, would let them ascend a couple of steps; and again, with a sudden gust, pin all up the shrouds the whole crawling line in attitudes of crucifixion. The other watch plunged down on the main deck to haul up the sail. Men's heads bobbed up as the water flung them irresistibly from side to side. Mr Baker grunted encouragingly in our midst, spluttering and blowing amongst the tangled ropes like an energetic porpoise. Favoured by an ominous and untrustworthy lull, the work was done without anyone being lost either off the deck or from the yard. For the moment the gale seemed to take off, and the ship, as if grateful for our efforts, plucked up heart and made better weather of it.

At eight the men off duty, watching their chance, ran forward over the flooded deck to get some rest. The other half of the crew remained aft for their turn of 'seeing her through her trouble', as they expressed it. The two mates urged the master to go below. Mr Baker grunted in his ear: 'Ough! surely now ... Ough! ... confidence in us ... nothing more to do ... she must lay it out or go. Ough! Ough!' Tall young Mr Creighton smiled down at him cheerfully: '... She's as right as a trivet! Take a spell, sir.' He looked at them stonily with bloodshot, sleepless eyes. The rims of his eyelids were scarlet, and he moved his jaw unceasingly with a slow effort, as though he had been masticating a lump of india-rubber. He shook his head. He repeated: 'Never mind me. I must see it out – I must see it out,' but he consented to sit down for a moment on the skylight, with his hard face turned unflinchingly to windward. The sea spat at it – and stoical, it streamed with water as though he had been weeping. On the weather side of the poop the watch, hanging on to the mizen rigging and to one another, tried to exchange encouraging words. Singleton, at the wheel, yelled out: 'Look out for yourselves!' His voice reached them in a warning whisper. They were startled.

A big, foaming sea came out of the mist; it made for the ship, roaring wildly, and in its rush it looked as mischievous and discomposing as a madman with an axe. One or two, shouting, scrambled up the rigging; most, with a convulsive catch of the breath, held on where they stood. Singleton dug his knees under the wheel-box, and carefully eased the helm to the headlong pitch of the ship, but without taking his eyes off the coming wave. It towered close-to and high, like a wall of green glass topped with snow. The ship rose to it as though she had soared on wings, for a moment rested poised upon the foaming crest as if she had been a great sea-bird. Before we could draw breath a heavy gust struck her, another roller took her unfairly under the weather bow, she gave a toppling lurch, and filled her decks. Captain Allistoun leaped up, and fell; Archie rolled over him, screaming: 'She will rise!' She gave another lurch to leeward; the lower deadeyes dipped heavily; the men's feet flew from under them, and they hung kicking above the slanting poop. They could see the ship putting her side in the water, and shouted all together: 'She's going!' Forward the forecastle doors flew open, and the watch below were seen leaping out one after another, throwing their arms up; and, falling on hands and knees, scrambled aft on all fours along the high side of the deck, sloping more than the roof of a house. From leeward the seas rose, pursuing them; they looked wretched in a hopeless struggle, like vermin fleeing before a flood; they fought up the weather ladder of the poop one after another, half naked and staring wildly; and as soon as they got up they shot to leeward in clusters, with closed eyes, till they brought up heavily with their ribs against the iron stanchions of the rail; then, groaning, they rolled in a confused mass. The immense volume of water thrown forward by the last scend of the ship had burst the lee door of the forecastle. They could see their chests, pillows, blankets, clothing, come out floating upon the sea. While they struggled back to windward they looked in dismay. The straw beds swam high, the blankets, spread out, undulated; while the chests, waterlogged and with a heavy list, pitched heavily like dismasted hulks, before they sank; Archie's big coat passed with outspread arms, resembling a drowned seaman floating with his head under water. Men were slipping down while trying to dig their fingers into the planks; others, jammed in corners, rolled enormous eyes. They all yelled unceasingly: 'The masts! Cut! Cut! . . .' A black squall howled low over the ship, that lay on her side with the weather yard-arms pointing to the clouds; while the tall masts, inclined nearly to the horizon, seemed to be of an immeasurable length. The carpenter let go his hold, rolled against the skylight, and began to crawl to the cabin entrance, where a big axe was kept ready for just such an emergency. At the moment the topsail sheet parted, the end of the heavy chain racketed aloft, and sparks of red fire streamed down through the flying sprays. The sail flapped once with a jerk that seemed to tear our hearts out through our teeth, and instantly changed into a bunch of fluttering narrow ribbons that tied themselves into knots and became quiet along the yard. Captain Allistoun struggled, managed to stand up with his face near the deck, upon which men swung on the ends of ropes, like nest robbers upon a cliff. One of his feet was on somebody's chest; his face was purple; his lips moved. He yelled also; he yelled, bending down: 'No! No!' Mr Baker, one leg over the binnacle-stand, roared out: 'Did you say no? Not cut?' He shook his head madly. 'No! No!' Between his legs the crawling carpenter heard, collapsed at once, and lay full length in the angle of the skylight. Voices took up the shout – 'No! No!' Then all became still. They waited for the ship to turn over altogether, and shake them out into the sea; and upon the terrific noise of wind and sea not a murmur of remonstrance came out from those men, who each would have given ever so many years of life to see 'them damned sticks go overboard!' They all believed it their only chance; but a little hard-faced man shook his grey head and shouted 'No!' without giving them as much as a glance. They were silent, and gasped. They gripped rails, they had wound ropes'-ends under their arms; they clutched ringbolts, they crawled in heaps where there was foothold; they held on with both arms, hooked themselves to anything to windward with elbows, with chins, almost with their teeth: and some, unable to crawl away from where they had been flung, felt the sea leap up, striking against their backs as they struggled upwards. Singleton had stuck to the wheel. His hair flew out in the wind; the gale seemed to take its life-long adversary by the beard and shake his old head. He wouldn't let go, and, with his knees forced between the spokes, flew up and down like a man on a bough. As Death appeared unready, they began to look about. Donkin, caught by one foot in a loop of some rope, hung, head down, below us, and yelled, with his face to the deck: 'Cut! Cut!' Two men lowered themselves cautiously to him; others hauled on the rope. They caught him up, shoved him into a safer place, held him. He shouted curses at the master, shook his fist at him with horrible blasphemies, called upon us in filthy words to 'Cut! Don't mind that murdering fool! Cut, some of you!' One of his rescuers struck him a back-handed blow over the mouth; his head banged on the deck, and he became suddenly very quiet, with a white face, breathing hard, and with a few drops of blood trickling from his cut lip. On the lee side another man could be seen stretched out as if stunned; only the washboard prevented him from going over the side. It was the steward. We had to sling him up like a bale for he was paralysed with fright. He had rushed up out of the pantry when he felt the ship go over, and had rolled down helplessly, clutching a china mug. It was not broken. With difficulty we tore it away from him, and when he saw it in our hands he was amazed. 'Where did you get that thing?' he kept on asking us in a trembling voice. His shirt was blown to shreds; the ripped sleeves flapped like wings. Two men made him fast, and, doubled over the rope that held him, he resembled a bundle of wet rags. Mr Baker crawled along the line of men, asking: 'Are you all there?' and looking them over. Some blinked vacantly, others shook convulsively; Wamibo's head hung over his breast; and in painful attitudes, cut by lashings, exhausted with clutching, screwed up in corners, they breathed heavily. Their lips twitched, and at every sickening heave of the overturned ship they opened them wide as if to shout. The cook, embracing a wooden stanchion, unconsciously repeated a prayer. In every short interval of the fiendish noises around he could be heard there, without cap or slippers, imploring in that storm the Master of our lives not to lead him into temptation. Soon he also became silent. In all that crowd of cold and hungry men, waiting wearily for a violent death, not a voice was heard; they were mute, and in sombre thoughtfulness listened to the horrible imprecations of the gale.

Hours passed. They were sheltered by the heavy inclination of the ship from the wind that rushed in one long unbroken moan above their heads, but cold rain showers fell at times into the uneasy calm of their refuge. Under the torment of that new infliction a pair of shoulders would writhe a little. Teeth chattered. The sky was clearing, and bright sunshine gleamed over the ship. After every burst of battering seas, vivid and fleeting rainbows arched over the drifting hull in the flick of sprays. The gale was ending in a clear blow, which gleamed and cut like a knife. Between two bearded shellbacks Charley, fastened with somebody's long muffler to a deck ring-bolt, wept quietly, with rare tears wrung out by bewilderment, cold, hunger, and general misery. One of his neighbours punched him in the ribs asking roughly: 'What's the matter with your cheek? In fine weather there's no holding you, youngster.' Turning about with prudence he worked himself out of his coat and threw it over the boy. The other man closed up, muttering: ' 'Twill make a bloomin' man of you, sonny.' They flung their arms over and pressed against him. Charley drew his feet up and his eyelids dropped. Sighs were heard, as men, perceiving that they were not to be 'drowned in a hurry', tried easier positions. Mr Creighton, who had hurt his leg, lay amongst us with compressed lips. Some fellows belonging to his watch set about securing him better. Without a word or a glance he lifted his arms one after another to facilitate the operation, and not a muscle moved in his stern, young face. They asked him with solicitude: 'Easier now, sir?' He answered with a curt: 'That'll do.' He was a hard young officer, but many of his watch used to say they liked him well enough because he had 'such a gentlemanly way of damning us up and down the deck'.

Others unable to discern such fine shades of refinement, respected him for his smartness. For the first time since the ship had gone on her beam ends Captain Allistoun gave a short glance down at his men. He was almost upright – one foot against the side of the skylight, one knee on the deck; and with the end of the vang round his waist swung back and forth with his gaze fixed ahead, watchful, like a man looking out for a sign. Before his eyes the ship, with half her deck below water, rose and fell on heavy seas that rushed from under her flashing in the cold sunshine. We began to think she was wonderfully buoyant – considering. Confident voices were heard shouting: 'She'll do, boys!' Belfast exclaimed with fervour. 'I would giv' a month's pay for a draw at a pipe!' One or two, passing dry tongues on their salt lips, muttered something about a 'drink of water'. The cook, as if inspired, scrambled up with his breast against the poop water-cask and looked in. There was a little at the bottom. He yelled, waving his arms, and two men began to crawl backwards and forwards with the mug. We had a good mouthful all round. The master shook his head impatiently, refusing. When it came to Charley one of his neighbours shouted: 'That bloomin' boy's asleep.' He slept as though he had been dosed with narcotics. They let him be. Singleton held to the wheel with one hand while he drank, bending down to shelter his lips from the wind. Wamibo had to be poked and yelled at before he saw the mug held before his eyes. Knowles said sagaciously: 'It's better'n a tot o' rum.' Mr Baker grunted: 'Thank ye.' Mr Creighton drank and nodded. Donkin gulped greedily, glaring over the rim. Belfast made us laugh when with grimacing mouth he shouted: 'Pass it this way. We're all taytottlers here.' The master, presented with the mug again by a crouching man, who screamed up at him: 'We all had a drink, captain,' groped for it without ceasing to look ahead, and handed it back stiffly as though he could not spare half a glance away from the ship. Faces brightened. We shouted to the cook: 'Well done, doctor!' He sat to leeward, propped by the water-cask and yelled back abundantly, but the seas were breaking in thunder just then, and we only caught snatches that sounded like: 'Providence' and 'born again'. He was at his old game of preaching. We made friendly but derisive gestures at him, and from below he lifted one arm, holding on with the other, moved his lips; he beamed up to us, straining his voice – earnest, and ducking his head before the sprays.

Suddenly someone cried: 'Where's Jimmy?' and we were appalled once more. On the end of the row the boatswain shouted hoarsely: 'Has anyone seed him come out?' Voices exclaimed dismally: 'Drowned – is he? ... No! In his cabin! ... Good Lord! ... Caught like a bloomin' rat in a trap.... Couldn't open his door ... Aye! She went over too quick and the water jammed it ... Poor beggar! ... No help for 'im.... Let's go and see ...' 'Damn him, who could go?' screamed Donkin. 'Nobody expects you to,' growled the man next to him: 'you're only a thing.' 'Is there half a chance to get at 'im?' inquired two or three men together. Belfast untied himself with blind impetuosity, and all at once shot down to leeward quicker than a flash of lightning. We shouted all together with dismay; but with his legs overboard he held and yelled for a rope. In our extremity nothing could be terrible; so we judged him funny kicking there, and with his scared face. Someone began to laugh, and, as if hysterically infected with screaming merriment, all those haggard men went off laughing, wild-eyed, like a lot of maniacs tied up on a wall. Mr Baker swung off the binnacle-stand and tendered him one leg. He scrambled up rather scared, and consigning us with abominable words to the 'divvle'. 'You are.... Ough! You're a foul-mouthed beggar, Craik,' grunted Mr Baker. He answered, stuttering with indignation: 'Look at 'em, sorr. The bloomin' dirty images! laughing at a chum going overboard. Call themselves men, too.' But from the break of the poop the boatswain called out: 'Come along,' and Belfast crawled away in a hurry to join him. The five men, poised and gazing over the edge of the poop, looked for the best way to get forward. They seemed to hesitate. The others, twisting in their lashings, turning painfully, stared with open lips. Captain Allistoun saw nothing; he seemed with his eyes to hold the ship up in a superhuman concentration of effort. The wind screamed loud in sunshine; columns of spray rose straight up; and in the glitter of rainbows bursting over the trembling hull the men went over cautiously, disappearing from sight with deliberate movements.

They went swinging from belaying pin to cleat above the seas that beat the half-submerged deck. Their toes scraped the planks. Lumps of green cold water toppled over the bulwark and on their heads. They hung for a moment on strained arms, with the breath knocked out of them, and with closed eyes – then, letting go with one hand, balanced with lolling heads, trying to grab some rope or stanchion further forward. The long-armed and athletic boatswain swung quickly, gripping things with a fist hard as iron, and remembering suddenly snatches of the last letter from his 'old woman'. Little Belfast scrambled in a rage spluttering 'cursed nigger'. Wamibo's tongue hung out with excitement; and Archie, intrepid and calm, watched his chance to move with intelligent coolness.

When above the side of the house, they let go one after another, and falling heavily, sprawled, pressing their palms to the smooth teak wood. Round them the backwash of waves seethed white and hissing. All the doors had become trapdoors, of course. The first was the galley door. The galley extended from side to side, and they could hear the sea splashing with hollow noises in there. The next door was that of the carpenter's shop. They lifted it, and looked down. The room seemed to have been devastated by an earthquake. Everything in it had tumbled on the bulkhead facing the door, and on the other side of that bulkhead there was Jimmy, dead or alive. The bench, a half-finished meat-safe, saws, chisels, wire rods, axes, crowbars, lay in a heap besprinkled with loose nails. A sharp adze stuck up with a shining edge that gleamed dangerously down there like a wicked smile. The men clung to one another peering. A sickening, sly lurch of the ship nearly sent them overboard in a body. Belfast howled 'Here goes!' and leaped down. Archie followed cannily, catching at shelves that gave way with him, and eased himself in a great crash of ripped wood. There was hardly room for three men to move. And in the sunshiny blue square of the door, the boatswain's face, bearded and dark, Wamibo's face, wild and pale, hung over – watching.

Together they shouted: 'Jimmy! Jim!' From above the boatswain contributed a deep growl: 'You . . . Wait!' In a pause, Belfast entreated: 'Jimmy, darlin', are ye aloive?' The boatswain said: 'Again! All together, boys!' All yelled excitedly.

Wamibo made noises resembling loud barks. Belfast drummed on the side of the bulkhead with a piece of iron. All ceased suddenly. The sound of screaming and hammering went on thin and distinct – like a solo after a chorus. He was alive. He was screaming and knocking below us with the fury of a man prematurely shut up in a coffin. We went to work. We attacked with desperation the abominable heap of things heavy, of things sharp, of things clumsy to handle. The boatswain crawled away to find somewhere a flying end of a rope; and Wamibo, held back by shouts: 'Don't jump! . . . Don't come in here, muddle-head!' – remained glaring above us – all shining eyes, gleaming fangs, tumbled hair; resembling an amazed and half-witted fiend gloating over the extraordinary agitation of the damned. The boatswain adjured us to 'bear a hand', and a rope descended. We made things fast to it and they went up spinning, never to be seen by man again. A rage to fling things overboard possessed us. We worked fiercely, cutting our hands and speaking brutally to one another. Jimmy kept up a distracting row; he screamed piercingly, without drawing breath, like a tortured woman; he banged with hands and feet. The agony of his fear wrung our hearts so terribly that we longed to abandon him, to get out of that place deep as a well and swaying like a tree, to get out of his hearing, back on the poop where we could wait passively for death in incomparable repose. We shouted to him to 'shut up, for God's sake'. He redoubled his cries. He must have fancied we could not hear him. Probably he heard his own clamour but faintly. We could picture him crouching on the edge of the upper berth, letting out with both fists at the wood, in the dark, and with his mouth wide open for that unceasing cry. Those were loathsome moments. A cloud driving across the sun would darken the doorway menacingly. Every movement of the ship was pain. We scrambled about with no room to breathe, and felt frightfully sick. The boatswain yelled down at us: 'Bear a hand! Bear a hand! We two will be washed away from here directly if you ain't quick!' Three times a sea leaped over the high side and flung bucketfuls of water on our heads. Then Jimmy, startled by the shock, would stop his noise for a moment – waiting for the ship to sink, perhaps – and began again, distressingly loud, as if invigorated by the gust of fear. At the bottom the nails lay in a layer several inches thick. It was ghastly. Every nail in the world, not driven in firmly somewhere, seemed to have found its way into that carpenter's shop. There they were, of all kinds, the remnants of stores from seven voyages. Tin-tacks, copper tacks (sharp as needles), pump nails, with big heads, like tiny mushrooms; nails without any heads (horrible); French nails polished and slim. They lay in a solid mass more inabordable than a hedgehog. We hesitated, yearning for a shovel, while Jimmy below us yelled as though he had been flayed. Groaning, we dug our fingers in, and very much hurt, shook our hands, scattered nails and drops of blood. We passed up our hats full of assorted nails to the boatswain, who, as if performing a mysterious and appeasing rite, cast them wide upon a raging sea.

We got to the bulkhead at last. Those were stout planks. She was a ship, well finished in every detail – the *Narcissus* was. They were the stoutest planks ever put into a ship's bulkhead – we thought – and then we perceived that, in our hurry, we had sent all the tools overboard. Absurd little Belfast wanted to break it down with his own weight, and with both feet leaped straight up like a springbok, cursing the Clyde shipwrights for not scamping their work. Incidentally he reviled all North Britain, the rest of the earth, the sea – and all his companions. He swore, as he alighted heavily on his heels, that he would never, never any more associate with any fool that 'hadn't savee enough to know his knee from his elbow'. He managed by his thumping to scare the last remnant of wits out of Jimmy. We could hear the object of our exasperated solicitude darting to and fro under the planks. He had cracked his voice at last, and could only squeak miserably. His back or else his head rubbed the planks, now here, now there, in a puzzling manner. He squeaked as he dodged the invisible blows. It was more heart-rending even than his yells. Suddenly Archie produced a crowbar. He had kept it back; also a small hatchet. We howled with satisfaction. He struck a mighty blow and small chips flew at our eyes. The boatswain above shouted: 'Look out! Look out there. Don't kill the man. Easy does it!' Wamibo, maddened with excitement, hung head down and insanely urged us: 'Hoo! Strook 'im! Hoo! Hoo!' We were afraid he would fall in and kill one of us and, hurriedly, we entreated the boatswain to 'shove the blamed Finn overboard'. Then, all together, we yelled down at the planks: 'Stand from under! Get forward,' and listened. We only heard the deep hum and moan of the wind above us, the mingled roar and hiss of the seas. The ship, as if overcome with despair, wallowed lifelessly, and our heads swam with that unnatural motion. Belfast clamoured: 'For the love of God, Jimmy, where are ye? ... Knock! Jimmy darlint! ... Knock! You bloody black beast! Knock!' He was as quiet as a dead man inside a grave; and, like men standing above a grave, we were on the verge of tears – but with vexation, the strain, the fatigue; with the great longing to be done with it, to get away, and lay down to rest somewhere where we could see our danger and breathe. Archie shouted: 'Gi'e me room!' We crouched behind him, guarding our heads, and he struck time after time in the joint of planks. They cracked. Suddenly the crowbar went half-way in through a splintered oblong hole. It must have missed Jimmy's head by less than an inch. Archie withdrew it quickly, and that infamous nigger rushed at the hole, put his lips to it, and whispered 'Help' in an almost extinct voice; he pressed his head to it, trying madly to get out through that opening one inch wide and three inches long. In our disturbed state we were absolutely paralysed by his incredible action. It seemed impossible to drive him away. Even Archie at last lost his composure. 'If ye don't clear oot I'll drive the crowbar thro' your head,' he shouted in a determined voice. He meant what he said, and his earnestness seemed to make an impression on Jimmy. He disappeared suddenly, and we set to prising and tearing at the planks with the eagerness of men trying to get at a mortal enemy, and spurred by the desire to tear him limb from limb. The wood split, cracked, gave way. Belfast plunged in head and shoulders and groped viciously. 'I've got 'im! Got 'im,' he shouted. 'Oh! There! ... He's gone; I've got 'im! ... Pull at my legs! ... Pull!' Wamibo hooted unceasingly. The boatswain shouted directions: 'Catch hold of his hair, Belfast; pull straight up, you two! ... Pull fair!' We pulled fair. We pulled Belfast out with a jerk, and dropped him with disgust. In a sitting posture, purple-faced, he sobbed despairingly: 'How can I hold on to 'is blooming short wool?' Suddenly

Jimmy's head and shoulders appeared. He stuck half-way, and with rolling eyes foamed at our feet. We flew at him with brutal impatience, we tore the shirt off his back, we tugged at his ears, we panted over him; and all at once he came away in our hands as though somebody had let go his legs. With the same movement, without a pause, we swung him up. His breath whistled, he kicked our upturned faces, he grasped two pairs of arms above his head, and he squirmed up with such precipitation that he seemed positively to escape from our hands like a bladder full of gas. Streaming with perspiration, we swarmed up the rope, and, coming into the blast of cold wind, gasped like men plunged into icy water. With burning faces we shivered to the very marrow of our bones. Never before had the gale seemed to us more furious, the sea more mad, the sunshine more merciless and mocking, and the position of the ship more hopeless and appalling. Every movement of her was ominous of the end of her agony and of the beginning of ours. We staggered away from the door, and, alarmed by a sudden roll, fell down in a bunch. It appeared to us that the side of the house was more smooth than glass and more slippery than ice. There was nothing to hang on to but a long brass hook used sometimes to keep back an open door. Wamibo held on to it and we held on to Wamibo, clutching our Jimmy. He had completely collapsed now. He did not seem to have the strength to close his hand. We stuck to him blindly in our fear. We were not afraid of Wamibo letting go (we remembered that the brute was stronger than any three men in the ship), but we were afraid of the hook giving way, and we also believed that the ship had made up her mind to turn over at last. But she didn't. A sea swept over us. The boatswain spluttered: 'Up and away. There's a lull. Away aft with you, or we will all go to the devil here.' We stood up surrounding Jimmy. We begged him to hold up, to hold on, at least. He glared with his bulging eyes, mute as a fish, and with all the stiffening knocked out of him. He wouldn't stand; he wouldn't even as much as clutch at our necks; he was only a cold black skin loosely stuffed with soft cotton wool; his arms and legs swung jointless and pliable; his head rolled about; the lower lip hung down, enormous and heavy. We pressed round him, bothered and dismayed; sheltering him we swung here and there in a body; and on the very brink of eternity we tottered all together with concealing and absurd gestures, like a lot of drunken men embraced with a stolen corpse.

Something had to be done. We had to get him aft. A rope was tied slack under his armpits, and, reaching up at the risk of our lives, we hung him on the foresheet cleet. He emitted no sound; he looked as ridiculously lamentable as a doll that had lost half its sawdust, and we started on our perilous journey over the main deck, dragging along with care that pitiful, that limp, that hateful burden. He was not very heavy, but had he weighed a ton he could not have been more awkward to handle. We literally passed him from hand to hand. Now and then we had to hang him up on a handy belaying-pin, to draw a breath and re-form the line. Had the pin broken he would have irretrievably gone into the Southern Ocean, but he had to take his chance of that; and after a little while, becoming apparently aware of it, he groaned slightly, and with a great effort whispered a few words. We listened eagerly. He was reproaching us with our carelessness in letting him run such risks: 'Now, after I got myself out from there,' he breathed out weakly. 'There' was his cabin. And he got himself out. We had nothing to do with it apparently! . . . No matter. . . . We went on and let him take his chances, simply because we could not help it; for though at that time we hated him more than ever – more than anything under heaven – we did not want to lose him. We had so far saved him; and it had become a personal matter between us and the sea. We meant to stick to him. Had we (by an incredible hypothesis) undergone similar toil and trouble for an empty cask, that cask would have become as precious to us as Jimmy was. More precious, in fact, because we would have had no reason to hate the cask. And we hated James Wait. We could not get rid of the monstrous suspicion that this astounding blackman was shamming sick, had been malingering heartlessly in the face of our toil, of our scorn, of our patience – and now was malingering in the face of our devotion – in the face of death. Our vague and imperfect morality rose with disgust at his unmanly lie. But he stuck to it manfully – amazingly. No! It couldn't be. He was at all extremity. His cantankerous temper was only the result of the provoking invincibleness of that death he felt by his side. Any man may be angry with such a masterful chum. But, then, what kind of men were we – with our thoughts! Indignation and doubt grappled within us in a scuffle that trampled upon the finest of our feelings. And we hated him because of the suspicion; we detested him because of the doubt. We could not scorn him safely – neither could we pity him without risk to our dignity. Se we hated him, and passed him carefully from hand to hand. We cried, 'Got him?' 'Yes. All right. Let go.' And he swung from one enemy to another, showing about as much of life as an old bolster would do. His eyes made two narrow white slits in the black face. The air escaped through his lips with a noise like the sound of bellows. We reached the poop ladder at last, and it being a comparatively safe place, we lay for a moment in an exhausted heap to rest a little. He began to mutter. We were always incurably anxious to hear what he had to say. This time he mumbled peevishly, 'It took you some time to come. I began to think the whole smart lot of you had been washed overboard. What kept you back? Hey? Funk?' We said nothing. With sighs we started again to drag him up. The secret and ardent desire of our hearts was the desire to beat him viciously with our fists about the head; and we handled him as tenderly as though he had been made of glass....

The return on the poop was like the return of wanderers after many years amongst people marked by the desolation of time. Eyes were turned slowly in their sockets glancing at us. Faint murmurs were heard, 'Have you got 'im after all?' The well-known faces looked strange and familiar; they seemed faded and grimy; they had a mingled expression of fatigue and eagerness. They seemed to have become much thinner during our absence, as if all these men had been starving for a long time in their abandoned attitudes. The captain, with a round turn of a rope on his wrist, and kneeling on one knee, swung with a face cold and stiff; but with living eyes he was still holding the ship up, heeding no one, as if lost in the unearthly effort of that endeavour. We fastened up James Wait in a safe place. Mr Baker scrambled along to lend a hand. Mr Creighton, on his back, and very pale, muttered, 'Well done,' and gave us, Jimmy, and the sky, a scornful glance, then closed his eyes slowly. Here and there a man stirred a little, but most of them remained apathetic, in cramped positions, muttering between shivers. The sun was setting. A sun enormous, unclouded and red, declining low as if bending down to look into their faces. The wind whistled across long sunbeams that, resplendent and cold, struck full on the dilated pupils of staring eyes without making them wink. The wisps of hair and the tangled beards were grey with the salt of the sea. The faces were earthy, and the dark patches under the eyes extended to the ears, smudged into the hollows of sunken cheeks. The lips were livid and thin, and when they moved it was with difficulty, as though they had been glued to the teeth. Some grinned sadly in the sunlight, shaking with cold. Others were sad and still. Charley, subdued by the sudden disclosure of the insignificance of his youth, darted fearful glances. The two smooth-faced Norwegians resembled decrepit children, staring stupidly. To leeward, on the edge of the horizon, black seas leaped up towards the glowing sun. It sank slowly, round and blazing, and the crests of waves splashed on the edge of the luminous circle. One of the Norwegians appeared to catch sight of it, and, after giving a violent start, began to speak. His voice, startling the others, made them stir. They moved their heads stiffly, or turning with difficulty, looked at him with surprise, with fear, or in grave silence. He chattered at the setting sun, nodding his head, while the big seas began to roll across the crimson disc; and over miles of turbulent waters the shadows of high waves swept with a running darkness the faces of men. A crested roller broke with a loud hissing roar, and the sun, as if put out, disappeared. The chattering voice faltered, went out together with the light. There were sighs. In the sudden lull that follows the crash of a broken sea a man said wearily, 'Here's that blooming Dutchman gone off his chump.' A seaman, lashed by the middle, tapped the deck with his open hand with unceasing quick flaps. In the gathering greyness of twilight a bulky form was seen rising aft, and began marching on all fours with the movements of some big cautious beast. It was Mr Baker passing along the line of men. He grunted encouragingly over every one, felt their fastenings. Some, with half-open eyes, puffed like men oppressed by heat; others mechanically and in dreamy voices answered him, 'Aye! aye! sir!' He went from one to another grunting, 'Ough! ... See her through it yet'; and unexpectedly, with loud angry outbursts, blew up Knowles for cutting off a long piece from the fall of the relieving tackle. 'Ough! ... Ashamed of yourself ... Relieving tackle ... Don't you know better! ... Ough! ... Able seaman! Ough!' The lame man was crushed. He muttered, 'Get som'think for a lashing for myself, sir.' Ough! Lashing ... yourself. Are you a tinker or a sailor ... What? Ough! ... May want that tackle directly.... Ough! ... More use to the ship than your lame carcass. Ough! ... Keep it! ... Keep it, now you've done it.' He crawled away slowly, muttering to himself about some men being 'worse than children'. It had been a comforting row. Low exclamations were heard: 'Hallo ... Hallo.' ... Those who had been painfully dozing asked with convulsive starts, 'What's up? ... What is it?' The answers came with unexpected cheerfulness: 'The mate is going bald-headed for lame Jack about something or other' – 'No!' – 'What 'as he done?' Someone even chuckled. It was like a whiff of hope, like a reminder of safe days. Donkin, who had been stupefied with fear, revived suddenly and began to shout: ''Ear 'im; that's the way they tawlk to us. Vy donch 'ee 'it 'im – one ov yer? 'It 'im. 'It 'im! Comin' the mate over us. We are as good men as 'ee! We're all goin' to 'ell now. We 'ave been starved in this rotten ship, an' now we're goin' to be drowned for them black 'earted bullies! 'It 'im!' He shrieked in the deepening gloom, he blubbered and sobbed, screaming: ''It 'im! 'It 'im!' The rage and fear of his disregarded right to live tried the steadfastness of hearts more than the menacing shadows of the night that advanced through the unceasing clamour of the gale. From aft Mr Baker was heard: 'Is one of you men going to stop him – must I come along?' 'Shut up!' ... 'Keep quiet!' cried various voices, exasperated, trembling with cold. 'You'll get one across the mug from me directly,' said an invisible seaman, in a weary tone. 'I won't let the mate have the trouble.' He ceased and lay still with the silence of despair. On the black sky the stars, coming out, gleamed over an inky sea that, speckled with foam, flashed back at them the evanescent and pale light of a dazzling whiteness born from the black turmoil of the waves. Remote in the eternal calm they glittered hard and cold above the uproar of the earth; they surrounded the vanquished and tormented ship on all sides; more pitiless than the eyes of a triumphant mob, and as unapproachable as the hearts of men.

The icy south wind howled exultingly under the sombre splendour of the sky. The cold shook the men with a resistless violence as though it had tried to shake them to pieces. Short moans were swept unheard off the stiff lips. Some complained in mutters of 'not feeling themselves below the waist'; while those who had closed their eyes, imagined they had a block of ice on their chests. Others, alarmed at not feeling any pain in their fingers, beat the deck feebly with their hands – obstinate and exhausted. Wamibo stared vacant and dreamy. The Scandinavians kept on a meaningless mutter through chattering teeth. The spare Scotchmen, with determined efforts, kept their lower jaws still. The West-country men lay big and stolid in an invulnerable surliness. A man yawned and swore in turns. Another breathed with a rattle in his throat. Two elderly hard-weather shellbacks, fast side by side, whispered dismally to one another about the landlady of a boarding-house in Sunderland, whom they both knew. They extolled her motherliness and her liberality; they tried to talk about the joint of beef and the big fire in the downstairs kitchen. The words dying faintly on their lips, ended in light sighs. A sudden voice cried into the cold night, 'Oh Lord!' No one changed his position or took any notice of the cry. One or two passed, with a repeated and vague gesture, their hand over their faces, but most of them kept very still. In the benumbed immobility of their bodies they were excessively wearied by their thoughts, which rushed with the rapidity and vividness of dreams. Now and then, by an abrupt and startling exclamation, they answered the weird hail of some illusion; then, again, in silence contemplated the vision of known faces and familiar things. They recalled the aspect of forgotten shipmates and heard the voice of dead and gone skippers. They remembered the noise of gaslit streets, the steamy heat of tap-rooms or the scorching sunshine of calm days at sea.

Mr Baker left his insecure place, and crawled, with stoppages, along the poop. In the dark and on all fours he resembled some carnivorous animal prowling amongst corpses. At the break, propped to windward of a stanchion, he looked down on the main deck. It seemed to him that the ship had a tendency to stand up a little more. The wind had eased a little, he thought, but the sea ran as high as ever. The waves foamed viciously, and the lee side of the deck disappeared under a hissing whiteness as of boiling milk, while the rigging sang steadily with a deep vibrating note, and, at every upward swing of the ship, the wind rushed with a long-drawn clamour amongst the spars. Mr Baker watched very still. A man near him began to make a blabbing noise with his lips, all at once and very loud, as though the cold had broken brutally through him. He went on: 'Ba – ba – ba – brrr – brr – ba – ba.' 'Stop that!' cried Mr Baker, groping in the dark. 'Stop it!' He went on shaking the leg he found under his hand. 'What is it, sir?' called out Belfast, in the tone of a man awakened suddenly; 'we are looking after that 'ere Jimmy.' 'Are you? Ough! Don't make that row then. Who's that near you?' 'It's me – the boatswain, sir,' growled the West-country man; 'we are trying to keep life in that poor devil.' 'Aye, aye!' said Mr Baker. 'Do it quietly, can't you.' 'He wants us to hold him up above the rail,' went on the boatswain, with irritation, 'says he can't breathe here under our jackets.' 'If we lift 'im, we drop 'im overboard,' said another voice, 'we can't feel our hands with cold.' 'I don't care. I am choking!' exclaimed James Wait in a clear tone. 'Oh, no, my son,' said the boatswain, desperately, 'you don't go till we all go on this fine night.' 'You will see yet many a worse,' said Mr Baker, cheerfully. 'It's no child's play, sir!' answered the boatswain. 'Some of us further aft, here, are in a pretty bad way.' 'If the blamed sticks had been cut out of her she would be running along on her bottom now like any decent ship, an' giv' us all a chance,' said someone, with a sigh. 'The old man wouldn't have it . . . much he cares for us,' whispered another. 'Care for you!' exclaimed Mr Baker, angrily. 'Why should he care for you? Are you a lot of women passengers to be taken care of? We are here to take care of the ship – and some of you ain't up to that. Ough! . . . What have you done so very smart to be taken care of? Ough! . . . Some of you can't stand a bit of a breeze without crying over it.' 'Come, sorr. We ain't so bad,' protested Belfast, in a voice shaken by shivers; 'we ain't . . . brrr . . .' 'Again,' shouted the mate, grabbing at the shadowy form; 'again! . . . Why, you're in your shirt! What have you done?' 'I've put my oilskin and jacket over that half-dead nayggur – and he says he chokes,' said Belfast, complainingly. 'You wouldn't call me nigger if I wasn't half dead, you Irish beggar!' boomed James Wait, vigorously. 'You ... brrr ... You wouldn't be white if you were ever so well ... I will fight you ... brrrr ... in fine weather ... brrr ... with one hand tied behind my back ... brrrrrr ..' 'I don't want your rags – I want air,' gasped out the other faintly, as if suddenly exhausted.

The sprays swept over whistling and pattering. Men disturbed in their peaceful torpor by the pain of quarrelsome shouts, moaned, muttering curses. Mr Baker crawled off a little way to leeward where a watercask loomed up big, with something white against it. 'Is it you, Podmore?' asked Mr Baker. He had to repeat the question twice before the cook turned, coughing feebly. 'Yes, sir. I've been praying in my mind for a quick deliverance; for I am prepared for any call. ... I—' 'Look here, cook,' interrupted Mr Baker, 'the men are perishing with cold.' 'Cold!' said the cook, mournfully; 'they will be warm enough before long.' 'What?' asked Mr Baker, looking along the deck into the faint sheen of frothing water. 'They are a wicked lot,' continued the cook solemnly, but in an unsteady voice, 'about as wicked as any ship's company in this sinful world! Now, I' – he trembled so that he could hardly speak; his was an exposed place, and in a cotton shirt, a thin pair of trousers, and with his knees under his nose, he received, quaking, the flicks of stinging, salt drops; his voice sounded exhausted – 'now, I – any time ... My eldest youngster, Mr Baker ... a clever boy ... last Sunday on shore before this voyage he wouldn't go to church, sir. Says I, "You go and clean yourself, or I'll know the reason why!" What does he do? ... Pond Mr Baker – fell into the pond in his best rig, sir! ... Accident? ... "Nothing will save you, fine scholar though you are!" says I.... Accident! ... I whopped him, sir, till I couldn't lift my arm....' His voice faltered. 'I whopped 'im!' he repeated, rattling his teeth; then, after a while, let out a mournful sound that was half a groan, half a snore. Mr Baker shook him by the shoulders. 'Hey! Cook! Hold up, Podmore! Tell me – is there any fresh water in the galley tank? The ship is lying along less, I think; I would try to get forward. A little water would do them good. Hallo! Look out! Look out!' The cook struggled. 'Not you, sir – not you!' He began to scramble to windward. 'Galley! . . . my business!' he shouted. 'Cook's going crazy now,' said several voices. He yelled: 'Crazy, am I? I am more ready to die than any of you, officers incloosive – there! As long as she swims I will cook! I will get you coffee.' 'Cook, ye are a gentleman!' cried Belfast. But the cook was already going over the weather-ladder. He stopped for a moment to shout back on the poop: 'As long as she swims I will cook!' and disappeared as though he had gone overboard. The men who had heard sent after him a cheer that sounded like a wail of sick children. An hour or more afterwards some one said distinctly: 'He's gone for good.' 'Very likely,' assented the boatswain; 'even in fine weather he was as smart about the deck as a milch-cow on her first voyage. We ought to go and see.' Nobody moved. As the hours dragged slowly through the darkness Mr Baker crawled back and forth along the poop several times. Some men fancied they had heard him exchange murmurs with the master, but at that time the memories were incomparably more vivid than anything actual, and they were not certain whether the murmurs were heard now or many years ago. They did not try to find out. A mutter more or less did not matter. It was too cold for curiosity, and almost for hope. They could not spare a moment or a thought from the great mental occupation of wishing to live. And the desire of life kept them alive, apathetic and enduring, under the cruel persistence of wind and cold; while the bestarred black dome of the sky revolved slowly above the ship, that drifted, bearing their patience and their suffering, through the stormy solitude of the sea.

Huddled close to one another, they fancied themselves utterly alone. They heard sustained loud noises, and again bore the pain of existence through long hours of profound silence. In the night they saw sunshine, felt warmth, and suddenly, with a start, thought that the sun would never rise upon a freezing world. Some heard laughter, listened to songs; others, near the end of the poop, could hear human shrieks, and opening their eyes, were surprised to hear them still, though very faint, and far away. The boatswain said: 'Why, it's the cook, hailing from forward, I think.' He hardly believed his own words or recognized his own voice. It was a long time before the man next to him gave a sign of life. He punched hard his other neighbour and said: 'The cook's shouting!' Many did not understand, others did not care; the majority further aft did not believe. But the boatswain and another man had the pluck to crawl away forward to see. They seemed to have been gone for hours, and were very soon forgotten. Then suddenly men who had been plunged in a hopeless resignation became as if possessed with a desire to hurt. They belaboured one another with fists. In the darkness they struck persistently anything soft they could feel near, and, with a greater effort than for a shout, whispered excitedly: 'They've got some hot coffee. . . . Bos'n got it. . . .' 'No! . . . Where?' – 'It's coming! Cook made it.' James Wait moaned. Donkin scrambled viciously, caring not where he kicked, and anxious that the officers should have none of it. It came in a pot, and they drank in turns. It was hot, and while it blistered the greedy palates, it seemed incredible. The men sighed out parting with the mug: 'How 'as he done it?' Some cried weakly: 'Bully for you, doctor!'

He had done it somehow. Afterwards Archie declared that the thing was 'meeraculous'. For many days we wondered, and it was the one ever-interesting subject of conversation to the end of the voyage. We asked the cook, in fine weather, how he felt when he saw his stove 'reared up on end'. We inquired, in the north-east trade and on serene evenings, whether he had to stand on his head to put things right somewhat. We suggested he had used his bread-board for a raft, and from there comfortably had stoked his grate; and we did our best to conceal our admiration under the wit of fine irony. He affirmed not to know anything about it, rebuked our levity, declared himself, with solemn animation, to have been the object of a special mercy for the saving of our unholy lives. Fundamentally he was right, no doubt; but he need not have been so offensively positive about it – he need not have hinted so often that it would have gone hard with us had he not been there, meritorious and pure, to receive the inspiration and the strength for the work of grace. Had we been saved by his recklessness or his agility, we could have at length become reconciled to the fact; but to admit our obligation to anybody's virtue and holiness alone was as difficult for us as for any other handful of mankind. Like many benefactors of humanity, the cook took himself too seriously, and reaped the reward of irreverence. We were not ungrateful, however. He remained heroic. His saying – *the* saying of his life – became proverbial in the mouths of men as are the sayings of conquerors or sages. Later, whenever one of us was puzzled by a task and advised to relinquish it, he would express his determination to persevere and to succeed by the words: 'As long as she swims I will cook!'

The hot drink helped us through the bleak hours that precede the dawn. The sky low by the horizon took on the delicate tints of pink and yellow like the inside of a rare shell. And higher, where it glowed with a pearly sheen, a small black cloud appeared, like a forgotten fragment of the night set in a border of dazzling gold. The beams of light skipped on the crests of waves. The eyes of men turned to the eastward. The sunlight flooded their weary faces. They were giving themselves up to fatigue as though they had done for ever with their work. On Singleton's black oilskin coat the dried salt glistened like hoar frost. He hung on by the wheel, with open and lifeless eyes. Captain Allistoun, unblinking, faced the rising sun. His lips stirred, opened for the first time in twenty-four hours, and with a fresh firm voice he cried, 'Wear ship!'

The commanding sharp tones made all these torpid men start like a sudden flick of a whip. Then again, motionless where they lay, the force of habit made some of them repeat the order in hardly audible murmurs. Captain Allistoun glanced down at his crew, and several, with fumbling fingers and hopeless movements, tried to cast themselves adrift. He repeated impatiently, 'Wear ship. Now then, Mr Baker, get the men along. What's the matter with them?' 'Wear ship. Do you hear there? – Wear ship!' thundered out the boatswain suddenly. His voice seemed to break through a deadly spell. Men began to stir and crawl. 'I want the fore-topmast staysail run up smartly,' said the master, very loudly; if you can't manage it standing up you must do it lying down – that's all. Bear a hand!' 'Come along! Let's give the old girl a chance,' urged the boatswain. 'Aye! aye! Wear ship!' exclaimed quavering voices. The forecastle men, with reluctant faces, prepared to go forward. Mr Baker pushed ahead grunting on all fours to show the way, and they followed him over the break. The others lay still with a vile hope in their hearts of not being required to move till they got saved or drowned in peace.

After some time they could be seen forward appearing on the forecastle head, one by one in unsafe attitudes; hanging on to the rails, clambering over the anchors; embracing the cross-head of the windlass or hugging the fore-capstan. They were restless with strange exertions, waved their arms, knelt, lay flat down, staggered up, seemed to strive their hardest to go overboard. Suddenly a small white piece of canvas fluttered amongst them, grew larger, beating. Its narrow head rose in jerks – and at last it stood distended and triangular in the sunshine. 'They have done it!' cried the voices aft. Captain Allistoun let go the rope he had round his wrist and rolled to leeward headlong. He could be seen casting the lee main braces off the pins while the back-wash splashed over him. 'Square the main yard!' he shouted up to us – who stared at him in wonder. We hesitated to stir. 'The main brace, men. Haul! haul anyhow! Lay on your backs and haul!' he screeched, half drowned down there. We did not believe we could move the main yard, but the strongest and the less discouraged tried to execute the order. Others assisted half-heartedly. Singleton's eyes blazed suddenly as he took a fresh grip of the spokes. Captain Allistoun fought his way up to windward. 'Haul men! Try to move it! Haul, and help the ship.' His hard face worked suffused and furious. 'Is she going off, Singleton?' he cried. 'Not a move yet, sir,' croaked the old seaman in a horribly hoarse voice. 'Watch the helm, Singleton,' spluttered the master. 'Haul men! Have you no more strength than rats? Haul, and earn your salt.' Mr Creighton, on his back, with a swollen leg and a face as white as a piece of paper, blinked his eyes; his bluish lips twitched. In the wild scramble men grabbed at him, crawled over his hurt leg, knelt on his chest. He kept perfectly still, setting his teeth without a moan, without a sigh. The master's ardour, the cries of that silent man inspired us. We hauled and hung in bunches on the rope. We heard him say with violence to Donkin, who sprawled abjectly on his stomach: 'I will brain you with this belaying pin if you don't catch hold of the brace,' and that victim of men's injustice, cowardly and cheeky, whimpered: 'Are you goin' to murder us now,' while with sudden desperation he gripped the rope. Men sighed, shouted, hissed meaningless words, groaned. The yards moved, came slowly square against the wind, that hummed loudly on the yard-arms. 'Going off, sir,' shouted Singleton, 'she's just started.' 'Catch a turn with that brace. Catch a turn!' clamoured the master. Mr Creighton, nearly suffocated and unable to move, made a mighty effort, and with his left hand managed to nip the rope. 'All fast!' cried someone. He closed his eyes as if going off into a swoon, while huddled together about the brace we watched with scared looks what the ship would do now.

She went off slowly as though she had been weary and disheartened like the men she carried. She paid off very gradually, making us hold our breath till we choked, and as soon as she had brought the wind abaft the beam she started to move, and fluttered our hearts. It was awful to see her, nearly overturned, begin to gather way and drag her submerged side through the water. The dead-eyes of the rigging churned the breaking seas. The lower half of the deck was full of mad whirlpools and eddies; and the long line of the lee rail could be seen showing black now and then in the swirls of a field of foam as dazzling and white as a field of snow. The wind sang shrilly amongst the spars; and at every slight lurch we expected her to slip to the bottom sideways from under our backs. When dead before it she made the first distinct attempt to stand up, and we encouraged her with a feeble and discordant howl. A great sea came running up aft and hung for a moment over us with a curling top; then crashed down under the counter and spread out on both sides into a great sheet of bursting froth. Above its fierce hiss we heard Singleton's croak: 'She is steering!' He had both his feet now planted firmly on the grating, and the wheel spun fast as he eased the helm. 'Bring the wind on the port quarter and steady her!' called out the master, staggering to his feet, the first man up from amongst our prostrate heap. One of two screamed with excitement: 'She rises!' Far away forward, Mr Baker and three others were seen erect and black on the clear sky, lifting their arms, and with open mouths as though they had been shouting all together. The ship trembled, trying to lift her side, lurched back, seemed to give up with a nerveless dip, and suddenly with an unexpected jerk swung violently to windward, as though she had torn herself out from a deadly grasp. The whole immense volume of water, lifted by her deck, was thrown bodily across to starboard. Loud cracks were heard. Iron ports breaking open thundered with ringing blows. The water topped over the starboard rail with the rush of a river falling over a dam. The sea on deck, and the seas on every side of her, mingled together in a deafening roar. She rolled violently. We got up and were helplessly run or flung about from side to side. Men, rolling over and over, yelled: 'The house will go!' – 'She clears herself!' Lifted by a towering sea she ran along with it for a moment, spouting thick streams of water through every opening of her wounded sides. The lee braces having been carried away or washed off the pins, all the ponderous yards on the fore swung from side to side and with appalling rapidity at every roll. The men forward were seen crouching here and there with fearful glances upwards at the enormous spars that whirled about over their heads. The torn canvas and the ends of broken gear streamed in the wind like wisps of hair. Through the clear sunshine, over the flashing turmoil and uproar of the seas, the ship ran blindly, dishevelled and headlong, as if fleeing for her life; and on the poop we spun, we tottered about, distracted and noisy. We all spoke at once in a thin babble; we had the aspect of invalids and the gestures of maniacs. Eyes shone, large and haggard, in smiling, meagre faces that seemed to have been dusted over with powdered chalk. We stamped, clapped our hands, feeling ready to jump and do anything; but in reality hardly able to keep on our feet. Captain Allistoun, hard and slim, gesticulated madly from the poop at Mr Baker: 'Steady these fore-yards! Steady them the best you can!' On the main deck, men excited by his cries, splashed, dashing aimlessly here and there with the foam swirling up to their waists. Apart, far aft, and alone by the helm, old Singleton had deliberately tucked his white beard under the top button of his glistening coat. Swaying upon the din and tumult of the seas, with the whole battered length of the ship launched forward in a rolling rush before his steady old eyes, he stood rigidly still, forgotten by all, and with an attentive face. In front of his erect figure only two arms moved crosswise with a swift and sudden readiness, to check or urge again the rapid stir of circling spokes. He steered with care.

4

On men reprieved by its disdainful mercy, the immortal sea confers in its justice the full privilege of desired unrest. Through the perfect wisdom of its grace they are not permitted to meditate at ease upon the complicated and acrid savour of existence. They must without pause justify their life to the eternal pity that commands toil to be hard and unceasing, from sunrise to sunset, from sunset to sunrise; till the weary succession of nights and days tainted by the obstinate clamour of sages, demanding bliss and an empty heaven, is redeemed at last by the vast silence of pain and labour, by the dumb fear and the dumb courage of men obscure, forgetful, and enduring.

The master and Mr Baker coming face to face stared for a moment, with the intense and amazed looks of men meeting unexpectedly after years of trouble. Their voices were gone, and they whispered desperately at one another. 'Anyone missing?' asked Captain Allistoun. 'No. All there.' 'Anybody hurt?' 'Only the second mate.' 'I will look after him directly. We're lucky.' 'Very,' articulated Mr Baker, faintly. He gripped the rail and rolled bloodshot eyes. The little grey man made an effort to raise his voice above a dull mutter, and fixed his chief mate with a cold gaze, piercing like a dart. 'Get sail on the ship,' he said, speaking authoritatively and with an inflexible snap of his thin lips. 'Get sail on her as soon as you can. This is a fair wind. At once, sir – Don't give the men time to feel themselves. They will get done up and stiff, and we will never ... We must get her along now ...' He reeled to a long heavy roll; the rail dipped into the glancing, hissing water. He caught a shroud, swung helplessly against the mate ... 'now we have a fair wind at last.... Make ... sail.' His head rolled from shoulder to shoulder. His eyelids began to beat rapidly. 'And the pumps ... pumps, Mr Baker.' He peered as though the face within a foot of his eyes had been half a mile off. 'Keep the men on the move to ... to get her 'long,' he mumbled in a drowsy tone, like a man going off into a doze. He pulled himself together suddenly. 'Mustn't stand. Won't do,' he said with a painful attempt at a smile. He let go his hold, and, propelled by the dip of the ship, ran aft unwillingly, with small steps, till he brought up against the binnacle stand. Hanging on there he looked up in an objectless manner at Singleton, who, unheeding him, watched anxiously the end of the jib-boom. 'Steering gear works all right?' he asked. There was a noise in the old seaman's throat, as though the words had been rattling together before they could come out. 'Steers ... like a little boat,' he said, at last, with hoarse tenderness, without giving the master as much as half a glance – then, watchfully, spun the wheel down, steadied, flung it back again. Captain Allistoun tore himself away from the delight of leaning against the binnacle, and began to walk the poop, swaying and reeling to preserve his balance....

The pump-rods, clanking, stamped in short jumps while the fly-wheels turned smoothly, with great speed, at the foot of the mainmast, flinging back and forth with a regular impetuosity two limp clusters of men clinging to the handles. They abandoned themselves, swaying from the hip with twitching faces and stony eyes. The carpenter, sounding from time to time, exclaimed mechanically: 'Shake her up! Keep her going!' Mr Baker could not speak, but found his voice to shout; and under the goad of his objurgations, men looked to the lashings, dragged out new sails; and thinking themselves unable to move, carried heavy blocks aloft – overhauled the gear. They went up the rigging with faltering and desperate efforts. Their heads swam as they shifted their hold, stepped blindly on the yards like men in the dark; or trusted themselves to the first rope at hand with the negligence of exhausted strength. The narrow escapes from falls did not disturb the languid beat of their hearts; the roar of the seas seething far below them sounded continuous and faint like an indistinct noise from another world: the wind filled their eyes with tears, and with heavy gusts tried to push them off from where they swayed in insecure positions. With streaming faces and blowing hair they flew up and down between sky and water, bestriding the ends of yard-arms, crouching on foot-ropes, embracing lifts to have their hands free, or standing up against chain ties. Their thoughts floated vaguely between the desire of rest and the desire of life, while their stiffened fingers cast off head-earrings, fumbled for knives, or held with tenacious grip against the violent shocks of beating canvas. They glared savagely at one another, made frantic signs with one hand while they held their life in the other, looked down on the narrow strip of flooded deck, shouted along to leeward: 'Light-to!' ... 'Haul out!' ... 'Make fast!' Their lips moved, their eyes started, furious and eager with the desire to be understood, but the wind tossed their words unheard upon the disturbed sea. In an unendurable and unending strain they worked like men driven by a merciless dream to toil in an atmosphere of ice or flame. They burnt and shivered in turns. Their eyeballs smarted as if in the smoke of a conflagration; their heads were ready to burst with every shout. Hard fingers seemed to grip their throats. At every roll they thought: Now I must let go. It will shake us all off – and thrown about aloft they cried wildly: 'Look out there – catch the end.' ... 'Reeve clear' ... 'Turn this block....' They nodded desperately; shook infuriated faces, 'No! No! From down up.' They seemed to hate one another with a deadly hate. The longing to be done with it all gnawed their breasts, and the wish to do things well was a burning pain. They cursed their fate, contemned their life, and wasted their breath in deadly imprecations upon one another. The sailmaker, with his bald head bared, worked feverishly, forgetting his intimacy with so many admirals. The boatswain, climbing up with marlinspikes and bunches of spunyarn rovings, or kneeling on the yard and ready to take a turn with the midship-stop, had acute and fleeting visions of his old woman and the youngsters in a moorland village. Mr Baker, feeling very weak, tottered here and there, grunting and inflexible, like a man of iron. He waylaid those who, coming from aloft, stood gasping for breath. He ordered, encouraged, scolded. 'Now then – to the main topsail now! Tally on to that gantline. Don't stand about there!' 'Is there no rest for us?' muttered voices. He spun round fiercely, with a sinking heart. 'No! No rest till the work is done. Work till you drop. That's what you're here for.' A bowed seaman at his elbow gave a short laugh. 'Do or die,' he croaked bitterly, then spat into his broad palms, swung up his long arms, and grasping the rope high above his head sent out a mournful, wailing cry for a pull all together. A sea boarded the quarter-deck and sent the whole lot sprawling to leeward. Caps, handspikes floated. Clenched hands, kicking legs, with here and there a spluttering face, stuck out of the white hiss of foaming water. Mr Baker, knocked down with the rest, screamed: 'Don't let go that rope! Hold on to it! Hold!' And sorely bruised by the brutal fling, they held on to it, as though it had been the fortune of their life. The ship ran, rolling heavily, and the topping crests glanced past port and starboard flashing their white heads. Pumps were freed. Braces were rove. The three topsails and foresail were set. She spurted faster over the water, outpacing the swift rush of waves. The menacing thunder of distanced seas rose behind her – filled the air with the tremendous vibrations of its voice. And devastated, battered, and wounded she drove foaming to the northward, as though inspired by the courage of a high endeavour....

The forecastle was a place of damp desolation. They looked at their dwelling with dismay. It was slimy, dripping; it hummed hollow with the wind, and was strewn with shapeless wreckage like a half-tide cavern in a rocky and exposed coast. Many had lost all they had in the world, but most of the starboard watch had preserved their chests; thin streams of water trickled out of them, however. The beds were soaked; the blankets spread out and saved by some nail squashed under foot. They dragged wet rags from evil-smelling corners, and wringing the water out, recognized their property. Some smiled stiffly. Others looked round blank and mute. There were cries of joy over old waistcoats, and groans of sorrow over shapeless things found among the splinters of smashed bed boards. One lamp was discovered jammed under the bowsprit. Charley whimpered a little. Knowles stumped here and there, sniffing, examining dark places for salvage. He poured dirty water out of a boot, and was concerned to find the owner. Those who, overwhelmed by their losses, sat on the forepeak hatch, remained elbows on knees, and, with a fist against each cheek, disdained to look up. He pushed it under their noses. 'Here's a good boot. Yours?' They snarled, 'No – get out.' One snapped at him, 'Take it to hell out of this.' He seemed surprised. 'Why? It's a good boot,' but remembering suddenly that he had lost every stitch of his clothing, he dropped his find and began to swear. In the dim light cursing voices clashed. A man came in and, dropping his arms, stood still, repeating from the door-step, 'Here's a bloomin' old go! Here's a bloomin' old go!' A few rooted anxiously in flooded chests for tobacco. They breathed hard, clamoured with heads down. 'Look at that Jack!' ... 'Here! Sam! Here's my shore-going rig spoilt for ever.' One blasphemed tearfully holding up a pair of dripping trousers. No one looked at him. The cat came out from somewhere. He had an ovation. They snatched him from hand to hand, caressed him in a murmur of pet names. They wondered where he had 'weathered it out'; disputed about it. A squabbling argument began. Two men brought in a bucket of fresh water, and all crowded round it; but Tom, lean and mewing, came up with every hair astir and had the first drink. A couple of hands went aft for oil and biscuits.

Then in the yellow light and in the intervals of mopping the deck they crunched hard bread, arranging to 'worry through somehow'. Men chummed as to beds. Turns were settled for wearing boots and having the use of oilskin coats. They called one another 'old man' and 'sonny' in cheery voices. Friendly slaps resounded. Jokes were shouted. One or two stretched on the wet deck, slept with heads pillowed on their bent arms, and several, sitting on the hatch, smoked. Their weary faces appeared through a thin blue haze, pacified and with sparkling eyes. The boatswain put his head through the door. 'Relieve the wheel, one of you' – he shouted inside – 'it's six. Blamme if that old Singleton hasn't been there more'n thirty hours. You are a fine lot.' He slammed the door again. 'Mate's watch on deck,' said someone. 'Hey, Donkin, it's your relief!' shouted three or four together. He had crawled into an empty bunk and on wet planks lay still. 'Donkin, your wheel.' He made no sound. 'Donkin's dead,' guffawed someone. 'Sell 'is bloomin' clothes,' shouted another. 'Donkin, if ye don't go to the bloomin' wheel they will sell your clothes – d'ye hear?' jeered a third. He groaned from his dark hole. He complained about pains in all his bones, he whimpered pitifully. 'He won't go,' exclaimed a contemptuous voice, 'your turn Davis.' The young seaman rose painfully squaring his shoulders. Donkin stuck his head out, and it appeared in the yellow light, fragile and ghastly. 'I will giv' yer a pound of tobaccer,' he whined in a conciliating voice, 'so soon as I draw it from aft. I will – s'elp me....' Davis swung his arm backhanded and the head vanished. 'I'll go,' he said, 'but you will pay for it.' He walked unsteady but resolute to the door. 'So I will,' yelped Donkin, popping out behind him. 'So I will – s'elp me ... a pound ... three bob they chawrge.' Davis flung the door open. 'You will pay my price ... in fine weather,' he shouted over his shoulder. One of the men unbuttoned his wet coat rapidly, threw it at his head. 'Here, Taffy – take that, you thief!' 'Thank you!' he cried from the darkness above the swish of rolling water. He could be heard splashing; a sea came on board with a thump. 'He's got his bath already,' remarked a grim shellback. 'Aye, aye!' grunted the others. Then, after a long silence, Wamibo made strange noises. 'Hallo, what's up with you?' said someone grumpily. 'He says he would have gone for Davy,' explained Archie, who was the Finn's interpreter generally. 'I believe him!' cried voices.... 'Never mind, Dutchy' ... 'You'll do, muddle-head.' ... 'Your turn will come soon enough.' ... 'You don't know when ye're well off.' They ceased, and all together turned their faces to the door. Singleton stepped in, made two paces, and stood swaying slightly. The sea hissed, flowed roaring past the bows, and the forecastle trembled, full of deep murmurs; the lamp flared, swinging like a pendulum. He looked with a dreamy and puzzled stare, as though he could not distinguish the still men from their restless shadows. There were awe-struck exclamations: 'Hallo, hallo' ... 'How does it look outside now, Singleton?' Those who sat on the hatch lifted their eyes in silence, and the next oldest seaman in the ship (those two understood one another, though they hardly exchanged three words in a day) gazed up at his friend attentively for a moment, then taking a short clay pipe out of his mouth, offered it without a word. Singleton put out his arm towards it, missed, staggered, and suddenly fell forward, crashing down, stiff and headlong like an uprooted tree. There was a swift rush. Men pushed, crying: 'He's done!' ... 'Turn him over!' ... 'Stand clear there!' Under a crowd of startled faces bending over him he lay on his back, staring upwards in a continuous and intolerable manner. In the breathless silence of a general consternation, he said in a grating murmur: 'I am all right,' and clutched with his hands. They helped him up. He mumbled despondently: 'I am geting old . . . old.' 'Not you,' cried Belfast, with ready tact. Supported on all sides, he hung his head. 'Are you better?' they asked. He glared at them from under his eyebrows with large black eyes, spreading over his chest the bushy whiteness of a beard long and thick. 'Old! old!' he repeated sternly. Helped along, he reached his bunk. There was in it a slimy soft heap of something that smelt, as does at dead low water a muddy foreshore. It was his soaked straw bed. With a convulsive effort he pitched himself on it, and in the darkness of the narrow place could be heard growling angrily, like an irritated and savage animal uneasy in its den: 'Bit of breeze . . . small thing . . . can't stand up . . . old!' He slept at last, high-booted, sou'wester on head, and his oilskin clothes rustled, when with a deep sighing groan he turned over. Men conversed about him in quiet, concerned whispers. 'This will break 'im up' . . . 'Strong as a horse' . . . 'Aye. But he ain't what he used to be.' . . . In sad murmurs they gave him up. Yet at midnight he turned out to duty as if nothing had been the matter, and answered to his name with a mournful 'Here!' He brooded alone more than ever, in an impenetrable silence and with a saddened face. For many years he had heard himself called 'Old Singleton', and had serenely accepted the qualification, taking it as a tribute of respect due to a man who through half a century had measured his strength against the favours and the rages of the sea. He had never given a thought to his mortal self. He lived unscathed, as though he had been indestructible, surrendering to all the temptations, weathering many gales. He had panted in sunshine, shivered in the cold; suffered hunger, thirst, debauch; passed through many trials – known all the furies. Old! It seemed to him he was broken at last. And like a man bound treacherously while he sleeps, he woke up fettered by the long chain of disregarded years. He had to take up at once the burden of all his existence, and found it almost too heavy for his strength. Old! He moved his arms, shook his head, felt his limbs. Getting old . . . and then? He looked upon the immortal sea with the awakened and groping perception of its heartless might; he saw it unchanged, black and foaming under the eternal scrutiny of the stars; he heard its impatient voice calling for him out of pitiless vastness full of unrest, or turmoil, and terror. He looked afar upon it, and he saw an immensity tormented and blind, moaning and furious, that claimed all the days of his tenacious life, and when life was over, would claim the worn-out body of its slave. . . .

*

This was the last of the breeze. It veered quickly, changed to a black south-easter, and blew itself out, giving the ship a famous shove to the northward into the joyous sunshine of the trade. Rapid and white she ran homewards in a straight path, under a blue sky and upon the plain of a blue sea. She carried Singleton's completed wisdom, Donkin's delicate susceptibilities, and the conceited folly of us all. The hours of ineffective turmoil were forgotten; the fear and anguish of these dark moments were never mentioned in the glowing peace of fine days. Yet from that time our life seemed to start afresh as though we had died and had been resuscitated. All the first part of the voyage, the Indian Ocean on the other side of the Cape, all that was lost in a haze, like an ineradicable suspicion of some previous existence. It had ended – then there were blank hours: a livid blurr – and again we lived! Singleton was possessed of sinister truth; Mr Creighton of a damaged leg; the cook of fame – and shamefully abused the opportunities of his distinction. Donkin had an added grievance. He went about repeating with insistence: ' 'E said 'e would brain me – did yer 'ear? They are goin' to murder us now for the least little thing.' We began at last to think it was rather awful. And we were conceited! We boasted of our pluck, of our capacity for work, of our energy. We remembered honourable episodes: our devotion, our indomitable perseverance – and were proud of them as though they had been the outcome of our unaided impulses. We remembered our danger, our toil – and conveniently forgot our horrible scare. We decried our officers – who had done nothing – and listened to the fascinating Donkin. His care for our rights, his disinterested concern for our dignity, were not discouraged by the invariable contumely of our words, by the disdain of our looks. Our contempt for him was unbounded – and we could not but listen with interest to that consummate artist. He told us we were good men – a 'bloomin' condemned lot of good men'. Who thanked us? Who took any notice of our wrongs? Didn't we lead a 'dorg's loife for two poun' ten a month?' Did we think that miserable pay enough to compensate us for the risk to our lives and for the loss of our clothes? 'We've lost every rag!' he cried. He made us forget that he, at any rate, had lost nothing of his own. The younger men listened, thinking – this 'ere Donkin's a long-headed chap, though no kind of man, anyhow. The Scandinavians were frightened at his audacities; Wamibo did not understand; and the older seamen thoughtfully nodded their heads making the thin gold earrings glitter in the fleshy lobes of hairy ears. Severe, sunburnt faces were propped meditatively on tattooed forearms. Veined, brown fists held in their knotted grip the dirty white clay of smouldering pipes. They listened, impenetrable, broad-backed, with bent shoulders, and in grim silence. He talked with ardour, despised and irrefutable. His picturesque and filthy loquacity flowed like a troubled stream from a poisoned source. His beady little eyes danced, glancing right and left, ever on the watch for the approach of an officer. Sometimes Mr Baker going forward to take a look at the head sheets would roll with his uncouth gait through the sudden stillness of the men; or Mr Creighton limped along, smooth-faced, youthful, and more stern than ever, piercing our short silence with a keen glance of his clear eyes. Behind his back Donkin would begin again darting stealthy, sidelong looks. ''Ere's one of 'em. Some of yer 'as made 'im fast that day. Much thanks yer got for it. Ain't 'ee a-drivin' yer wusse'n ever? . . . Let 'im slip overboard. . . . Vy not? It would 'ave been less trouble. Vy not?' He advanced confidentially, backed away with great effect; he whispered, he screamed, waved his miserable arms no thicker than pipestems – stretched his lean neck – spluttered – squinted. In the pauses of his impassioned orations the wind sighed quietly aloft, the calm sea unheeded murmured in a warning whisper along the ship's side. We abominated the creature and could not deny the luminous truth of his contentions. It was all so obvious. We were indubitably good men; our deserts were great and our pay small. Through our exertions we had saved the ship and the skipper would get the credit of it. What had he done? we wanted to know. Donkin asked: 'What 'ee could do without hus?' and we could not answer. We were oppressed by the injustice of the world, surprised to perceive how long we had lived under its burden without realizing our unfortunate state, annoyed by the uneasy suspicion of our undiscerning stupidity. Donkin assured us it was all our 'good 'eartedness', but we would not be consoled by such shallow sophistry. We were men enough to courageously admit to ourselves our intellectual shortcomings; though from that time we refrained from kicking him, tweaking his nose, or from accidentally knocking him about, which last, after we had weathered the Cape, had been rather a popular amusement. Davis ceased to talk to him provokingly about black eyes and flattened noses. Charley, much subdued since the gale, did not jeer at him. Knowles deferentially and with a crafty air propounded questions such as: 'Could we all have the same grub as the mates? Could we all stop ashore till we got it? What would be the next thing to try for if we got that?' He answered readily with contemptuous certitude; he strutted with assurance in clothes that were much too big for him as though he had tried to disguise himself. These were Jimmy's clothes mostly – though he would accept anything from anybody; but nobody, except Jimmy, had anything to spare. His devotion to Jimmy was unbounded. He was for ever dodging in the little cabin, ministering to Jimmy's wants, humouring his whims, submitting to his exacting peevishness, often laughing with him. Nothing could keep him away from the pious work of visiting the sick, especially when there was some heavy hauling to be done on deck. Mr Baker had on two occasions jerked him out from there by the scruff of the neck to our inexpressible scandal. Was a sick chap to be left without attendance? Were we to be ill-used for attending a shipmate? 'What?' growled Mr Baker, turning menacingly at the mutter, and the whole half-circle like one man stepped back a pace. 'Set the topmast stunsail. Away aloft, Donkin, overhaul the gear,' ordered the mate inflexibly. 'Fetch the sail along; bend the down-haul clear. Bear a hand.' Then, the sail set, he would go slowly aft and stand looking at the compass for a long time, careworn, pensive, and breathing hard as if stifled by the taint of unaccountable ill-will that pervaded the ship. 'What's up amongst them?' he thought. 'Can't make out this hanging back and growling. A good crowd, too, as they go nowadays.' On deck the men exchanged bitter words, suggested by a silly exasperation against something unjust and irremediable that would not be denied, and would whisper into their ears long after Donkin had ceased speaking. Our little world went on its curved and unswerving path carrying a discontented and aspiring population. They found comfort of a gloomy kind in an interminable and conscientious analysis of their unappreciated worth; and inspired by Donkin's hopeful doctrines they dreamed enthusiastically of the time when every lonely ship would travel over a serene sea, manned by a wealthy and well-fed crew of satisfied skippers.

It looked as if it would be a long passage. The south-east trades, light and unsteady, were left behind; and then, on the equator and under a low grey sky, the ship, in close heat, floated upon a smooth sea that resembled a sheet of ground glass. Thunder squalls hung on the horizon, circled round the ship, far off and growling angrily, like a troop of wild beasts afraid to charge home. The invisible sun, sweeping above the upright masts, made on the clouds a blurred stain of rayless light, and a similar patch of faded radiance kept pace with it from east to west over the unglittering level of the waters. At night, through the impenetrable darkness of earth and heaven, broad sheets of flame waved noiselessly; and for half a second the becalmed craft stood out with its masts and rigging, with every sail and every rope distinct and black in the centre of a fiery outburst, like a charred ship enclosed in a globe of fire. And, again, for long hours she remained lost in a vast universe of night and silence where gentle sighs wandering here and there like forlorn souls, made the still sails flutter as in sudden fear, and the ripple of a beshrouded ocean whisper its compassion afar – in a voice mournful, immense, and faint....

*

When the lamp was put out, and through the door thrown wide open, Jimmy, turning on his pillow, could see vanishing beyond the straight line of top-gallant rail, the quick, repeated visions of a fabulous world made up of leaping fire and sleeping water. The lightning gleamed in his big sad eyes that seemed in a red flicker to burn themselves out in his black face, and then he would lie blinded and invisible in the midst of an intense darkness. He could hear on the quiet deck soft footfalls, the breathing of some man lounging on the doorstep; the low creak of swaying masts; or the calm voice of the watch-officer reverberating aloft, hard and loud, amongst the unstirring sails. He listened with avidity, taking a rest in the attentive perception of the slightest sound from the fatiguing wanderings of his sleeplessness. He was cheered by the rattling of blocks, reassured by the stir and murmur of the watch, soothed by the slow yawn of some sleepy and weary seaman settling himself deliberately for a snooze on the planks. Life seemed an indestructible thing. It went on in darkness, in sunshine, in sleep; tireless, it hovered affectionately round the imposture of his ready death. It was bright, like the twisted flare of lightning, and more full of surprises than the dark night. It made him safe, and the calm of its overpowering darkness was as precious as its restless and dangerous light.

But in the evening, in the dog-watches, and even far into the first night-watch, a knot of men could always be seen congregated before Jimmy's cabin. They leaned on each side of the door peacefully interested and with crossed legs; they stood astride the doorstep discoursing, or sat in silent couples on his sea-chest; while against the bulwark along the spare topmast, three or four in a row stared meditatively; with their simple faces lit up by the projected glare of Jimmy's lamp. The little place, repainted white, had, in the night, the brilliance of a silver shrine where a black idol, reclining stiffly under a blanket, blinked its weary eyes and received our homage. Donkin officiated. He had the air of a demonstrator showing a phenomenon, a manifestation bizarre, simple, and meritorious that, to the beholders, should be a profound and an everlasting lesson. 'Just look at 'im, 'ee knows what's what – never fear!' he exclaimed now and then, flourishing a hand hard and fleshless like the claw of a snipe. Jimmy, on his back, smiled with reserve and without moving a limb. He affected the languor of extreme weakness, so as to make it manifest to us that our delay in hauling him out from his horrible confinement, and then that night spent on the poop among our selfish neglect of his needs, had 'done for him'. He rather liked to talk about it, and of course we were always interested. He spoke spasmodically, in fast rushes with long pauses between, as a tipsy man walks.... 'Cook had just given me a pannikin of hot coffee. ... Slapped it down there, on my chest – banged the door to. ... I felt a heavy roll coming; tried to save my coffee, burnt my fingers ... and fell out of my bunk.... She went over so quick. ... Water came in through the ventilator.... I couldn't move the door ... dark as a grave ... tried to scramble up into the upper berth.... Rats ... a rat bit my finger as I got up.... I could hear him swimming below me.... I thought you would never come.... I thought you were all gone overboard ... of course ... Could hear nothing but the wind.... Then you came ... to look for the corpse, I suppose. A little more and ...'

'Man! But ye made a rare lot of noise in here,' observed Archie, thoughtfully.

'You chaps kicked up such a confounded row above.... Enough to scare anyone.... I didn't know what you were up to.... Bash in the blamed planks ... my head.... Just what a silly, scary gang of fools would do.... Not much good to me anyhow.... Just as well ... drown.... Pah.'

He groaned, snapped his big white teeth, and gazed with scorn. Belfast lifted a pair of dolorous eyes, with a broken-hearted smile, clenched his fists stealthily; blue-eyed Archie caressed his red whiskers with a hesitating hand; the boatswain at the door stared a moment, and brusquely went away with a loud guffaw. Wamibo dreamed.... Donkin felt all over his sterile chin for the few rare hairs, and said, triumphantly, with a sidelong glance at Jimmy: 'Look at 'im! Wish I was 'arf has 'ealthy as 'ee is – I do.' He jerked a short thumb over his shoulder towards the after end of the ship. 'That's the blooming way to do 'em!' he yelped, with forced heartiness. Jimmy said: 'Don't be a damn fool,' in a pleasant voice. Knowles, rubbing his shoulder against the doorpost, remarked shrewdly: 'We can't all go an' be took sick – it would be mutiny.' 'Mutiny – gawn!' jeered Donkin, 'there's no bloomin' law against bein' sick.' 'There's six week's hard for refoosing dooty,' argued Knowles. 'I mind I once seed in Cardiff the crew of an overloaded ship – leastways she weren't overloaded, only a fatherly old gentleman with a white beard and an umbreller came along the quay and talked to the hands. Said as how it was crool hard to be drownded in winter just for the sake of a few pounds more for the owner – he said. Nearly cried over them – he did; and he had a square mainsail coat, and a gaff-topsail hat too – all proper. So they chaps they said they wouldn't go to be drownded in winter – depending upon that 'ere Plimsoll man to see 'em through the court. They thought to have a bloomin' lark and two or three days' spree. And the beak giv' 'em six weeks – coss the ship warn't overloaded. Anyways they made it out in court that she wasn't. There wasn't one overloaded ship in Penarth Dock at all. 'Pears that old coon he was only on pay and allowance from some kind people, under orders to look for overloaded ships, and he couldn't see no further than the length of his umbreller. Some of us in the boarding-house, where I live when I'm looking for a ship in Cardiff, stood by to duck that old weeping spunger in the dock. We kept a good look-out too – but he topped his boom directly he was outside the court. . . . Yes. They got six weeks' hard. . . .'

They listened, full of curiosity, nodding in the pauses their rough pensive faces. Donkin opened his mouth once or twice, but restrained himself. Jimmy lay still with open eyes and not at all interested. A seaman emitted the opinion that after a verdict of atrocious partiality 'the bloomin' beaks go an' drink at the skipper's expense'. Others assented. It was clear, of course. Donkin said: 'Well, six weeks ain't much trouble. You sleep all night in, reg'lar, in hokey. Do it on my 'ead.' 'You are used to it ainch'ee, Donkin?' asked somebody. Jimmy condescended to laugh. It cheered up everyone wonderfully. Knowles, with surprising mental agility, shifted his ground. 'If we all went sick what would become of the ship? eh?' He posed the problem and grinned all round. 'Let 'er go to 'ell,' sneered Donkin. 'Damn 'er. She ain't yourn.' 'What? Just let her drift?' insisted Knowles in a tone of unbelief. 'Aye! Drift, an' be blowed,' affirmed Donkin with fine recklessness. The other did not see it – meditated. 'The stores would run out,' he muttered, 'and . . . never get anywhere . . . and what about pay-day?' he added with greater assurance. 'Jack likes a good pay-day,' exclaimed a listener on the doorstep. 'Aye, because then the girls put one arm round his neck an' t'other in his pocket, and call him ducky. Don't they, Jack?' – 'Jack, you're a terror with the gals' – 'He takes three of 'em in tow to once, like one of 'em Watkinses two-funnel tugs waddling away with three schooners behind' – 'Jack, you're a lame scamp' – 'Jack, tell us about that one with a blue eye and a black one. Do' – 'There's plenty of girls with one black eye along the Highway by . . .' – 'No, that's a speshul one – come Jack.' Donkin looked severe and disgusted; Jimmy very bored; a grey-haired sea-dog shook his head slightly, smiling at the bowl of his pipe, discreetly amused. Knowles turned about bewildered; stammered first at one, then at another. 'No! . . . I never! . . . can't talk sensible sense midst you. . . . Always on the kid.' He retired bashfully – muttering and pleased. They laughed hooting in the crude light, around Jimmy's bed, where on a white pillow his hollowed black face moved to and fro restlessly. A puff of wind came, made the flame of the lamp leap, and outside, high up, the sails fluttered, while near by the block of the foresheet struck a ringing blow on the iron bulwark. A voice far off cried, 'Helm up!' another, more faint, answered, 'Hard-up, sir!' They became silent – waited expectantly. The grey-haired seaman knocked his pipe on the doorstep and stood up. The ship leaned over gently and the sea seemed to wake up, murmuring drowsily. 'Here's a little wind comin',' said someone very low. Jimmy turned over slowly to face the breeze. The voice in the night cried loud and commanding: 'Haul the spanker out.' The group before the door vanished out of the light. They could be heard tramping aft while they repeated with varied intonations: 'Spanker out!' . . . 'Out spanker, sir!' Donkin remained alone with Jimmy. There was a silence. Jimmy opened and shut his lips several times as if swallowing draughts of fresher air; Donkin moved the toes of his bare feet and looked at them thoughtfully.

'Ain't you going to give them a hand with the sail?' asked Jimmy.

'No. If six ov 'em ain't 'nough beef to set that blamed, rotten spanker, they ain't fit to live,' answered Donkin in a bored, faraway voice, as though he had been talking from the bottom of a hole. Jimmy considered the conical, fowl-like profile with a queer kind of interest; he was leaning out of his bunk with the calculating, uncertain expression of a man who reflects how best to lay hold of some strange creature that looks as though it could sting or bite. But he said only: 'The mate will miss you – and there will be ructions.'

Donkin got up to go. 'I will do for 'im some dark night; see if I don't,' he said over his shoulder.

Jimmy went on quickly. 'You're like a poll-parrot, like a screechin' poll-parrot.' Donkin stopped and cocked his head attentively on one side. His big ears stood out, transparent and veined, resembling the thin wings of a bat.

'Yuss?' he said, with his back towards Jimmy.

'Yes! Chatter out all you know – like . . . like a dirty white cockatoo.'

Donkin waited. He could hear the other's breathing, long and slow; the breathing of a man with a hundredweight or so on the breastbone. Then he asked calmly: 'What do I know?'

'What? . . . What I tell you . . . not much. What do you want . . . to talk about my health so. . . .'

'It's a blooming imposyshun. A bloomin', stinkin', first-class imposychun – but it don't tyke me in. Not it.'

Jimmy kept still. Donkin put his hands in his pockets, and in one slouching stride came up to the bunk.

'I talk – what's the odds. They ain't men 'ere – sheep they are. A driven lot of sheep. I 'old you up . . . Vy not? You're well orf.'

'I am . . . I don't say anything about that. . . .'

'Well. Let 'em see it. Let 'em larn what a man can do. I am a man, I know all about yer. . . .' Jimmy threw himself further away on the pillow; the other stretched out his skinny neck, jerked his bird face down at him as though pecking at the eyes. 'I am a man. I've seen the inside of every chokey in the Colonies rather'n give up my rights. . . .'

'You are a jail-prop,' said Jimmy, weakly.

'I am . . . an' proud of it, too. You! You 'aven't the bloomin' nerve – so you inventyd this 'ere dodge. . . .' He paused; then with marked afterthought accentuated slowly: 'Yer ain't sick – are yer?'

'No,' said Jimmy, firmly. 'Been out of sorts now and again this year,' he mumbled with a sudden drop in his voice.

Donkin closed one eye, amicable and confidential. He whispered: 'Ye 'ave done this afore 'aven'tchee?' Jimmy smiled – then as if unable to hold back he let himself go: 'Last ship – yes. I was out of sorts on the passage. See? It was easy. They paid me off in Calcutta, and the skipper made no bones about it either. . . . I got my money all right. Laid up fifty-eight days! The fools! O Lord! The fools! Paid right off.' He laughed spasmodically. Donkin chimed in giggling. Then Jimmy coughed violently. 'I am as well as ever,' he said, as soon as he could draw breath.

Donkin made a derisive gesture. 'In course,' he said, profoundly, 'anyone can see that.' 'They don't,' said Jimmy, gasping like a fish. 'They would swallow any yarn,' affirmed Donkin. 'Don't you let on too much,' admonished Jimmy in an exhausted voice. 'You're little gyme? Eh?' commented Donkin, jovially. Then with sudden disgust: 'Yer all for yerself, s'long as ye're right. . . .'

So charged with egoism James Wait pulled the blanket up to his chin and lay still for awhile. His heavy lips protruding in an everlasting black pout .'Why are you so hot on making trouble?' he asked without much interest.

' 'Cos it's a bloomin' shayme. We are put about . . . bad food, bad pay . . . I want us to kick up a bloomin' row; a blamed 'owling row that would make 'em remember! Knocking people about . . . brains us . . . indeed! Ain't we men?' His altruistic indignation blazed. Then he said calmly: 'I've been airing yer clothes.' 'All right,' said Jimmy, languidly, 'bring them in.' 'Giv' us the key of your chest, I'll put 'em away for yer,' said Donkin with friendly eagerness. 'Bring 'em in, I will put them away myself,' answered James Wait with severity. Donkin looked down, muttering. . . . 'What d'you say? What d'you say?' inquired Wait anxiously. 'Nothink. The night's dry, let 'em 'ang out till the morning,' said Donkin, in a strangely trembling voice, as though restraining laughter or rage. Jimmy seemed satisfied. 'Give me a little water for the night in my mug – there,' he said. Donkin took a stride over the doorstep. 'Git it yerself,' he replied in a surly tone. 'You can do it, unless you *are* sick.' 'Of course I can do it,' said Wait, 'only . . .' 'Well, then, do it,' said Donkin, viciously, 'if yer can look after yer clothes, yer can look after yerself.' He went on deck without a look back.

Jimmy reached out for the mug. Not a drop. He put it back gently with a faint sigh – and closed his eyes. He thought: That lunatic Belfast will bring me some water if I ask. Fool. I am very thirsty.... It was very hot in the cabin, and it seemed to turn slowly round, detach itself from the ship, and swing out smoothly into a luminous, arid space where a black sun shone, spinning very fast. A place without water! No water! A policeman with the face of Donkin drank a glass of beer by the side of an empty well, and flew away flapping vigorously. A ship whose mastheads protruded through the sky and could not be seen, was discharging grain, and the wind whirled the dry husks in spirals along the quay of a dock with no water in it. He whirled along with the husks – very tired and light. All his inside was gone. He felt lighter than the husks – and more dry. He expanded his hollow chest. The air streamed in carrying away in its rush a lot of strange things that resembled houses, trees, people, lamp-posts.... No more! There was no more air – and he had not finished drawing his long breath. But he was in jail! They were locking him up. A door slammed. They turned the key twice, flung a bucket of water over him – Phoo! What for?

He opened his eyes, thinking the fall had been very heavy for an empty man – empty – empty. He was in his cabin. Ah! All right! His face was streaming with perspiration, his arms heavier than lead. He saw the cook standing in the doorway, a brass key in one hand and a bright tin hook-pot in the other.

'I have locked up the galley for the night,' said the cook, beaming benevolently. 'Eight bells just gone. I brought you a pot of cold tea for your night's drinking, Jimmy. I sweetened it with some white cabin sugar, too. Well – it won't break the ship.'

He came in, hung the pot on the edge of the bunk, asked perfunctorily, 'How goes it?' and sat down on the box. 'H'm,' grunted Wait, inhospitably. The cook wiped his face with a dirty cotton rag, which, afterwards, he tied round his neck. 'That's how them firemen do in steamboats,' he said, serenely, and much pleased with himself. 'My work is as heavy as theirs – I'm thinking – and longer hours. Did you ever see them down the stokehold? Like fiends they look – firing – firing – firing – down there.'

He pointed his forefinger at the deck. Some gloomy thought darkened his shining face, fleeting, like the shadow of a travelling cloud over the light of a peaceful sea. The relieved watch tramped noisily forward, passing in a body across the sheen of the doorway. Someone cried, 'Good night!' Belfast stopped for a moment and looked at Jimmy, quivering and speechless with repressed emotion. He gave the cook a glance charged with dismal foreboding, and vanished. The cook cleared his throat. Jimmy stared upwards and kept as still as a man in hiding.

The night was clear, with a gentle breeze. Above the mastheads the resplendent curve of the Milky Way spanned the sky like a triumphal arch of eternal light, thrown over the dark pathway of the earth. On the forecastle head a man whistled with loud precision a lively jig, while another could be heard faintly, shuffling and stamping in time. There came from forward a confused murmur of voices, laughter – snatches of song. The cook shook his head, glanced obliquely at Jimmy, and began to mutter. 'Aye. Dance and sing. That's all they think of. I am surprised that Providence don't get tired.... They forget the day that's sure to come ... but you....'

Jimmy drank a gulp of tea, hurriedly, as though he had stolen it, and shrank under his blanket, edging away towards the bulkhead. The cook got up, closed the door, then sat down again and said distinctly:

'Whenever I poke my galley fire I think of you chaps – swearing, stealing, lying, and worse – as if there was no such thing as another world.... Not bad fellows, either, in a way,' he conceded, slowly; then, after a pause of regretful musing, he went on in a resigned tone: 'Well, well. They will have a hot time of it. Hot! Did I say? The furnaces of one of them White Star boats ain't nothing to it.'

He kept very quiet for a while. There was a great stir in his brain; an addled vision of bright outlines; an exciting row of rousing songs and groans of pain. He suffered, enjoyed, admired, approved. He was delighted, frightened, exalted – as on that evening (the only time in his life – twenty-seven years ago; he loved to recall the number of years) when as a young man he had – through keeping bad company – become intoxicated in an East End music-hall. A tide of sudden feeling swept him clean out of his body. He soared. He contemplated the secret of the hereafter. It commended itself to him. It was excellent; he loved it, himself, all hands, and Jimmy. His heart overflowed with tenderness, with comprehension, with the desire to meddle, with anxiety for the soul of that black man, with the pride of possessed eternity, with the feeling of might. Snatch him up in his arms and pitch him right into the middle of salvation. . . . The black soul – blacker – body – rot – Devil. No! Talk – strength – Samson. . . . There was a great din as of cymbals in his ears; he flashed through an ecstatic jumble of shining faces, lilies, prayer-books, unearthly joy, white shirts, gold harps, black coats, wings. He saw flowing garments, clean-shaved faces, a sea of light – a lake of pitch. There were sweet scents, a smell of sulphur – red tongues of flame licking a white mist. An awesome voice thundered! . . . It lasted three seconds.

'Jimmy!' he cried in an inspired tone. Then he hesitated. A spark of human pity glimmered yet through the infernal fog of his supreme conceit.

'What?' said James Wait, unwillingly. There was a silence. He turned his head just the least bit, and stole a cautious glance. The cook's lips moved without a sound; his face was rapt, his eyes turned up. He seemed to be mentally imploring deck beams, the brass hook of the lamp, two cockroaches.

'Look here,' said Wait, 'I want to go to sleep. I think I could.'

'This is no time for sleep!' exclaimed the cook, very loud. He had prayerfully divested himself of the last vestige of his humanity. He was a voice – a fleshless and sublime thing, as on that memorable night – the night when he went walking over the sea to make coffee for perishing sinners. 'This is no time for sleeping,' he repeated with exaltation. '*I* can't sleep.'

'Don't care damn,' said Wait, with factitious energy. 'I can. Go an' turn in.'

'Swear . . . in the very jaws! . . . In the very jaws! Don't you see the everlasting fire . . . don't you feel it? Blind, chock-full of sin! Repent, repent! I can't bear to think of you. I hear the call to save you. Night and day. Jimmy, let me save you!' The words of entreaty and menace broke out of him in a roaring torrent. The cockroaches ran away. Jimmy perspired, wriggling stealthily under the blanket. The cook yelled. . . . 'Your days are numbered! . . .' 'Get out of this,' boomed Wait, courageously. 'Pray with me! . . .' 'I won't! . . .' The little cabin was as hot as an oven. It contained an immensity of fear and pain; an atmosphere of shrieks and moans; prayers vociferated like blasphemies and whispered curses. Outside, the men called by Charley, who informed them in tones of delight that there was a holy row going on in Jimmy's place, crowded before the closed door, too startled to open it. All hands were there. The watch below had jumped out on deck in their shirts, as after a collision. Men running up, asked: 'What is it?' Others said: 'Listen!' The muffled screaming went on: 'On your knees! On your knees!' – 'Shut up!' – 'Never! You are delivered into my hands. . . . Your life has been saved. . . . Purpose. . . . Mercy. . . . Repent.' 'You are a crazy fool! . . .' 'Account of you . . . you . . . Never sleep in this world, if I . . .' 'Leave off.' 'No! . . . stokehold . . . only think! . . .' Then an impassioned screeching babble where words pattered like hail. 'No!' shouted Wait. 'Yes. You are! . . . No help. . . . Everybody says so.' 'You lie!' 'I see you dying this minyt . . . before my eyes . . . as good as dead already.' 'Help!' shouted Jimmy, piercingly. 'Not in this valley. . . . look upwards,' howled the other. 'Go away! Murder! Help!' clamoured Jimmy. His voice broke. There were moanings, low mutters, a few sobs.

'What's the matter now?' said a seldom-heard voice. 'Fall back, men! Fall back, there!' repeated Mr Creighton, sternly, pushing through. 'Here's the old man,' whispered some. 'The cook's in there, sir,' exclaimed several, backing away. The door clattered open; a broad stream of light darted out on wondering faces; a warm whiff of vitiated air passed. The two mates towered head and shoulders above the spare, grey-haired man who stood revealed between them, in shabby clothes, stiff and angular, like a small carved figure, and with a thin, composed face. The cook got up from his knees. Jimmy sat high in the bunk, clasping his drawn-up legs. The tassel of the blue night-cap almost imperceptibly trembled over his knees. They gazed astonished at his long, curved back, while the white corner of one eye gleamed blindly at them. He was afraid to turn his head, he shrank within himself; and there was an aspect astounding and animal-like in the perfection of his expectant immobility. A thing of instinct – the unthinking stillness of a scared brute.

'What are you doing here?' asked Mr Baker, sharply. 'My duty,' said the cook, with ardour. 'Your ... what?' began the mate. Captain Allistoun touched his arm lightly. 'I know his caper,' he said, in a low voice. 'Come out of that, Podmore,' he ordered, aloud.

The cook wrung his hands, shook his fists above his head and his arms dropped as if too heavy. For a moment he stood distracted and speechless. 'Never,' he stammered, 'I ... he ... I.' 'What – do – you – say?' pronounced Captain Allistoun. 'Come out at once – or ...' 'I am going,' said the cook, with a hasty and sombre resignation. He strode over the doorstep firmly – hesitated – made a few steps. They looked at him in silence. 'I make you responsible!' he cried, desperately, turning half round. 'That man is dying. I make you ...' 'You there yet?' called the master in a threatening tone. 'No, sir,' he exclaimed, hurriedly, in a startled voice. The boatswain led him away by the arm; someone laughed; Jimmy lifted his head for a stealthy glance, and in one unexpected leap sprang out of his bunk; Mr Baker made a clever catch and felt him very limp in his arms; the group at the door grunted with surprise. 'He lies,' gasped Wait, 'he talked about black devils – he is a devil – a white devil – I am all right.' He stiffened himself, and Mr Baker, experimentally, let him go. He staggered a pace or two; Captain Allistoun watched him with a quiet and penetrating gaze; Belfast ran to his support. He did not appear to be aware of anyone near him; he stood silent for a moment, battling single-handed with a legion of nameless terrors, amidst the eager looks of excited men who watched him far off, utterly alone in the impenetrable solitude of his fear. The sea gurgled through the scuppers as the ship heeled over to a short puff of wind.

'Keep away from me,' said James Wait at last in his fine baritone voice, and leaning with all his weight on Belfast's neck. 'I've been better this last week ... I am well ... I was going back to duty ... tomorrow – now if you like – Captain.' Belfast hitched his shoulders to keep him upright.

'No,' said the master, looking at him, fixedly.

Under Jimmy's armpit Belfast's red face moved uneasily. A

row of eyes gleaming stared on the edge of light. They pushed one another with elbows, turned their heads, whispered. Wait let his chin fall on his breast and, with lowered eyelids, looked round in a suspicious manner.

'Why not?' cried a voice from the shadows, 'the man's all right, sir.'

'I am all right,' said Wait, with eagerness. 'Been sick ... better ... turn-to now.' He sighed. 'Howly Mother!' exclaimed Belfast with a heave of the shoulders, 'stand up, Jimmy.' 'Keep away from me then,' said Wait, giving Belfast a petulant push, and reeling fetched against the doorpost. His cheek-bones glistened as though they had been varnished. He snatched off his night-cap, wiped his perspiring face with it, flung it on the deck. 'I am coming out,' he declared without stirring.

'No. You don't,' said the master, curtly. Bare feet shuffled, disapproving voices murmured all round; he went on as if he had not heard: 'You have been skulking nearly all the passage and now you want to come out. You think you are near enough to the pay-table now. Smell the shore, hey?'

'I've been sick ... now – better,' mumbled Wait, glaring in the light. 'You have been shamming sick,' retorted Captain Allistoun with severity; 'Why ...' he hesitated for less than half a second. 'Why, anybody can see that. There's nothing the matter with you, but you choose to lie-up to please yourself – and now you shall lie-up to please me. Mr Baker, my orders are that this man is not to bc allowed on deck to the end of the passage.'

There were exclamations of surprise, triumph, indignation. The dark group of men swung across the light. 'What for?' – 'Told you so ...' – 'Bloomin' shame....' 'We've got to say somethink about that,' screeched Donkin from the rear. 'Never mind, Jim – we will see you righted,' cried several together. An elderly seaman stepped to the front. 'D'ye mean to say, sir,' he asked, ominously, 'that a sick chap ain't allowed to get well in this 'ere hooker?' Behind him Donkin whispered excitedly amongst a staring crowd where no one spared him a glance, but Captain Allistoun shook a forefinger at the angry bronzed face of the speaker. 'You – you hold your tongue,' he said, warningly. 'This isn't the way,' clamoured two or three younger men.

'Are we bloomin' masheens?' inquired Donkin in a piercing tone, and dived under the elbows of the front rank. 'Soon show 'im we ain't boys . . .' – 'The man's a man if he is black' – 'We ain't goin' to work this bloomin' ship shorthanded if Snowball's all right . . .' – 'He says he is' – 'Well, then, strike, boys, strike!' – 'That's the bloomin' ticket.' Captain Allistoun said sharply to the second mate: 'Keep quiet, Mr Creighton,' and stood composed in the tumult, listening with profound attention to mixed growls and screeches, to every exclamation and every curse of the sudden outbreak. Somebody slammed the cabin door to with a kick; the darkness full of menacing mutters leaped with a short clatter over the streak of light, and the men became gesticulating shadows that growled, hissed, laughed excitedly. Mr Baker whispered: 'Get away from them, sir.' The big shape of Mr Creighton hovered silently about the slight figure of the master. 'We have been hymposed upon all this voyage,' said a gruff voice, 'but this 'ere fancy takes the cake.' 'That man is a shipmate' – 'Are we bloomin' kids?' – 'The port watch will refuse duty.' Charley carried away by his feeling whistled shrilly, then yelped: 'Giv' us our Jimmy!' This seemed to cause a variation in the disturbance. There was a fresh outburst of squabbling uproar. A lot of quarrels were set going at once. 'Yes' – 'No' – 'Never been sick' – 'Go for them to once' – 'Shut yer mouth, youngster – this is men's work.' 'Is it?' muttered Captain Allistoun, bitterly. Mr Baker grunted: 'Ough! They're gone silly. They've been simmering for the last month.' 'I did notice,' said the master. 'They have started a row amongst themselves now,' said Mr Creighton with disdain, 'better get aft, sir. We will soothe them.' 'Keep your temper, Creighton,' said the master. And the three men began to move slowly towards the cabin door.

In the shadows of the fore rigging a dark mass stamped, eddied, advanced, retreated. There were words of reproach, encouragement, unbelief, execration. The elder seamen, bewildered and angry, growled their determination to go through with something or other; but the younger school of advanced thought exposed their and Jimmy's wrongs with confused shouts, arguing amongst themselves. They clustered round that moribund carcass, the fit emblem of their aspirations, and encouraging one another they swayed, they tramped on one spot, shouting that they would not be 'put upon'. Inside the cabin, Belfast, helping Jimmy into his bunk, twitched all over in his desire not to miss all the row, and with difficulty restrained the tears of his facile emotion. James Wait, flat on his back under the blanket, gasped complaints. 'We will back you up, never fear,' assured Belfast, busy about his feet. 'I'll come out tomorrow morning . . . take my chance . . . you fellows must . . .' mumbled Wait, 'I come out tomorrow . . . skipper or no skipper.' He lifted one arm with great difficulty, passed the hand over his face; 'Don't you let that cook . . .' he breathed out. 'No, no,' said Belfast, turning his back on the bunk, 'I will put a head on him if he comes near you.' 'I will smash his mug!' exclaimed Wait faintly, enraged and weak; 'I don't want to kill a man, but . . .' He panted fast like a dog after a run in sunshine. Someone just outside the door shouted, 'He's as fit as any ov us!' Belfast put his hand on the door-handle. 'Here!' called James Wait, hurriedly, and in such a clear voice that the other spun round with a start. James Wait, stretched out black and deathlike in the dazzling light, turned his head on the pillow. His eyes stared at Belfast, appealing and impudent. 'I am rather weak from lying-up so long,' he said, distinctly. Belfast nodded. 'Getting quite well now,' insisted Wait. 'Yes. I noticed you getting better this . . . last month,' said Belfast, looking down. 'Hallo! What's this?' he shouted and ran out.

He was flattened directly against the side of the house by two men who lurched against him. A lot of disputes seemed to be going on all around. He got clear and saw three indistinct figures standing alone in the fainter darkness under the arched foot of the mainsail, that rose above their heads like a convex wall of a high edifice. Donkin hissed: 'Go for them . . . it's dark!' The crowd took a short run aft in a body – then there was a check. Donkin, agile and thin, flitted past with his right arm going like a windmill – and then stood still suddenly with his arm pointing rigidly above his head. The hurtling flight of some heavy object was heard; it passed between the heads of the two mates, bounded heavily along the deck, struck the after hatch with a ponderous and deadened blow. The bulky shape of Mr Baker grew distinct. 'Come to your senses, men!' he cried, advancing at the arrested crowd. 'Come back, Mr Baker!' called the master's quiet voice. He obeyed unwillingly. There was a minute of silence, then a deafening hubbub arose. Above it Archie was heard energetically: 'If ye do oot ageen I wull tell!' There were shouts. 'Don't!' – 'Drop it!' – 'We ain't that kind!' The black cluster of human forms reeled against the bulwark, back again towards the house. Ringbolts rang under stumbling feet. 'Drop it!' – 'Let me!' – 'No!' – 'Curse you . . . hah!' Then sounds as of someone's face being slapped; a piece of iron fell on the deck; a short scuffle, and someone's shadowy body scuttled rapidly across the main hatch before the shadow of a kick. A raging voice sobbed out a torrent of filthy language. . . . 'Throwing things – good God!' grunted Mr Baker in dismay. 'That was meant for me,' said the master, quietly; 'I felt the wind of that thing; what was it – an iron belaying-pin?' 'By Jove!' muttered Mr Creighton. The confused voices of men talking amidships mingled with the wash of the sea, ascended between the silent and distended sails – seemed to flow away into the night, further than the horizon, higher than the sky. The stars burned steadily over the inclined mastheads. Trails of light lay on the water, broke before the advancing hull, and, after she had passed, trembled for a long time as if in awe of the murmuring sea.

Meantime the helmsman, anxious to know what the row was about, had let go the wheel, and, bent double, ran with long, stealthy footsteps to the break of the poop. The *Narcissus*, left to herself, came up gently to the wind without anyone being aware of it. She gave a slight roll, and the sleeping sails woke suddenly, coming all together with a mighty flap against the masts, then filled again one after another in a quick succession of loud reports that ran down the lofty spars, till the collapsed mainsail flew out last with a violent jerk. The ship trembled from trucks to keel; the sails kept on rattling like a discharge of musketry; the chain sheets and loose shackles jingled aloft in a thin peal; the gin blocks groaned. It was as if an invisible hand had given the ship an angry shake to recall the men that peopled her decks to the sense of reality, vigilance, and duty. 'Helm up!' cried the master, sharply. 'Run aft, Mr Creighton, and see what that fool there is up to.' 'Flatten in the head sheets. Stand by the weather fore-braces,' growled Mr Baker. Startled men ran swiftly repeating the orders. The watch below, abandoned all at once by the watch on deck, drifted towards the forecastle in twos and threes, arguing noisily as they went: 'We shall see tomorrow!' cried a loud voice, as if to cover with a menacing hint an inglorious retreat. And then only orders were heard, the falling of heavy coils of rope, the rattling of blocks. Singleton's white head flitted here and there in the night, high above the deck, like the ghost of a bird. 'Going off, sir!' shouted Mr Creighton from aft. 'Full again' – 'All right....' 'Ease off the head sheets. That will do the braces. Coil the ropes up,' grunted Mr Baker, bustling about.

Gradually the tramping noises, the confused sound of voices, died out, and the officers, coming together on the poop, discussed the events. Mr Baker was bewildered and grunted; Mr Creighton was calmly furious; but Captain Allistoun was composed and thoughtful. He listened to Mr Baker's growling argumentation, to Creighton's interjected and severe remarks, while looking down on the deck he weighed in his hand the iron belaying-pin – that a moment ago had just missed his head – as if it had been the only tangible fact of the whole transaction. He was one of those commanders who speak little, seem to hear nothing, look at no one – and know everything, hear every whisper, see every fleeting shadow of their ship's life. His two big officers towered above his lean, short figure; they talked over his head; they were dismayed, surprised, and angry, while between them the little quiet man seemed to have found his taciturn serenity in the profound depths of a larger experience. Lights were burning in the forecastle; now and then a loud gust of babbling chatter came from forward, swept over the decks, and became faint, as if the unconscious ship, gliding gently through the great peace of the sea, had left behind and for ever the foolish noise of turbulent mankind. But it was renewed again and again. Gesticulating arms, profiles of heads with open mouths appeared for a moment in the illuminated squares of doorways; black fists darted – withdrew ... 'Yes. It was most damnable to have such an unprovoked row sprung on one,' assented the master. ... A tumult of yells rose in the light, abruptly ceased.... He didn't think there would be any further trouble just then.... A bell struck aft, another, forward, answered in a deeper tone, and the clamour of ringing metal spread round the ship in a circle of wide vibrations that ebbed away into the immeasurable night of an empty sea.... Didn't he know them! Didn't he! In past years. Better men, too. Real men to stand by one in a tight place. Worse than devils too sometimes – downright, horned devils. Pah! This – nothing. A miss as good as a mile.... The wheel was being relieved in the usual way. 'Full and by,' said, very loud, the man going off. 'Full and by,' repeated the other, catching hold of the spokes. 'This head wind is my trouble,' exclaimed the master, stamping his foot in sudden anger; 'head wind! all the rest is nothing.' He was calm again in a moment. 'Keep them on the move tonight, gentlemen; just to let them feel we've got hold all the time – quietly, you know. Mind you keep your hands off them, Creighton. Tomorrow I will talk to them like a Dutch Uncle. A crazy crowd of tinkers! Yes, tinkers! I could count the real sailors amongst them on the fingers of one hand. Nothing will do but a row – if – you – please.' He paused. 'Did you think I had gone wrong there, Mr Baker?' He tapped his forehead, laughed short. 'When I saw him standing there, three parts dead and so scared – black amongst that gaping lot – no grit to face what's coming to us all – the notion came to me all at once, before I could think. Sorry for him – like you would be for a sick brute. If ever creature was in a mortal funk to die! ... I thought I would let him go out in his own way. Kind of impulse. It never came into my head, those fools.... H'm! Stand to it now – of course.' He stuck the belaying-pin in his pocket, seemed ashamed of himself, then sharply: 'If you see Podmore at his tricks again tell him I will have him put under the pump. Had to do it once before. The fellow breaks out like that now and then. Good cook tho'.' He walked away quickly, came back to the companion. The two mates followed him through the starlight with amazed eyes. He went down three steps, and changing his tone, spoke with his head near the deck: 'I shan't turn in tonight, in case of anything; just call out if ... Did you see the eyes of that sick nigger, Mr Baker? I fancied he begged me for something. What? Past all help. One lone black beggar amongst the lot of us, and he seemed to look through me into the very hell. Fancy, this wretched Podmore! Well, let him die in peace. I am master here after all. Let him be. He might have been half a man once. . . . Keep a good look-out.' He disappeared down below, leaving his mates facing one another, and more impressed than if they had seen a stone image shed a miraculous tear of compassion over the incertitudes of life and death. . . .

In a blue mist spreading from twisted threads that stood upright in the bowls of pipes, the forecastle appeared as vast as a hall. Between the beams a heavy cloud stagnated; and the lamps surrounded by halos burned each at the core of a purple glow in two lifeless flames without rays. Wreaths drifted in denser wisps. Men sprawled about on the deck, sat in negligent poses, or, bending a knee, drooped with one shoulder against a bulkhead. Lips moved, eyes flashed, waving arms made sudden eddies in the smoke. The murmur of voices seemed to pile itself higher as if unable to run out quick enough through the narrow doors. The watch below in their shirts, and striding on long white legs, resembled raving somnambulists; while now and then one of the watch on deck would rush in, looking strangely over-dressed, listen a moment, fling a rapid sentence into the noise, and run out again; but a few remained near the door, fascinated, and with one ear turned to the deck. 'Stick together, boys,' roared Davis. Belfast tried to make himself heard. Knowles grinned in a slow, dazed way. A short fellow with a thick clipped beard kept on yelling periodically. 'Who's afeard? Who's afeard?' Another one jumped up, excited, with glazing eyes, sent out a string of unattached curses and sat down quietly. Two men discussed familiarity, striking one another's breast in turn, to clinch arguments. Three others, with their heads in a bunch, spoke all together with a confidential air, and at the top of their voices. It was a stormy chaos of speech where intelligible fragments tossing, struck the ear. One could hear: 'In the last ship' – 'Who cares? Try it on any one of us if—' – 'Knock under' – 'Not a hand's turn' – 'He says he is all right' – 'I always thought' – 'Never mind. . . .' Donkin, crouching all in a heap against the bowsprit, hunched his shoulderblades as high as his ears, and hanging a peaked nose, resembled a sick vulture with ruffled plumes. Belfast, straddling his legs, had a face red with yelling, and with arms thrown up, figured a Maltese cross. The two

Scandinavians, in a corner, had the dumbfounded and distracted aspect of men gazing at a cataclysm. And, beyond the light, Singleton stood in the smoke, monumental, indistinct, with his head touching the beam; like a statue of heroic size in the gloom of a crypt.

He stepped forward, impassive and big. The noise subsided like a broken wave: but Belfast cried once more with uplifted arms: 'The man is dying I tell ye!' then sat down suddenly on the hatch and took his head between his hands. All looked at Singleton, gazing upwards from the deck, staring out of dark corners, or turning their heads with curious glances. They were expectant and appeased as if that old man, who looked at no one, had possessed the secret of their uneasy indignations and desires, a sharper vision, a clearer knowledge. And indeed standing there amongst them, he had the uninterested appearance of one who had seen multitudes of ships, had listened many times to voices such as theirs, had already seen all that could happen on the wide seas. They heard his voice rumble in his broad chest as though the words had been rolling towards them out of a rugged past. 'What do you want to do?' he asked. No one answered. Only Knowles muttered – 'Aye, aye,' and somebody said low: 'It's a bloomin' shame.' He waited, made a contemptuous gesture. 'I have seen rows aboard ship before some of you were born,' he said, slowly, 'for something or nothing; but never for such a thing.' 'The man is dying, I tell ye,' repeated Belfast, woefully, sitting at Singleton's feet. 'And a black fellow, too,' went on the old seaman, 'I have seen them die like flies.' He stopped, thoughtful, as if trying to recollect gruesome things, details, of horrors, hecatombs of niggers. They looked at him fascinated. He was old enough to remember slavers, bloody mutinies, pirates perhaps; who could tell through what violences and terrors he had lived! What would he say? He said: 'You can't help him; die he must.' He made another pause. His moustache and beard stirred. He chewed words, mumbled behind tangled white hairs; incomprehensible and exciting, like an oracle behind a veil.... 'Stop ashore ... sick ... Instead ... bringing all this head wind. Afraid. The sea will have her own.... Die in sight of land. Always so. They know it ... long passage ... more days, more dollars.... You keep quiet....

What do you want? Can't help him.' He seemed to wake up from a dream. 'You can't help yourselves,' he said, austerely. 'Skipper's no fool. He has something in his mind. Look out – I say! I know 'em!' With eyes fixed in front he turned his head from right to left, from left to right, as if inspecting a long row of astute skippers. ''Ee said 'ee would brain me!' cried Donkin in a heartrending tone. Singleton peered downwards with puzzled attention, as though he couldn't find him. 'Damn you!' he said, vaguely, giving it up. He radiated unspeakable wisdom, hard unconcern, the chilling air of resignation. Round him all the listeners felt themselves somehow completely enlightened by their disappointment, and mute, they lolled about with the careless ease of men who can discern perfectly the irremediable aspect of their existence. He, profound and unconscious, waved his arm once, and strode out on deck without another word.

Belfast was lost in a round-eyed meditation. One or two vaulted heavily into upper berths, and, once there, sighed; others dived head first inside lower bunks – swift, and turning round instantly upon themselves, like animals going into lairs. The grating of a knife scraping burnt clay was heard. Knowles grinned no more. Davies said, in a tone of ardent conviction: 'Then our skipper's looney.' Archie muttered: 'My faith! we haven't heard the last of it yet!' Four bells was struck. 'Half our watch below gone!' cried Knowles in alarm, then reflected. 'Well, two hours' sleep is something towards a rest,' he observed, consolingly. Some already pretended to slumber; and Charley, sound asleep, suddenly said a few slurred words in an arbitrary, blank voice. 'This blamed boy has worrums!' commented Knowles from under a blanket, in a learned manner. Belfast got up and approached Archie's berth. 'We pulled him out,' he whispered, sadly. 'What?' said the other, with sleepy discontent. 'And now we will have to chuck him overboard,' went on Belfast, whose lower lip trembled. 'Chuck what?' asked Archie. 'Poor Jimmy,' breathed out Belfast. 'He be blowed!' said Archie with untruthful brutality, and sat up in his bunk; 'It's all through him. If it hadn't been for me, there would have been murder on board this ship!' ''Taint his fault, is it?' argued Belfast, in a murmur; 'I've put him to bed ... an' he ain't no heavier than an empty beef-cask,' he added, with tears in his eyes. Archie looked at him steadily, then turned his nose to the ship's side with determination. Belfast wandered about as though he had lost his way in the dim forecastle, and nearly fell over Donkin. He contemplated him from on high for a while. 'Ain't ye going to turn in?' he asked. Donkin looked up hopelessly. 'That black 'earted Scotch son of a thief kicked me!' he whispered from the floor, in a tone of utter desolation. 'And a good job, too!' said Belfast, still very depressed; 'You were as near hanging as damn-it tonight, sonny. Don't you play any of your murthering games around my Jimmy! You haven't pulled him out. You just mind! 'Cos if I start to kick you' – he brightened up a bit – 'if I start to kick you, it will be Yankee fashion – to break something!' He tapped lightly with his knuckles the top of the bowed head. 'You moind that, my bhoy!' he concluded, cheerily. Donkin let it pass. 'Will they split on me?' he asked, with pained anxiety. 'Who – split?' hissed Belfast, coming back a step. 'I would split your nose this minyt if I hadn't Jimmy to look after! Who d'ye think we are?' Donkin rose and watched Belfast's back lurch through the doorway. On all sides invisible men slept, breathing calmly. He seemed to draw courage and fury from the peace around him. Venomous and thin-faced, he glared from the ample misfit of borrowed clothes as if looking for something he could smash. His heart leaped wildly in his hollow chest. They slept! He wanted to wring necks, gouge eyes, spit on faces. He shook a dirty pair of meagre fists at the smoking lights. 'Ye're no men!' he cried, in a deadened tone. No one moved. 'Yer 'aven't the pluck of a mouse!' His voice rose to a husky screech. Wamibo darted out a dishevelled head, and looked at him wildly. 'Ye're sweepings ov ships! I 'ope you will all rot before you die!' Wamibo blinked, uncomprehending but interested. Donkin sat down heavily; he blew with force through quivering nostrils, he ground and snapped his teeth, and, with the chin pressed hard against the breast, he seemed busy gnawing his way through it, as if to get at the heart within....

*

In the morning the ship, beginning another day of her wandering life, had an aspect of sumptuous freshness, like the springtime of the earth. The washed decks glistened in a long clear stretch; the oblique sunlight struck the yellow brasses in dazzling splashes, darted over the polished rods in lines of gold, and the single drops of salt water forgotten here and there along the rail were as limpid as drops of dew, and sparkled more than scattered diamonds. The sails slept, hushed by a gentle breeze. The sun, rising lonely and splendid in the blue sky, saw a solitary ship gliding close-hauled on the blue sea.

The men pressed three deep abreast of the mainmast and opposite the cabin-door. They shuffled, pushed, had an irresolute mien and stolid faces. At every slight movement Knowles lurched heavily on his short leg. Donkin glided behind backs, restless and anxious, like a man looking for an ambush. Captain Allistoun came out on the quarter-deck suddenly. He walked to and fro before the front. He was grey, slight, alert, shabby in the sunshine, and as hard as adamant. He had his right hand in the side-pocket of his jacket, and also something heavy in there that made folds all down that side. One of the seamen cleared his throat ominously. 'I haven't till now found fault with you men,' said the master, stopping short. He faced them with his worn, steely gaze, that by an universal illusion looked straight into every individual pair of the twenty pairs of eyes before his face. At his back Mr Baker, gloomy, and bull-necked, grunted low; Mr Creighton, fresh as paint, had rosy cheeks and a ready, resolute bearing. 'And I don't now,' continued the master; 'but I am here to drive this ship and keep every man-jack aboard of her up to the mark. If you knew your work as well as I do mine, there would be no trouble. You've been braying in the dark about "See tomorrow morning!" Well, you see me now. What do you want?' He waited, stepping quickly to and fro, giving them searching glances. What did they want? They shifted from foot to foot, they balanced their bodies; some, pushing back their caps, scratched their heads. What did they want? Jimmy was forgotten; no one thought of him, alone forward in his cabin, fighting great shadows, clinging to brazen lies, chuckling painfully over his transparent deceptions. No, not Jimmy; he was more forgotten than if he had been dead. They wanted great things. And suddenly all the simple words they knew seemed to be lost for ever in the immensity of their vague and burning desire. They knew what they wanted, but they could not find anything worth saying. They stirred on one spot, swinging, at the end of muscular arms, big tarry hands with crooked fingers. A murmur died out. 'What is it – food?' asked the master, 'you know the stores have been spoiled off the Cape.' 'We know that, sir,' said a bearded shell-back in the front rank. 'Work too hard – eh? Too much for your strength?' he asked again. There was an offended silence. 'We don't want to go shorthanded, sir,' began at last Davies in a wavering voice, 'and this 'ere black . . .' 'Enough!' cried the master. He stood scanning them for a moment, then walking a few steps this way and that began to storm at them coldly, in gusts violent and cutting like the gales of those icy seas that had known his youth. 'Tell you what's the matter? Too big for your boots. Think yourselves damn good men. Know half your work. Do half your duty. Think it too much. If you did ten times as much it wouldn't be enough.' 'We did our best by her, sir,' cried someone with shaky exasperation. 'Your best,' stormed on the master: 'You hear a lot on shore, don't you? They don't tell you there your best isn't much to boast of. I tell you – your best is no better than bad. You can do no more? No, I know, and say nothing. But you stop your caper or I will stop it for you. I am ready for you! Stop it!' He shook a finger at the crowd. 'As to that man,' he raised his voice very much; 'as to that man, if he puts his nose out on deck without my leave I will clap him in irons. There!' The cook heard him forward, ran out of the galley lifting his arms, horrified, unbelieving, amazed, and ran in again. There was a moment of profound silence during which a bow-legged seaman, stepping aside, expectorated decorously into the scupper. 'There is another thing,' said the master, calmly. He made a quick stride and with a swing took an iron belaying-pin out of his pocket. 'This!' His movement was so unexpected and sudden that the crowd stepped back. He gazed fixedly at their faces, and some at once put on a surprised air as though they had never seen a belaying-pin before. He held it up. 'This is my affair. I don't ask you any questions, but you all know it; it has got to go where it came from.' His eyes became angry. The crowd stirred uneasily. They looked away from the piece of iron, they appeared shy, they were embarrassed and shocked as though it had been something horrid, scandalous, or indelicate, that in common decency should not have been flourished like this in broad daylight. The master watched them attentively. 'Donkin,' he called out in a short, sharp tone.

Donkin dodged behind one, then behind another, but they looked over their shoulders and moved aside. The ranks kept on opening before him, closing behind, till at last he appeared alone before the master as though he had come up through the deck. Captain Allistoun moved close to him. They were much of a size, and at short range the master exchanged a deadly glance with the beady eyes. They wavered. 'You know this,' asked the master. 'No, I don't,' answered the other with cheeky trepidation. 'You are a cur. Take it,' ordered the master. Donkin's arms seemed glued to his thighs; he stood, eyes front, as if drawn on parade. 'Take it,' repeated the master, and stepped closer; they breathed on one another. 'Take it,' said Captain Allistoun again, making a menacing gesture. Donkin tore away one arm from his side. 'Vy are yer down on me?' he mumbled with effort and as if his mouth had been full of dough. 'If you don't ...' began the master. Donkin snatched at the pin as though his intention had been to run away with it, and remained stock still holding it like a candle. 'Put it back where you took it from,' said Captain Allistoun, looking at him fiercely. Donkin stepped back opening wide eyes. 'Go, you blackguard, or I will make you,' cried the master, driving him slowly backwards by a menacing advance. He dodged, and with the dangerous iron tried to guard his head from a threatening fist. Mr Baker ceased grunting for a moment. 'Good! By Jove,' murmured appreciatively Mr Creighton in the tone of a connoisseur. 'Don't tech me,' snarled Donkin, backing away. 'Then go. Go faster.' 'Don't yer 'it me.... I will pull yer up afore the magistryt.... I'll show yer up.' Captain Allistoun made a long stride, and Donkin, turning his back fairly, ran off a little, then stopped and over his shoulder showed yellow teeth. 'Further on, fore-rigging,' urged the master, pointing with his arm. 'Are yer goin' to stand by and see me bullied,' screamed Donkin at the silent crowd that watched him. Captain Allistoun walked at him smartly. He started off again with a leap, dashed at the fore-rigging, rammed the pin into its hole violently. 'I'll be even with yer yet,' he screamed at the ship at large and vanished beyond the foremast. Captain Allistoun spun round and walked back aft with a composed face, as though he had already forgotten the scene. Men moved out of his way. He looked at no one. 'That will do, Mr Baker. Send the watch below,' he said, quietly. 'And you men try to walk straight for the future,' he added in a calm voice. He looked pensively for a while at the backs of the impressed and retreating crowd. 'Breakfast, steward,' he called in a tone of relief through the cabin door. 'I didn't like to see you – Ough! – give that pin to that chap, sir,' observed Mr Baker; 'he could have bust – Ough! – bust you head like an eggshell with it.' 'O! he!' muttered the master absently. 'Queer lot,' he went on in a low voice. 'I suppose it's all right now. Can never tell tho', nowadays, with such a . . . Years ago; I was a young master then – one China voyage I had a mutiny; real mutiny, Baker. Differen men tho'. I knew what they wanted: they wanted to broach the cargo and get at the liquor. Very simple. . . . We knocked them about for two days, and when they had enough – gentle as lambs. Good crew. And a smart trip I made.' He glanced aloft at the yards braced sharp up. 'Head wind day after day,' he exclaimed, bitterly. 'Shall we never get a decent slant this passage?' 'Ready, sir,' said the steward, appearing before them as if by magic and with a stained napkin in his hand. 'Ah! All right. Come along, Mr Baker – it's late – with all this nonsense.'

5

A heavy atmosphere of oppressive quietude pervaded the ship. In the afternoon men went about washing clothes and hanging them out to dry in the unprosperous breeze with the meditative languor of disenchanted philosophers. Very little was said. The problem of life seemed too voluminous for the narrow limits of human speech, and by common consent it was abandoned to the great sea that had from the beginning enfolded it in its immense grip; to the sea that knew all, and would in time infallibly unveil to each the wisdom hidden in all the errors, the certitude that lurks in doubts, the realm of safety and peace beyond the frontiers of sorrow and fear. And in the confused current of impotent thoughts that set unceasingly this way and that through bodies of men, Jimmy bobbed up upon the surface, compelling attention, like a black buoy chained to the bottom of a muddy stream. Falsehood triumphed. It triumphed through doubt, through stupidity, through pity, through sentimentalism. We set ourselves to bolster it up, from compassion, from recklessness, from a sense of fun. Jimmy's steadfastness to his untruthful attitude in the face of the inevitable truth had the proportions of a colossal enigma – of a manifestation grand and incomprehensible that at times inspired a wondering awe; and there was also, to many, something exquisitely droll in fooling him thus to the top of his bent. The latent egoism of tenderness to suffering appeared in the developing anxiety not to see him die. His obstinate non-recognition of the only certitude whose approach we could watch from day to day was as disquieting as the failure of some law of nature. He was so utterly wrong about himself that one could not but suspect him of having access to some source of supernatural knowledge. He was absurd to the point of inspiration. He was unique, and as fascinating as only something inhuman could be; he seemed to shout his denials already from beyond the awful border. He was becoming immaterial like an apparition; his cheekbones rose, the forehead slanted more; the face was all hollows, patches of shade; and the fleshless head resembled a disinterred black skull, fitted with two restless globes of silver in the sockets of eyes. He was demoralizing. Through him we were becoming highly humanized, tender, complex, excessively decadent: we understood the subtlety of his fear, sympathized with all his repulsions, shrinkings, evasions, delusions – as though we had been over-civilized, and rotten, and without any knowledge of the meaning of life. We had the air of being initiated in some infamous mysteries; we had the profound grimaces of conspirators, exchanged meaning glances, significant short words. We were inexpressibly vile and very much pleased with ourselves. We lied to him with gravity, with emotion, with unction, as if performing some moral trick with a view to an eternal reward. We made a chorus of affirmation to his wildest assertions, as though he had been a millionaire, a politician, or a reformer – and we a crowd of ambitious lubbers. When we ventured to question his statements we did it after the manner of obsequious sycophants, to the end that his glory should be augmented by the flattery of our dissent. He influenced the moral tone of our world as though he had it in his power to distribute honours, treasures, or pain; and he could give us nothing but his contempt. It was immense; it seemed to grow gradually larger, as his body day by day shrank a little more, while we looked. It was the only thing about him – of him – that gave the impression of durability and vigour. It lived within him with an unquenchable life. It spoke through the eternal pout of his black lips; it looked at us through the impertinent mournfulness of his languid and enormous stare. We watched him intently. He seemed unwilling to move, as if distrustful of his own solidity. The slightest gesture must have disclosed to him (it could not surely be otherwise) his bodily weakness, and caused a pang of mental suffering. He was chary of movements. He lay stretched out, chin on blanket, in a kind of sly, cautious immobility. Only his eyes roamed over faces: his eyes disdainful, penetrating, and sad.

It was at that time that Belfast's devotion – and also his pugnacity – secured universal respect. He spent every moment of his spare time in Jimmy's cabin. He tended him, talked to him; was as gentle as a woman, as tenderly gay as an old philanthropist, as sentimentally careful of his nigger as a model slave-owner. But outside he was irritable, explosive as gunpowder, sombre, suspicious, and never more brutal than when most sorrowful. With him it was a tear and a blow: a tear for Jimmy, a blow for anyone who did not seem to take a scrupulously orthodox view of Jimmy's case. We talked about nothing else. The two Scandinavians, even, discussed the situation – but it was impossible to know in what spirit, because they quarrelled in their own language. Belfast suspected one of them of irreverence, and this incertitude thought that there was no option but to fight them both. They became very much terrified by his truculence, and henceforth lived amongst us, dejected, like a pair of mutes. Wamibo never spoke intelligibly, but he was as smileless as an animal – seemed to know much less about it all than the cat – and consequently was safe. Moreover, he had belonged to the chosen band of Jimmy's rescuers, and was above suspicion. Archie was silent generally, but often spent an hour or so talking to Jimmy quietly with an air of proprietorship. At any time of the day and often through the night some man could be seen sitting on Jimmy's box. In the evening, between six and eight, the cabin was crowded, and there was an interested group at the door. Everyone stared at the nigger.

He basked in the warmth of our interest. His eyes gleamed ironically, and in a weak voice he reproached us with our cowardice. He would say, 'If you fellows had stuck out for me I would be now on deck.' We hung our heads. 'Yes, but if you think I am going to let them put me in irons just to show you sport. . . . Well, no. . . . It ruins my health, this lying-up, it does. You don't care.' We were as abashed as if it had been true. His superb impudence carried all before it. We would not have dared to revolt. We didn't want to, really. We wanted to keep him alive till home – to the end of the voyage.

Singleton as usual held aloof, appearing to scorn the insignificant events of an ended life. Once only he came along, and unexpectedly stopped in the doorway. He peered at Jimmy in profound silence, as if desirous to add that black image to the crowd of Shades that peopled his old memory. We kept very quiet, and for a long time Singleton stood there as though he had come by appointment to call for someone, or to see some important event. James Wait lay perfectly still, and apparently not aware of the gaze scrutinizing him with a steadiness full of expectation. There was a sense of a contest in the air. We felt the inward strain of men watching a wrestling bout. At last Jimmy with perceptible apprehension turned his head on the pillow. 'Good evening,' he said in a conciliating tone. 'H'm,' answered the old seaman grumpily. For a moment longer he looked at Jimmy with severe fixity, then suddenly went away. It was a long time before anyone spoke in the little cabin, though we all breathed more freely as men do after an escape from some dangerous situation. We all knew the old man's ideas about Jimmy, and nobody dared to combat them. They were unsettling, they caused pain; and, what was worse, they might have been true for all we knew. Only once did he condescend to explain them fully, but the impression was lasting. He said that Jimmy was the cause of head winds. Mortally sick men – he maintained – linger till the first sight of land, and then die; and Jimmy knew that the very first land would draw his life from him. It is so in every ship. Didn't we know it? He asked us with austere contempt: what did we know? What would we doubt next? Jimmy's desire encouraged by us and aided by Wamibo's (he was a Finn – wasn't he? Very well!) by Wamibo's spells delayed the ship in the open sea. Only lubberly fools couldn't see it. Whoever heard of such a run of calms and head winds? It wasn't natural.... We could not deny that it was strange. We felt uneasy. The common saying, 'More days, more dollars', did not give the usual comfort because the stores were running short. Much had been spoiled off the Cape, and we were on half allowance of biscuit. Peas, sugar and tea had been finished long ago. Salt meat was giving out. We had plenty of coffee but very little water to make it with. We took up another hole in our belts and went on scraping, polishing, painting the ship from morning to night. And soon she looked as though she had come out of a band-box; but hunger lived on board of her. Not dead starvation, but steady, living hunger that stalked about the decks, slept in the forecastle; the tormentor of waking moments, the disturber of dreams. We looked to windward for signs of change. Every few hours of night and day we put her round with the hope that she would come up on that tack at last! She didn't. She seemed to have forgotten the way home; she rushed to and fro, heading north-west, heading east; she ran backwards and forwards, distracted like a timid creature at the foot of a wall. Sometimes, as if tired to death, she would wallow languidly for a day in the smooth swell of an unruffled sea. All up the swinging masts the sails trashed furiously through the hot stillness of the calm. We were weary, hungry, thirsty; we commenced to believe Singleton, but with unshaken fidelity dissembled to Jimmy. We spoke to him with jocose allusiveness, like cheerful accomplices in a clever plot; but we looked to the westward over the rail with longing eyes for a sign of hope, for a sign of fair wind; even if its first breath should bring death to our reluctant Jimmy. In vain! The universe conspired with James Wait. Light airs from the northward sprang up again; the sky remained clear; and round our weariness the glittering sea, touched by the breeze, basked voluptuously in the great sunshine, as though it had forgotten our life and trouble.

Donkin looked out for a fair wind along with the rest. No one knew the venom of his thoughts now. He was silent, and appeared thinner, as if consumed slowly by an inward rage at the injustice of men and of fate. He was ignored by all and spoke to no one, but his hate for every man dwelt in his furtive eyes. He talked with the cook only, having somehow persuaded the good man that he – Donkin – was a much calumniated and persecuted person. Together they bewailed the immorality of the ship's company. There could be no greater criminals than we, who by our lives conspired to send the unprepared soul of a poor ignorant black man to everlasting perdition. Podmore cooked what there was to cook, remorsefully, and felt all the time that by preparing the food of such sinners he imperilled his own salvation. As to the Captain – he had sailed with him for seven years, now, he said, and would not have believed it possible that such a man ... 'Well. Well ... There it was.... Can't get out of it. Judgement capsized all in a minute.... Struck in all his pride.... More like a sudden visitation than anything else.' Donkin, perched sullenly on the coal-locker, swung his legs and concurred. He paid in the coin of spurious assent for the privilege to sit in the galley; he was disheartened and scandalized; he agreed with the cook; could find no words severe enough to criticize our conduct; and when in the heat of reprobation he swore at us, Podmore, who would have liked to swear also if it hadn't been for his principles, pretended not to hear. So Donkin, unrebuked, cursed enough for two, cadged for matches, borrowed tobacco, loafed for hours and very much at home before the stove. From there he could hear us on the other side of the bulkhead, talking to Jimmy. The cook knocked the saucepans about, slammed the oven door, muttered prophecies of damnation for all the ship's company; and Donkin, who did not admit of any hereafter (except for purposes of blasphemy) listened, concentrated and angry, gloated fiercely over a called-up image of infinite torment – as men gloat over the accursed images of cruelty and revenge, of greed and of power. . . .

On clear evenings the silent ship, under the cold sheen of the dead moon, took on a false aspect of passionless repose resembling the winter of the earth. Under her a long band of gold barred the black disc of the sea. Footsteps echoed on her quiet decks. The moonlight clung to her like a frosted mist, and the white sails stood out in dazzling cones as of stainless snow. In the magnificence of the phantom rays the ship appeared pure like a vision of ideal beauty, illusive like a tender dream of serene peace. And nothing in her was real, nothing was distinct and solid but the heavy shadows that filled her decks with their unceasing and noiseless stir: the shadows darker than the night and more restless than the thoughts of men.

Donkin prowled spiteful and alone amongst the shadows, thinking that Jimmy too long delayed to die. That evening land had been reported from aloft, and the master, while adjusting the tubes of the long glass, had observed with quiet bitterness to Mr Baker that, after fighting our way inch by inch to the Western Islands, there was nothing to expect now but a spell of calm. The sky was clear and the barometer high. The light breeze dropped with the sun, and an enormous stillness, forerunner of a night without wind, descended upon the heated waters of the ocean. As long as daylight lasted, the hands collected on the forecastle-head watched on the eastern sky the island of Flores, that rose above the level expanse of the sea with irregular and broken outlines like a sombre ruin upon a vast and deserted plain. It was the first land seen for nearly four months. Charley was excited, and in the midst of general indulgence took liberties with his betters. Men strangely elated without knowing why, talked in groups, and pointed with bared arms. For the first time that voyage Jimmy's sham existence seemed for a moment forgotten in the face of a solid reality. We had got so far anyhow. Belfast discoursed, quoting imaginary examples of short homeward runs from the Islands. 'Them smart fruit schooners do it in five days,' he affirmed. 'What do you want? – only a good little breeze.' Archie maintained that seven days was the record passage, and they disputed amicably with insulting words. Knowles declared he could already smell home from there, and with a heavy list on his short leg laughed fit to split his sides. A group of grizzled sea-dogs looked out for a time in silence and with grim absorbed faces. One said suddenly: ''Tain't far to London now.' 'My first night ashore, blamme if I haven't steak and onions for supper ... and a pint of bitter,' said another. 'A barrel ye mean,' shouted someone. 'Ham an' eggs three times a day. That's the way I live!' cried an excited voice. There was a stir, appreciative murmurs; eyes began to shine; jaws champed; short, nervous laughs were heard. Archie smiled with a reserve all to himself. Singleton came up, gave a careless glance, and went down again without saying a word, indifferent, like a man who had seen Flores an incalculable number of times. The night travelling from the East blotted out of the limpid sky the purple stain of the high land. 'Dead calm,' said somebody quietly. The murmur of lively talk suddenly wavered, died out; the clusters broke up; men began to drift away one by one, descending the ladders slowly and with serious faces as if sobered by that reminder of their dependence upon the invisible. And when the big yellow moon ascended gently above the sharp rim of the clear horizon it found the ship wrapped up in a breathless silence; a fearless ship that seemed to sleep profoundly, dreamlessly on the bosom of the sleeping and terrible sea.

Donkin chafed at the peace – at the ship – at the sea that stretching away on all sides merged into the illimitable silence of all creation. He felt himself pulled up sharp by unrecognized grievances. He had been physically cowed, but his injured dignity remained indomitable, and nothing could heal his lacerated feelings. Here was land already – home very soon – a bad pay-day – no clothes – more hard work. How offensive all this was. Land. The land that draws away life from sick sailors. That nigger there had money – clothes – easy times; and would not die. Land draws life away.... He felt tempted to go and see whether it did. Perhaps already ... It would be a bit of luck. There was money in the beggar's chest. He stepped briskly out of the shadows into the moonlight, and, instantly, his craving, hungry face from sallow became livid. He opened the door of the cabin and had a shock. Sure enough, Jimmy was dead! He moved no more than a recumbent figure with clasped hands, carved on the lid of a stone coffin. Donkin glared with avidity. Then Jimmy, without stirring, blinked his eyelids, and Donkin had another shock. Those eyes were rather startling. He shut the door behind his back with gentle care, looking intently the while at James Wait as though he had come in there at a great risk to tell some secret of startling importance. Jimmy did not move but glanced languidly out of the corners of his eyes. 'Calm?' he asked. 'Yuss,' said Donkin, very disappointed, and sat down on the box.

Jimmy was used to such visits at all times of night or day. Men succeeded one another. They spoke in clear voices, pronounced cheerful words, repeated old jokes, listened to him; and each, going out, seemed to leave behind a little of his own vitality, surrender some of his own strength, renew the assurance of life – the indestructible thing! He did not like to be alone in his cabin, because, when he was alone, it seemed to him as if he hadn't been there at all. There was nothing. No pain. Not now. Perfectly right – but he couldn't enjoy his healthful repose unless someone was by to see it. This man would do as well as anybody. Donkin watched him stealthily. 'Soon home now,' observed Wait. 'Vy d'yer whisper?' asked Donkin with interest, 'can't yer speak up?' Jimmy looked annoyed and said nothing for a while; then in a lifeless, unringing voice: 'Why should I shout? You ain't deaf that I know.' 'Oh! I can 'ear right enough,' answered Donkin in a low tone, and looked down. He was thinking sadly of going out when Jimmy spoke again. 'Time we did get home ... to get something decent to eat.... I am always hungry.' Donkin felt angry all of a sudden. 'What about me,' he hissed, 'I am 'ungry too an' got ter work.

You, 'ungry!' 'Your work won't kill you,' commented Wait, feebly; 'there's a couple of biscuits in the lower bunk there – you may have one. I can't eat them.' Donkin dived in, groped in the corner and when he came up again his mouth was full. He munched with ardour. Jimmy seemed to doze with open eyes. Donkin finished his hard bread and got up. 'You're not going?' asked Jimmy, staring at the ceiling. 'No,' said Donkin, impulsively, and instead of going out leaned his back against the closed door. He looked at James Wait, and saw him long, lean, dried up, as though all his flesh had shrivelled on his bones in the heat of a white furnace; the meagre fingers of one hand moved lightly upon the edge of the bunk playing an endless tune. To look at him was irritating and fatiguing; he could last like this for days; he was outrageous – belonging wholly neither to death nor life, and perfectly invulnerable in his apparent ignorance of both. Donkin felt tempted to enlighten him. 'What are yer thinkin' of?' he asked, surlily. James Wait had a grimacing smile that passed over the death-like impassiveness of his bony face, incredible and frightful as would, in a dream, have been the sudden smile of a corpse.

'There is a girl,' whispered Wait.... 'Canton Street girl.... She chucked a third engineer of a Rennie boat... for me. Cooks oysters just as I like.... She says... she would chuck... any toff... for a coloured gentleman.... That's me. I am kind to wimmen,' he added, a shade louder.

Donkin could hardly believe his ears. He was scandalized – 'Would she? Yer wouldn't be any good to 'er,' he said with unrestrained disgust. Wait was not there to hear him. He was swaggering up the East India Dock Road; saying kindly, 'Come along for a treat,' pushing glass swing-doors, posing with superb assurance in the gaslight above a mahogany counter. 'D'yer think yer will ever get ashore?' asked Donkin angrily. Wait came back with a start. 'Ten days,' he said, promptly, and returned at once to the regions of memory that know nothing of time. He felt untired, calm, and safely withdrawn within himself beyond the reach of every grave incertitude. There was something of the immutable quality of eternity in the slow moments of his complete restfulness. He was very quiet and easy amongst his vivid reminiscences which he mistook joyfully for images of an undoubted future. He cared for no one. Donkin felt this vaguely like a blind man feeling in his darkness the fatal antagonism of all the surrounding existences, that to him shall for ever remain irrealizable, unseen and enviable. He had a desire to assert his importance, to break, to crush; to be even with everybody for everything; to tear the veil, unmask, expose, leave no refuge – a perfidious desire of truthfulness! He laughed in a mocking splutter and said:

'Ten days. Strike me blind if I ever! . . . You will be dead by this time tomorrow p'r'aps. Ten days!' He waited for a while. 'D'ye 'ear me? Blamme if yer don't look dead already.'

Wait must have been collecting his strength for he said almost aloud: 'You're a stinking, cadging liar. Everyone knows you.' And sitting up, against all probability, startled his visitor horribly. But very soon Donkin recovered himself. He blustered:

'What? What? Who's a liar? You are – the crowd are – the skipper – everybody. I ain't! Putting on airs! Who's yer?' He nearly choked himself with indignation. 'Who's yer to put on airs,' he repeated, trembling. ''Ave one – 'ave one, says 'ee – an' cawn't eat 'em 'isself. Now I'll 'ave both. By Gawd – I will! Yer nobody!'

He plunged into the lower bunk, rooted in there, and brought to light another dusty biscuit. He held it up before Jimmy – then took a bite defiantly.

'What now?' he asked with feverish impudence. 'Yer may take one – says yer. Why not giv' me both? No. I'm a mangy dorg. One fur a mangy dorg. I'll tyke both. Can yer stop me? Try. Come on. Try.'

Jimmy was clasping his legs and hiding his face on the knees. His shirt clung to him. Every rib was visible. His emaciated back was shaken in repeated jerks by the panting catches of his breath.

'Yer won't? You can't! What did I say?' went on Donkin, fiercely. He swallowed another dry mouthful with a hasty effort. The other's silent helplessness, his weakness, his shrinking attitude exasperated him. 'Ye're done!' he cried. 'Who's yer to be lied to; to be waited on 'and an' foot like a bloomin' ymperor. Yer nobody. Yer no one at all!' he spluttered with such a strength of unerring conviction that it shook him from head to foot in coming out, and left him vibrating like a released string.

James Wait rallied again. He lifted his head and turned bravely at Donkin, who saw a strange face, an unknown face, a fantastic and grimacing mask of despair and fury. Its lips moved rapidly; and hollow, moaning, whistling sounds filled the cabin with a vague mutter full of menace, complaint, and desolation, like the far-off murmur of a rising wind. Wait shook his head; rolled his eyes; he denied, cursed, threatened – and not a word had the strength to pass beyond the sorrowful pout of those black lips. It was incomprehensible and disturbing; a gibberish of emotions, a frantic dumb show of speech pleading for impossible things, promising a shadowy vengeance. It sobered Donkin into a scrutinizing watchfulness.

'Yer can't oller. See? What did I tell yer?' he said, slowly, after a moment of attentive examination. The other kept on headlong and unheard, nodding passionately, grinning with grotesque and appalling flashes of big white teeth. Donkin, as if fascinated by the dumb eloquence and anger of that black phantom, approached, stretching his neck out with distrustful curiosity; and it seemed to him suddenly that he was looking only at the shadow of a man crouching high in the bunk on the level with his eyes. 'What? What?' he said. He seemed to catch the shape of some words in the continuous panting hiss. 'Yer will tell Belfast! Will yer? Are yer a bloomin' kid!' He trembled with alarm and rage, 'Tell yer gran'mother! Yer afeard! Who's yer ter be afeard more'n anyone?' His passionate sense of his own importance ran away with a last remnant of caution. 'Tell an' be damned! Tell, if yer can!' he cried. 'I've been treated worser'n a dorg by your blooming back-lickers. They 'as set me on, only to turn aginst me. I am the only man 'ere. They clouted me, kicked me – an' yer laffed – yer black, rotten incumbrance, you! You will pay fur it. They giv' yer their grub, their water – yer will pay fur it to me, by Gawd! Who axed me ter 'ave a drink of water? They put their bloomin' rags on yer that night, an' what did they giv' ter me – a clout on the bloomin' mouth – blast their . . . S'elp me! . . . Yer will pay fur it with yer money. I'm goin' ter 'ave it in a minyt; as soon has ye're dead, yer bloomin' useless fraud. That's the man I am. An' ye're a thing – a bloody thing. Yah – you corpse!'

He flung at Jimmy's head the biscuit he had been all the time clutching hard, but it only grazed, and striking with a loud crack the bulkhead beyond burst like a hand-grenade into flying pieces. James Wait, as if wounded mortally, fell back on the pillow. His lips ceased to move and the rolling eyes became quiet and stared upwards with an intense and steady persistence. Donkin was surprised; he sat suddenly on the chest, and looked down, exhausted and gloomy. After a moment, he began to mutter to himself, 'Die, you beggar – die. Somebody'll come in. . . . I wish I was drunk. . . . Ten days . . . oysters . . .' He looked up and spoke louder. 'No . . . No more for yer . . . no more bloomin' gals that cook oysters . . . Who's yer? It's my turn now. . . . I wish I was drunk; I would soon giv' you a leg up. That's where yer bound to go. Feet fust, through a port. . . . Splash! Never see yer any more. Overboard! Good 'nuff fur yer.'

Jimmy's head moved slightly and he turned his eyes to Donkin's face; a gaze unbelieving, desolated, and appealing, of a child frightened by the menace of being shut up alone in the dark. Donkin observed him from the chest with hopeful eyes; then, without rising, tried the lid. Locked. 'I wish I was drunk,' he muttered and getting up listened anxiously to the distant sound of footsteps on the deck. They approached – ceased. Someone yawned interminably just outside the door, and the footsteps went away shuffling lazily. Donkin's fluttering heart eased its pace, and when he looked towards the bunk again Jimmy was staring as before at the white beam. ' 'Ow d'yer feel now?' he asked. 'Bad,' breathed out Jimmy.

Donkin sat down patient and purposeful. Every half-hour the bells spoke to one another ringing along the whole length of the ship. Jimmy's respiration was so rapid that it couldn't be counted, so faint that it couldn't be heard. His eyes were terrified as though he had been looking at unspeakable horrors; and by his face one could see that he was thinking of abominable things. Suddenly with an incredibly strong and heart-breaking voice he sobbed out:

'Overboard! . . . I! . . . My God!'

Donkin writhed a little on the box. He looked unwillingly. James Wait was mute. His two long bony hands smoothed the blanket upwards, as though he had wished to gather it all up under his chin. A tear, a big solitary tear, escaped from the corner of his eye and, without touching the hollow cheek, fell on the pillow. His throat rattled faintly.

And Donkin, watching the end of that hateful nigger, felt the anguishing grasp of a great sorrow on his heart at the thought that he himself, some day, would have to go through it all – just like this – perhaps! His eyes became moist. 'Poor beggar,' he murmured. The night seemed to go by in a flash; it seemed to him he could hear the irremediable rush of precious minutes. How long would this blooming affair last? Too long surely. No luck. He could not restrain himself. He got up and approached the bunk. Wait did not stir. Only his eyes appeared alive and his hands continued their smoothing movement with a horrible and tireless industry. Donkin bent over.

'Jimmy,' he called low. There was no answer, but the rattle stopped. 'D'yer see me?' he asked, trembling. Jimmy's chest heaved. Donkin, looking away, bent his ear to Jimmy's lips, and heard a sound like the rustle of a single dry leaf driven along the smooth sand of a beach. It shaped itself.

'Light . . . the lamp . . . and . . . go,' breathed out Wait.

Donkin, instinctively, glanced over his shoulder at the brilliant flame; then, still looking away, felt under the pillow for a key. He got it at once and for the next few minutes remained on his knees shakily but swiftly busy inside the box. When he got up, his face – for the first time in his life – had a pink flush – perhaps of triumph.

He slipped the key under the pillow again, avoiding to glance at Jimmy, who had not moved. He turned his back squarely from the bunk, and started to the door as though he were going to walk a mile. At his second stride he had his nose against it. He clutched the handle cautiously, but at that moment he received the irresistible impression of something happening behind his back. He spun round as though he had been tapped on the shoulder. He was just in time to see Wait's eyes blaze up and go out at once, like two lamps overturned together by a sweeping blow. Something resembling a scarlet thread hung down his chin out of the corner of his lips – and he had ceased to breathe.

Donkin closed the door behind him gently but firmly. Sleeping men, huddled under jackets, made on the lighted deck shapeless dark mounds that had the appearance of neglected graves. Nothing had been done all through the night and he hadn't been missed. He stood motionless and perfectly astounded to find the world outside as he had left it; there was the sea, the ship – sleeping men; and he wondered absurdly at it, as though he had expected to find the men dead, familiar things gone for ever: as though, like a wanderer returning after many years, he had expected to see bewildering changes. He shuddered a little in the penetrating freshness of the air, and hugged himself forlornly. The declining moon drooped sadly in the western board as if withered by the cold touch of a pale dawn. The ship slept. And the immortal sea stretched away, immense and hazy, like the image of life, with a glittering surface and lightless depths. Donkin gave it a defiant glance and slunk off noiselessly as if judged and cast out by the august silence of its might.

*

Jimmy's death, after all, came as a tremendous surprise. We did not know till then how much faith we had put in his delusions. We had taken his chances of life so much at his own valuation that his death, like the death of an old belief, shook the foundations of our society. A common bond was gone; the strong, effective, and respectable bond of a sentimental lie. All that day we mooned at our work, with suspicious looks and a disabused air. In our hearts we thought that in the matter of his departure Jimmy had acted in a perverse and unfriendly manner. He didn't back us up, as a shipmate should. In going he took away with himself the gloomy and solemn shadow in which our folly had posed, with humane satisfaction, as a tender arbiter of fate. And now we saw it was no such thing. It was just common foolishness; a silly and ineffectual meddling with issues of majestic import – that is, if Podmore was right. Perhaps he was? Doubt survived Jimmy; and, like a community of banded criminals disintegrated by a touch of grace, we were profoundly scandalized with each other. Men spoke unkindly to their best chums. Others refused to speak at all. Singleton only was not surprised. 'Dead – is he? Of course,' he said, pointing at the island right abeam; for the calm still held the ship spell-bound within sight of Flores. Dead – of course. *He* wasn't surprised. Here was the land, and there, on the fore-hatch and waiting for the sailmaker – there was that corpse. Cause and effect. And for the first time that voyage, the old seaman became quite cheery and garrulous, explaining and illustrating from the stores of experience how, in sickness, the sight of an island (even a very small one) is generally more fatal than the view of a continent. But he couldn't explain why.

Jimmy was to be buried at five, and it was a long day till then – a day of mental disquiet and even of physical disturbance. We took no interest in our work and, very properly, were rebuked for it. This, in our constant state of hungry irritation, was exasperating. Donkin worked with his brow bound in a dirty rag, and looked so ghastly that Mr Barker was touched with compassion at the sight of this plucky suffering. 'Ough! You, Donkin! Put down your work and go lay-up this watch. You look ill.' 'I am bad, sir – in my 'ead,' he said in a subdued voice, and vanished speedily. This annoyed many, and they thought the mate 'bloomin' soft today'. Captain Allistoun could be seen on the poop watching the sky to the south-west, and it soon got to be known about the decks that the barometer had begun to fall in the night, and that a breeze might be expected before long. This, by a subtle association of ideas, led to violent quarreling as to the exact moment of Jimmy's death. Was it before or after 'that 'ere glass started down'? It was impossible to know, and it caused much contemptuous growling at one another. All of a sudden there was a great tumult forward. Pacific Knowles and good-tempered Davies had come to blows over it. The watch below interfered with spirit, and for ten minutes there was a noisy scrimmage round the hatch, where, in the balancing shade of the sails, Jimmy's body wrapped up in a white blanket, was watched over by the sorrowful Belfast, who, in his desolation, disdained the fray. When the noise had ceased, and the passions had calmed into surly silence, he stood up at the head of the swathed body, lifting both arms on high, cried with pained indignation: 'You ought to be ashamed of yourselves! ...' We were.

Belfast took his bereavement very hard. He gave proofs of unextinguishable devotion. It was he, and no other man, who would help the sailmaker to prepare what was left of Jimmy for a solemn surrender to the insatiable sea. He arranged the weights carefully at the feet: two holystones, an old anchor-shackle without its pin, some broken links of a worn-out stream cable. He arranged them this way, then that. 'Bless my soul! you aren't afraid he will chafe his heel?' said the sailmaker, who hated the job. He pushed the needle, puffing furiously, with his head in a cloud of tobacco smoke; he turned the flaps over, pulled at the stitches, stretched at the canvas. 'Lift his shoulders. . . . Pull to you a bit. . . . So – o – o. Steady.' Belfast obeyed, pulled, lifted, overcome with sorrow, dropping tears on the tarred twine. 'Don't you drag the canvas too taut over his poor face, Sails,' he entreated tearfully. 'What are you fashing yourself for? He will be comfortable enough,' assured the sailmaker, cutting the thread after the last stitch, which came about the middle of Jimmy's forehead. He rolled up the remaining canvas, put away the needles. 'What makes you take on so?' he asked. Belfast looked down at the long package of grey sailcloth. 'I pulled him out,' he whispered, 'and he did not want to go. If I had sat up with him last night he would have kept alive for me . . . but something made me tired.' The sailmaker took vigorous draws at his pipe and mumbled: 'When I . . . West India Station . . . In the *Blanche* frigate . . . Yellow Jack . . . sewed in twenty men a week . . . Portsmouth–Devonport men – townies – knew their fathers, mothers, sisters – the whole boiling of 'em. Thought nothing of it. And these niggers like this one – you don't know where it comes from. Got nobody. No use to nobody. Who will miss him?' 'I do – I pulled him out,' mourned Belfast dismally.

On two planks nailed together and apparently resigned and still under the folds of the Union Jack with a white border, James Wait, carried aft by four men, was deposited slowly, with his feet pointing at an open port. A swell had set in from the westward, and following on the roll of the ship, the red ensign, at half-mast, darted out and collapsed again on the grey sky, like a tongue of flickering fire; Charley tolled the bell; and at every swing to starboard the whole vast semi-circle of steely waters visible on that side seemed to come up with a rush to the edge of the port, as if impatient to get at our Jimmy. Everyone was there but Donkin, who was too ill to come; the Captain and Mr Creighton stood bareheaded on the break of the poop; Mr Baker, directed by the master, who had said to him gravely: 'You know more about the prayer book than I do,' came out of the cabin door quickly and a little embarrassed. All the caps went off. He began to read in a low tone, and with his usual harmlessly menacing utterance, as though he had been for the last time reproving confidentially that dead seaman at his feet. The men listened in scattered groups; they leaned on the fife rail, gazing on the deck; they held their chins in their hands thoughtfully, or, with crossed arms and one knee slightly bent, hung their heads in an attitude of upright meditation. Wamibo dreamed. Mr Baker read on, grunting reverently at the turn of every page. The words, missing the unsteady hearts of men, rolled out to wander without a home upon the heartless sea; and James Wait, silenced for ever, lay uncritical and passive under the hoarse murmur of despair and hopes.

Two men made ready and waited for those words that send so many of our brothers to their last plunge. Mr Baker began the passage. 'Stand by,' muttered the boatswain. Mr Baker read out: 'To the deep,' and paused. The men lifted the inboard end of the planks, the boatswain snatched off the Union Jack, and James Wait did not move. 'Higher,' muttered the boatswain angrily. All the heads were raised; every man stirred uneasily, but James Wait gave no sign of going. In death and swathed up for all eternity, he yet seemed to cling to the ship with the grip of an undying fear. 'Higher! Lift!' whispered the boatswain, fiercely. 'He won't go,' stammered one of the men, shakily, and both appeared ready to drop everything. Mr Baker waited, burying his face in the book, and shuffling his feet nervously. All the men looked profoundly disturbed; from their midst a faint humming noise spread out – growing louder. . . . 'Jimmy!' cried Belfast in a wailing tone, and there was a second of shuddering dismay.

'Jimmy, be a man!' he shrieked, passionately. Every mouth was wide open, not an eyelid winked. He stared wildly, twitching all over; he bent his body forward like a man peering at a horror. 'Go!' he shouted, and sprang out of the crowd with his arm extended. 'Go, Jimmy! – Jimmy, go; Go!' His fingers touched the head of the body, and the grey package started reluctantly to whizz off the lifted planks all at once, with the suddenness of a flash of lightning. The crowd stepped forward like one man; a deep Ah – h – h! came out vibrating from the broad chests. The ship rolled as if relieved of an unfair burden; the sails flapped. Belfast, supported by Archie, gasped hysterically; and Charley, who anxious to see Jimmy's last dive, leaped headlong on the rail, was too late to see anything but the faint circle of a vanishing ripple.

Mr Baker, perspiring abundantly, read out the last prayer in a deep rumour of excited men and fluttering sails. 'Amen!' he said in an unsteady growl, and closed the book.

'Square the yards!' thundered a voice above his head. All hands gave a jump; one or two dropped their caps; Mr Baker looked up surprised. The master, standing on the break of the poop, pointed to the westward. 'Breeze coming,' he said. 'Man the weather braces.' Mr Baker crammed the book hurriedly into his pocket. 'Forward, there – let go the foretack!' he hailed joyfully, bareheaded and brisk; 'Square the foreyard, you port-watch!' 'Fair wind – fair wind,' muttered the men going to the braces. 'What did I tell you?' mumbled old Singleton, flinging down coil after coil with hasty energy; 'I knowed it – he's gone and here it comes.'

It came with the sound of a lofty and powerful sigh. The sails filled, the ship gathered way, and the waking sea began to murmur sleepily of home to the ears of men.

That night, while the ship rushed foaming to the northward before a freshening gale, the boatswain unbosomed himself to the petty officers' berth: 'The chap was nothing but trouble,' he said, 'from the moment he came aboard – d'ye remember – that night in Bombay? Been bullying all that softy crowd – cheeked the old man – we had to go fooling all over a half-drowned ship to save him. Dam' nigh a mutiny all for him – and now the mate abused me like a pickpocket for forgetting to dab a lump of grease on them planks. So I did, but you ought to have known better, too, than to leave a nail sticking up – hey, Chips?'

'And you ought to have known better than to chuck all my tools overboard for 'im, like a skeary greenhorn,' retorted the morose carpenter. 'Well – he's gone after 'em now,' he added in an unforgiving tone. 'On the China Station, I remember once, the Admiral he says to me . . .' began the sailmaker.

*

A week after the *Narcissus* entered the chops of the Channel.

Under white wings she skimmed low over the blue sea like a great tired bird speeding to its nest. The clouds raced with her mastheads; they rose astern enormous and white, soared to the zenith, flew past, and, falling down the wide curve of the sky, seemed to dash headlong into the sea – the clouds swifter than the ship, more free, but without a home. The coast to welcome her stepped out of space into the sunshine. The lofty headlands trod masterfully into the sea; the wide bays smiled in the light; the shadows of homeless clouds ran along the sunny plains, leaped over valleys, without a check darted up the hills, rolled down the slopes; and the sunshine pursued them with patches of running brightness. On the brows of dark cliffs white lighthouses shone in pillars of light. The Channel glittered like a blue mantle shot with gold and starred by the silver of the capping seas. The *Narcissus* rushed past the headlands and the bays. Outward- bound vessels crossed her track, lying over, and with their masts stripped for a slogging fight with the hard sou'-wester. And, inshore, a string of smoking steamboats waddled, hugging the coast, like migrating and amphibious monsters, distrustful of the restless waves.

At night the headlands retreated, the bays advanced into one unbroken line of gloom. The lights of the earth mingled with the lights of heaven; and above the tossing lanterns of a trawling fleet a great lighthouse shone steadily, like an enormous riding light burning above a vessel of fabulous dimensions. Below its steady glow, the coast, stretching away straight and black, resembled the high side of an indestructible craft riding motionless upon the immortal and unresting sea. The dark land lay alone in the midst of waters, like a mighty ship bestarred with vigilant lights – a ship carrying the burden of millions of lives – a ship freighted with dross and with jewels, with gold and with steel. She towered up immense and strong, guarding priceless traditions and untold suffering, sheltering glorious memories and base forgetfulness, ignoble virtues and splendid transgressions. A great ship! For ages had the ocean battered in vain her enduring sides; she was there when the world was vaster and darker, when the sea was great and mysterious, and ready to surrender the prize of fame to audacious men. A ship mother of fleets and nations! The great flagship of the race; stronger than the storms! and anchored in the open sea.

The *Narcissus*, heeling over to off-shore gusts, rounded the South Foreland, passed through the Downs, and, in tow, entered the river. Shorn of the glory of her white wings, she wound obediently after the tug through the maze of invisible channels. As she passed them the red-painted light-vessels, swung at their moorings, seemed for an instant to sail with great speed in the rush of tide, and the next moment were left hopelessly behind. The big buoys on the tails of banks slipped past her sides very low, and, dropping in her wake, tugged at their chains like fierce watch-dogs. The reach narrowed; from both sides, the land approached the ship. She went steadily up the river. On the riverside slopes the houses appeared in groups – seemed to stream down the declivities at a run to see her pass, and, checked by the mud of the foreshore, crowded on the banks. Farther on, the tall factory chimneys appeared in insolent bands and watched her go by, like a straggling crowd of slim giants, swaggering and upright under the black plummets of smoke, cavalierly aslant. She swept round the bends; an impure breeze shrieked a welcome between her stripped spars; and the land, closing in, stepped between the ship and the sea.

A low cloud hung before her – a great opalescent and tremulous cloud, that seemed to rise from the steaming brows of millions of men. Long drifts of smoky vapours soiled it with livid trails; it throbbed to the beat of millions of hearts, and from it came an immense and lamentable murmur – the murmur of millions of lips praying, cursing, sighing, jeering – the undying murmur of folly, regret, and hope exhaled by the crowds of the anxious earth. The *Narcissus* entered the cloud; the shadows deepened; on all sides there was the clang of iron, the sound of mighty blows, shrieks, yells. Black barges drifted stealthily on the murky stream. A mad jumble of begrimed walls loomed up vaguely in the smoke, bewildering and mournful, like a vision of disaster. The tugs backed and filled in the stream, to hold the ship steady at the dock-gates; from her bows two lines went through the air whistling, and struck at the land viciously, like a pair of snakes. A bridge broke in two before her, as if by enchantment; big hydraulic capstans began to turn all by themselves, as though animated by a mysterious and unholy spell. She moved through a narrow lane of water between two low walls of granite, and men with check-ropes in their hands kept pace with her, walking on the broad flag-stones. A group waited impatiently on each side of the vanished bridge: rough heavy men in caps; sallow-faced men in high hats; two bareheaded women; ragged children, fascinated, and with wide eyes. A cart coming at a jerky trot pulled up sharply. One of the women screamed at the silent ship: 'Hallo, Jack!' without looking at anyone in particular, and all hands looked at her from the forecastle head. 'Stand clear! Stand clear of that rope!' cried the dockmen, bending over the stone posts. The crowd murmured, stamped where they stood. 'Let go your quarter-checks! Let go!' sang out a ruddy-faced old man on the quay. The ropes splashed heavily falling in the water, and the *Narcissus* entered the dock.

The stony shores ran away right and left in straight lines, enclosing a sombre and rectangular pool. Brick walls rose high above the water – soulless walls, staring through hundreds of windows as troubled and dull as the eyes of over-fed brutes. At their base monstrous iron cranes crouched, with chains hanging from their long necks, balancing cruel-looking hooks over the decks of lifeless ships. A noise of wheels rolling over stones, the thump of heavy things falling, the racket of feverish winches, the grinding of strained chains, floated on the air. Between high buildings the dust of all the continents soared in short flights; and a penetrating smell of perfumes and dirt, of spices and hides, of things costly and of things filthy, pervaded the space, made for it an atmosphere precious and disgusting. The *Narcissus* came gently into her berth; the shadows of soulless walls fell upon her, the dust of all the continents leaped upon her deck, and a swarm of strange men, clambering up her sides, took possession of her in the name of the sordid earth. She had ceased to live.

A toff in a black coat and high hat scrambled with agility, came up to the second mate, shook hands, and said: 'Hallo

Herbert.' It was his brother. A lady appeared suddenly. A real lady, in a black dress and with a parasol. She looked extremely elegant in the midst of us, and as strange as if she had fallen there from the sky. Mr Baker touched his cap to her. It was the master's wife. And very soon the Captain, dressed very smartly and in a white shirt, went with her over the side. We didn't recognize him at all till, turning on the quay, he called to Mr Baker: 'Don't forget to wind up the chronometers tomorrow morning.' An underhand lot of seedy-looking chaps with shifty eyes wandered in and out of the forecastle looking for a job – they said. 'More likely for something to steal,' commented Knowles, cheerfully. Poor beggars. Who cared? Weren't we home! But Mr Baker went for one of them who had given him some cheek, and we were delighted. Everything was delightful. 'I've finished aft, sir,' called out Mr Creighton. 'No water in the well, sir,' reported for the last time the carpenter, sounding-rod in hand. Mr Baker glanced along the decks at the expectant group of sailors, glanced aloft at the yards. 'Ough! That will do, men,' he grunted. The group broke up. The voyage was ended.

Rolled-up beds went flying over the rail; lashed chests went sliding down the gangway – mighty few of both at that. 'The rest is having a cruise off the Cape,' explained Knowles enigmatically to a dock-loafer with whom he had struck a sudden friendship. Men ran, calling to one another, hailing utter strangers to 'lend a hand with the dunnage', then with sudden decorum approached the mate to shake hands before going ashore. 'Good-bye, sir,' they repeated in various tones. Mr Baker grasped hard palms, grunted in a friendly manner at everyone, his eyes twinkled. 'Take care of your money, Knowles. Ough! Soon get a nice wife if you do.' The lame man was delighted. 'Good-bye, sir,' said Belfast, with emotion, wringing the mate's hand, and looked up with swimming eyes. 'I thought I would take 'im ashore with me,' he went on, plaintively. Mr Baker did not understand, but said kindly: 'Take care of yourself, Craik,' and the bereaved Belfast went over the rail mourning and alone.

Mr Baker, in the sudden peace of the ship, moved about solitary and grunting, trying door-handles, peering into dark places, never done – a model chief mate! No one waited for him ashore. Mother dead; father and two brothers, Yarmouth fishermen, drowned on the Dogger Bank; sister married and unfriendly. Quite a lady. Married to the leading tailor of a little town, and its leading politician, who did not think his sailor brother-in-law quite respectable enough for him. Quite a lady, he thought, sitting down for a moment's rest on the quarter-hatch. Time enough to go ashore and get a bite and sup, and a bed somewhere. He didn't like to part with a ship. No one to think about then. The darkness of a misty evening fell, cold and damp, upon the deserted deck; and Mr Baker sat smoking, thinking of all the successive ships to whom through many long years he had given the best of a seaman's care. And never a command in sight. Not once! 'I haven't somehow the cut of a skipper about me,' he meditated, placidly, while the shipkeeper (who had taken possession of the galley), a wizened old man with bleared eyes, cursed him in whispers for 'hanging about so'. 'Now, Creighton,' he pursued the unenvious train of thought, 'quite a gentleman . . . swell friends . . . will get on. Fine young fellow . . . a little more experience.' He got up and shook himself. 'I'll be back first thing tomorrow morning for the hatches. Don't let them touch anything before I come, shipkeeper,' he called out. Then, at last, he also went ashore – a model chief mate!

The men scattered by the dissolving contact of the land came together once more in the shipping office. 'The *Narcissus* pays off,' shouted outside a glazed door a brass-bound old fellow with a crown and the capitals B. T. on his cap. A lot trooped in at once but many were late. The room was large, whitewashed, and bare; a counter surmounted by a brass-wire grating fenced off a third of the dusty space, and behind the grating a pasty-faced clerk with his hair parted in the middle, had the quick, glittering eyes and the vivacious, jerky movements of a caged bird. Poor Captain Allistoun also in there, and sitting before a little table with piles of gold and notes on it, appeared subdued by his captivity. Another Board of Trade bird was perching on a high stool near the door: an old bird that did not mind the chaff of elated sailors. The crew of the *Narcissus*, broken up into knots, pushed in the corners. They had new shore togs, smart jackets that looked as if they had been shaped with an axe, glossy trousers that seemed made of crumpled sheet-iron, collarless flannel shirts, shiny new boots. They tapped on shoulders, button-holed one another, asked: 'Where did you sleep last night?' whispered gaily, slapped their thighs with bursts of subdued laughter. Most had clean, radiant faces; only one or two turned up dishevelled and sad; the two young Norwegians looked tidy, meek, and altogether of a promising material for the kind ladies who patronize the Scandinavian Home. Wamibo, still in his working clothes, dreamed, upright and burly in the middle of the room, and, when Archie came in, woke up for a smile. But the wide-awake clerk called out a name, and the paying-off business began.

One by one they came up to the pay-table to get the wages of their glorious and obscure toil. They swept the money with care into the broad palms, rammed it trustfully into trousers' pockets, or, turning their backs on the table, reckoned with difficulty in the hollow of their stiff hands. 'Money right? Sign the release. There – there,' repeated the clerk, impatiently. 'How stupid those sailors are!' he thought. Singleton came up, venerable – and uncertain as to daylight; brown drops of tobacco juice hung in his white beard; his hands, that never hesitated in the great light of the open sea, could hardly find the small pile of gold in the profound darkness of the shore. 'Can't write?' said the clerk, shocked. 'Make a mark, then.' Singleton painfully sketched a heavy cross, blotted the page. 'What a disgusting old brute,' muttered the clerk. Somebody opened the door for him, and the patriachial seaman passed through unsteadily, without as much as a glance at any of us.

Archie displayed a pocket-book. He was chaffed. Belfast, who looked wild, as though he had already luffed up through a public-house or two, gave signs of emotion and wanted to speak to the Captain privately. The master was surprised. They spoke through the wires, and we could hear the Captain saying: 'I've given it up to the Board of Trade.' 'I should 've liked to get something of his,' mumbled Belfast. 'But you can't, my man. It's given up, locked and sealed, to the Marine office,' expostulated the master; and Belfast stood back, with drooping mouth and troubled eyes. In a pause of the business we heard the master and the clerk talking. We caught: 'James Wait – deceased – found no papers of any kind – no relations – no trace – the Office must hold his wages then.' Donkin entered. He seemed out of breath, was grave, full of business. He went straight to the desk, talked with animation to the clerk, who thought him an intelligent man. They discussed the account dropping h's against one another as if for a wager – very friendly. Captain Allistoun paid. 'I give you a bad discharge,' he said quietly. Donkin raised his voice: 'I don't want your bloomin' discharge – keep it. I'm goin' ter 'ave a job ashore.' He turned to us. 'No more bloomin' sea fur me,' he said, aloud. All looked at him. He had better clothes, had an easy air, appeared more at home than any of us; he stared with assurance, enjoying the effect of his declaration. 'Yuss. I 'ave friends well off. That's more'n you got. But I am a man. Yer shipmates for all that. Who's comin' fur a drink?'

No one moved. There was a silence; a silence of blank faces and stony looks. He waited a moment, smiled bitterly, and went to the door. There he faced round once more. 'You won't? You bloomin' lot of yrpocrits. No? What 'ave I done to yer? Did I bully yer? Did I 'urt yer? Did I? . . . You won't drink? . . . No! . . . Then may yer die of thirst, every mother's son of yer! Not one of yer 'as the sperrit of a bug. Ye're the scum of the world. Work and starve!'

He went out, and slammed the door with such violence that the old Board of Trade bird nearly fell off his perch.

'He's mad,' declared Archie. 'No! No! He's drunk,' insisted Belfast, lurching about, and in a maudlin tone. Captain Allistoun sat smiling thoughtfully at the cleared pay-table.

*

Outside, on Tower Hill, they blinked, hesitated clumsily, as if blinded by the strange quality of the hazy light, as if discomposed by the view of so many men; and they who could hear one another in the howl of gales seemed deafened and distracted by the dull roar of the busy earth. 'To the Black Horse! To the Black Horse!' cried some. 'Let us have a drink together before we part.' They crossed the road, clinging to one another. Only Charley and Belfast wandered off alone. As I came up I saw a red-faced, blowsy woman, in a grey shawl, and with dusty, fluffy hair, fall on Charley's neck. It was his mother. She slobbered over him: 'O, my boy! My boy!' 'Leggo of me,' said Charley. 'Leggo, mother!' I was passing him at the time, and over the untidy head of the blubbering woman he gave me a humorous smile and a glance ironic, courageous, and profound, that seemed to put all my knowledge of life to shame. I nodded and passed on, but heard him say again, good-naturedly: 'If you leggo of me this minyt – ye shall 'ave a bob for a drink out of my pay.' In the next few steps I came upon Belfast. He caught my arm with tremulous enthusiasm. 'I couldn't go wi' 'em,' he stammered, indicating by a nod our noisy crowd, that drifted slowly along the other sidewalk. 'When I think of Jimmy ... Poor Jim! When I think of him I have no heart for drink. You were his chum, too ... but I pulled him out ... didn't I? Short wool he had.... Yes. And I stole the blooming pie.... He wouldn't go.... He wouldn't go for nobody.' He burst into tears. 'I never touched him – never – never!' he sobbed. 'He went for me like ... like ... a lamb.'

I disengaged myself gently. Belfast's crying fits generally ended in a fight with someone, and I wasn't anxious to stand the brunt of his inconsolable sorrow. Moreover, two bulky policemen stood near by, looking at us with a disapproving and incorruptible gaze. 'So long!' I said, and went on my way.

But at the corner I stopped to take my last look at the crew of the *Narcissus*. They were swaying irresolute and noisy on the broad flagstones before the Mint. They were bound for the Black Horse, where men in fur caps, with brutal faces and in shirt sleeves, dispense out of varnished barrels the illusions of strength, mirth, happiness; the illusion of splendour and poetry of life, to the paid-off crews of southern-going ships. From afar I saw them discoursing, with jovial eyes and clumsy gestures, while the sea of life thundered into their ears ceaseless and unheeded. And swaying about there on the white stones, surrounded by the hurry and clamour of men, they appeared to be creatures of another kind – lost, alone, forgetful, and doomed; they were like castaways, like reckless and joyous castaways, like mad castaways making merry in the storm and upon an insecure ledge of a treacherous rock. The roar of the town resembled the roar of topping breakers, merciless and strong, with a loud voice and cruel purpose; but overhead the clouds broke; a flood of sunshine streamed down the walls of grimy houses. The dark knot of seamen drifted in sunshine. To the left of them the trees in Tower Gardens sighed. The stones of the Tower gleaming, seemed to stir in the play of light, as if remembering suddenly all the great joys and sorrows of the past, the fighting prototypes of these men; press-gangs; mutinous cries; the wailing of women by the riverside, and the shouts of men welcoming victories. The sunshine of heaven fell like a gift of grace on the mud of the earth, on the remembering and mute stones, on greed, selfishness; on the anxious faces of forgetful men. And to the right of the dark group the stained front of the Mint, cleansed by the flood of light, stood out for a moment dazzling and white like a marble place in a fairy tale. The crew of the *Narcissus* drifted out of sight.

I never saw them again. The sea took some, the steamers took others, the graveyards of the earth will account for the rest. Singleton had no doubt taken with him the long record of his faithful work into the peaceful depths of a hospitable sea. And Donkin, who never did a decent day's work in his life, no doubt earns his living by discoursing with filthy eloquence upon the right of labour to live. So be it! Let the earth and the sea each have its own.

A gone shipmate, like any other man, is gone for ever; and I never met one of them again. But at times the spring-flood of memory sets with force up the dark River of the Nine Bends. Then on the waters of the forlorn stream drifts a ship – a shadowy ship manned by a crew of Shades. They pass and make a sign, in a shadowy hail. Haven't we, together and upon the immortal sea, wrung out a meaning from our sinful lives? Good-bye, brothers! You were a good crowd. As good a crowd as ever fisted with wild cries the beating canvas of a heavy foresail; or tossing aloft, invisible in the night, gave back yell for yell to a westerly gale.

Youth

'Youth': a Narrative

This could have occurred nowhere but in England, where men and sea interpenetrate, so to speak – the sea entering into the life of most men, and the men knowing something or everything about the sea, in the way of amusement, of travel, or of bread-winning.

We were sitting round a mahogany table that reflected the bottle, the claret-glasses, and our faces as we leaned on our elbows. There was a director of companies, an accountant, a lawyer, Marlow, and myself. The director had been a *Conway* boy, the accountant had served four years at sea, the lawyer – a fine crusted Tory, High Churchman, the best of old fellows, the soul of honour – had been chief officer in the P. & O. service in the good old days when mail-boats were square-rigged at least on two masts, and used to come down the China Sea before a fair monsoon with stun'sails set alow and aloft. We all began life in the merchant service. Between the five of us there was the strong bond of the sea, and also the fellowship of the craft, which no amount of enthusiasm for yachting, cruising, and so on can give, since one is only the amusement of life and the other is life itself.

Marlow (at least I think that is how he spelt his name) told the story, or rather the chronicle, of a voyage:

'Yes, I have seen a little of the Eastern seas; but what I remember best is my first voyage there. You fellows know there are those voyages that seem ordered for the illustration of life, that might stand for a symbol of existence. You fight, work, sweat, nearly kill yourself, sometimes do kill yourself, trying to accomplish something – and you can't. Not from any fault of yours. You simply can do nothing, neither great nor little – not a thing in the world – not even marry an old maid, or get a wretched 600-ton cargo of coal to its port of destination.

'It was altogether a memorable affair. It was my first voyage to the East, and my first voyage as second mate; it was also my skipper's first command. You'll admit it was time. He was sixty if a day; a little man, with a broad, not very straight back, with bowed shoulders and one leg more bandy than the other, he had that queer twisted-about appearance you see so often in men who work in the fields. He had a nut-cracker face – chin and nose trying to come together over a sunken mouth – and it was framed in iron-grey fluffy hair, that looked like a chin-strap of cotton-wool sprinkled with coal-dust. And he had blue eyes in that old face of his, which were amazingly like a boy's, with that candid expression some quite common men preserve to the end of their days by a rare internal gift of simplicity of heart and rectitude of soul. What induced him to accept me was a wonder. I had come out of a crack Australian clipper, where I had been third officer, and he seemed to have a prejudice against crack clippers as aristocratic and high-toned. He said to me, "You know, in this ship you will have to work." I said I had to work in every ship I had ever been in. "Ah, but this is different, and you gentlemen out of them big ships; ... but there! I dare say you will do. Join tomorrow."

'I joined tomorrow. It was twenty-two years ago; and I was just twenty. How time passes! It was one of the happiest days of my life. Fancy! Second mate for the first time – a really responsible officer! I wouldn't have thrown up my new billet for a fortune. The mate looked me over carefully. He was also an old chap, but of another stamp. He had a Roman nose, a snow-white, long beard, and his name was Mahon, but he insisted that it should be pronounced Mann. He was well connected; yet there was something wrong with his luck, and he had never got on.

'As to the captain, he had been for years in coasters, then in the Mediterranean, and last in the West Indian trade. He had never been round the Capes. He could just write a kind of sketchy hand, and didn't care for writing at all. Both were thorough good seamen of course, and between those two old chaps I felt like a small boy between two grandfathers.

'The ship also was old. Her name was the *Judea*. Queer name, isn't it? She belonged to a man Wilmer, Wilcox – some name like that; but he has been bankrupt and dead these twenty years or more, and his name don't matter. She had been laid up in Shadwell basin for ever so long. You may imagine her state. She was all rust, dust, grime – soot aloft, dirt on deck. To me it was like coming out of a palace into a ruined cottage. She was about 400 tons, had a primitive windlass, wooden latches to the doors, not a bit of brass about her, and a big square stern. There was on it, below her name in big letters, a lot of scroll-work, with the gilt off, and some sort of a coat of arms, with the motto "Do or Die" underneath. I remember it took my fancy immensely. There was a touch of romance in it, something that made me love the old thing – something that appealed to my youth!

'We left London in ballast – sand ballast – to load a cargo of coal in a northern port for Bankok. Bankok! I thrilled. I had been six years at sea, but had only seen Melbourne and Sydney, very good places, charming places in their way – but Bankok!

'We worked out of the Thames under canvas, with a North Sea pilot on board. His name was Jermyn, and he dodged all day long about the galley drying his handkerchief before the stove. Apparently he never slept. He was a dismal man, with a perpetual tear sparkling at the end of his nose, who either had been in trouble, or was in trouble, or expected to be in trouble – couldn't be happy unless something went wrong. He mistrusted my youth, my commonsense, and my seamanship, and made a point of showing it in a hundred little ways. I dare say he was right. It seems to me I knew very little then, and I know not much more now; but I cherish a hate for that Jermyn to this day.

'We were a week working up as far as Yarmouth Roads, and then we got into a gale – the famous October gale of twenty-two years ago. It was wind, lightning, sleet, snow, and a terrific sea. We were flying light, and you may imagine how bad it was when I tell you we had smashed bulwarks and a flooded deck. On the second night she shifted her ballast into the lee bow, and by that time we had been blown off somewhere on the Dogger Bank. There was nothing for it but go below with shovels and try to right her, and there we were in that vast hold, gloomy like a cavern, the tallow dips stuck and flickering on the beams, the gale howling above, the ship tossing about like mad on her side; there we all were, Jermyn, the captain, every one, hardly able to keep our feet, engaged on that gravedigger's work, and trying to toss shovelfuls of wet sand up to windward.

At every tumble of the ship you could see vaguely in the dim light men falling down with a great flourish of shovels. One of the ship's boys (we had two), impressed by the weirdness of the scene, wept as if his heart would break. We could hear him blubbering somewhere in the shadows.

'On the third day the gale died out, and by-and-by a north country tug picked us up. We took sixteen days in all to get from London to the Tyne! When we got into dock we had lost our turn for loading, and they hauled us off to a tier where we remained for a month. Mrs Beard (the captain's name was Beard) came from Colchester to see the old man. She lived on board. The crew of runners had left, and there remained only the officers, one boy and the steward, a mulatto who answered to the name of Abraham. Mrs Beard was an old woman, with a face all wrinkled and ruddy like a winter apple, and the figure of a young girl. She caught sight of me once, sewing on a button, and insisted on having my shirts to repair. This was something different from the captains' wives I had known on board crack clippers. When I brought her the shirts, she said: "And the socks? They want mending, I am sure, and John's – Captain Beard's – things are all in order now. I would be glad of something to do." Bless the old woman. She overhauled my outfit for me, and meantime I read for the first time *Sartor Resartus* and Burnaby's *Ride to Khiva*. I didn't understand much of the first then; but I remember I preferred the soldier to the philosopher at the time; a preference which life has only confirmed. One was a man, and the other was either more – or less. However, they are both dead and Mrs Beard is dead, and youth, strength, genius, thoughts, achievements, simple hearts – all dies. . . . No matter.

'They loaded us at last. We shipped a crew. Eight able seamen and two boys. We hauled off one evening to the buoys at the dock-gates, ready to go out, and with a fair prospect of beginning the voyage next day. Mrs Beard was to start for home by a late train. When the ship was fast we went to tea. We sat rather silent through the meal – Mahon, the old couple, and I. I finished first, and slipped away for a smoke, my cabin being in a deck-house just against the poop. It was high water, blowing fresh with a drizzle; the double dock-gates were opened, and the steam-colliers were going in and out in the darkness with their lights burning bright, a great plashing of propellers, rattling of winches, and a lot of hailing on the pier-heads. I watched the procession of head-lights gliding high and of green lights gliding low in the night, when suddenly a red gleam flashed at me, vanished, came into view again, and remained. The fore-end of a steamer loomed up close. I shouted down the cabin, "Come up, quick!" and then heard a startled voice saying afar in the dark, "Stop her, sir." A bell jingled. Another voice cried warningly. "We are going right into that barque, sir." The answer to this was a gruff "All right," and the next thing was a heavy crash as the steamer struck a glancing blow with the bluff of her bow about our fore-rigging. There was a moment of confusion, yelling, and running about. Steam roared. Then somebody was heard saying, "All clear, sir." ... "Are you all right?" asked the gruff voice. I had jumped forward to see the damage, and hailed back, "I think so." "Easy astern," said the gruff voice. A bell jingled. "What steamer is that?" screamed Mahon. By that time she was no more to us than a bulky shadow manœuvring a little way off. They shouted at us some name – a woman's name, Miranda or Melissa – or some such thing. "This means another month in this beastly hole," said Mahon to me, as we peered with lamps about the splintered bulwarks and broken braces. "But where's the captain?"

'We had not heard or seen anything of him all that time. We went aft to look. A doleful voice arose hailing somewhere in the middle of the dock, "*Judea* ahoy!" ... How the devil did he get there? ... "Hallo!" we shouted. "I am adrift in our boat without oars," he cried. A belated water-man offered his services, and Mahon struck a bargain with him for half-a-crown to tow our skipper alongside; but it was Mrs Beard that came up the ladder first. They had been floating about the dock in that mizzly cold rain for nearly an hour. I was never so surprised in my life.

'It appears that when he heard my shout "Come up" he understood at once what was the matter, caught up his wife, ran on deck, and across, and down into our boat, which was fast to the ladder. Not bad for a sixty-year-old. Just imagine that old fellow saving heroically in his arms that old woman – the woman of his life. He set her down on a thwart, and was ready to climb back on board when the painter came adrift somehow, and away they went together. Of course in the confusion we did not hear him shouting. He looked abashed. She said cheerfully, "I suppose it does not matter my losing the train now?" "No, Jenny – you go below and get warm," he growled. Then to us: "A sailor has no business with a wife – I say. There I was, out of the ship. Well, no harm done this time. Let's go and look at what that fool of a steamer smashed."

'It wasn't much, but it delayed us three weeks. At the end of that time, the captain being engaged with his agents, I carried Mrs Beard's bag to the railway-station and put her all comfy into a third-class carriage. She lowered the window to say, "You are a good young man. If you see John – Captain Beard – without his muffler at night, just remind him from me to keep his throat well wrapped up." "Certainly, Mrs Beard," I said. "You are a good young man; I noticed how attentive you are to John – to Captain—" The train pulled out suddenly; I took my cap off to the old woman: I never saw her again. . . . Pass the bottle.

'We went to sea next day. When we made that start for Bankok we had been already three months out of London. We had expected to be a fortnight or so – at the outside.

'It was January, and the weather was beautiful – the beautiful sunny winter weather that has more charm than in the summer-time, because it is unexpected, and crisp, and you know it won't, it can't, last long. It's like a windfall, like a godsend, like an unexpected piece of luck.

'It lasted all down the North Sea, all down Channel; and it lasted till we were three hundred miles or so to the westward of the Lizards: then the wind went round to the sou'west and began to pipe up. In two days it blew a gale. The *Judea*, hove to, wallowed on the Atlantic like an old candle-box. It blew day after day: it blew with spite, without interval, without mercy, without rest. The world was nothing but an immensity of great foaming waves rushing at us, under a sky low enough to touch with the hand and dirty like a smoked ceiling. In the stormy space surrounding us there was as much flying spray as air. Day after day and night after night there was nothing round the ship but the howl of the wind, the tumult of the sea, the noise of water pouring over her deck. There was no rest for her and no rest for us. She tossed, she pitched, she stood on her head, she sat on her tail, she rolled, she groaned, and we had to hold on while on deck and cling to our bunks when below, in a constant effort of body and worry of mind.

'One night Mahon spoke through the small window of my berth. It opened right into my very bed, and I was lying there sleepless, in my boots, feeling as though I had not slept for years, and could not if I tried. He said excitedly –

' "You got the sounding-rod in here, Marlow? I can't get the pumps to suck. By God; it's no child's play."

'I gave him the sounding-rod and lay down again, trying to think of various things – but I thought only of the pumps. When I came on deck they were still at it, and my watch relieved at the pumps. By the light of the lantern brought on deck to examine the sounding-rod I caught a glimpse of their weary, serious faces. We pumped all the four hours. We pumped all night, all day, all the week – watch and watch. She was working herself loose, and leaked badly – not enough to drown us at once, but enough to kill us with the work at the pumps. And while we pumped the ship was going from us piecemeal: the bulwarks went, the stanchions were torn out, the ventilators smashed, the cabin-door burst in. There was not a dry spot in the ship. She was being gutted bit by bit. The long-boat changed, as if my magic, into matchwood where she stood in her gripes. I had lashed her myself, and was rather proud of my handiwork, which had withstood so long the malice of the sea. And we pumped. And there was no break in the weather. The sea was white like a sheet of foam, like a caldron of boiling milk; there was not a break in the clouds, no – not the size of a man's hand – no, not for so much as ten seconds. There was for us no sky, there were for us no stars, no sun, no universe – nothing but angry clouds and an infuriated sea. We pumped watch and watch, for dear life; and it seemed to last for months, for years, for all eternity, as though we had been dead and gone to a hell for sailors. We forgot the day of the week, the name of the month, what year it was, and whether we had ever been ashore. The sails blew away, she lay broadside on under a weather-cloth, the ocean poured over her, and we did not care. We turned those handles, and had the eyes of idiots. As soon as we had crawled on deck I used to take a round turn with a rope about the men, the pumps, and the mainmast, and we turned, we turned incessantly, with the water to our waists, to our necks, over our heads. It was all one. We had forgotten how it felt to be dry.

'And there was somewhere in me the thought: By Jove! this is the deuce of an adventure – something you read about; and it is my first voyage as second mate – and I am only twenty – and here I am lasting it out as well as any of these men, and keeping my chaps up to the mark. I was pleased. I would not have given up the experience for worlds. I had moments of exultation. Whenever the old dismantled craft pitched heavily with her counter high in the air, she seemed to me to throw up, like an appeal, like a defiance, like a cry to the clouds without mercy, the words written on her stern: "*Judea*, London. Do or Die."

'O youth! The strength of it, the faith of it, the imagination of it! To me she was not an old rattletrap carting about the world a lot of coal for a freight – to me she was the endeavour, the test, the trial of life. I think of her with pleasure, with affection, with regret – as you would think of someone dead you have loved. I shall never forget her. . . . Pass the bottle.

'One night when tied to the mast, as I explained, we were pumping on, deafened with the wind, and without spirit enough in us to wish ourselves dead, a heavy sea crashed aboard and swept clean over us. As soon as I got my breath I shouted, as in duty bound, "Keep on, boys!" when suddenly I felt something hard floating on deck strike the calf of my leg. I made a grab at it and missed. It was so dark we could not see each other's faces within a foot – you understand.

'After the thump the ship kept quiet for a while, and the thing, whatever it was, struck my leg again. This time I caught it – and it was a saucepan. At first, being stupid with fatigue and thinking of nothing but the pumps, I did not understand what I had in my hand. Suddenly it dawned upon me, and I shouted, "Boys, the house on deck is gone. Leave this, and let's look for the cook."

'There was a deck-house forward, which contained the galley, the cook's berth, and the quarters of the crew. As we had expected for days to see it swept away, the hands had been ordered to sleep in the cabin – the only safe place in the ship. The steward, Abraham, however, persisted in clinging to his berth, stupidly, like a mule – from sheer fright I believe, like an animal that won't leave a stable falling in an earthquake. So we went to look for him. It was chancing death, since once out of our lashings we were as exposed as if on a raft. But we went. The house was shattered as if a shell had exploded inside. Most of it had gone overboard – stove, men's quarters, and their property, all was gone; but two posts, holding a portion of the bulkhead to which Abraham's bunk was attached, remained as if by a miracle. We groped in the ruins and came upon this, and there he was, sitting in his bunk, surrounded by foam and wreckage, jabbering cheerfully to himself. He was out of his mind; completely and for ever mad, with this sudden shock coming upon the fag-end of his endurance. We snatched him up, lugged him aft, and pitched him head-first down the cabin companion. You understand there was no time to carry him down with infinite precautions and wait to see how he got on. Those below would pick him up at the bottom of the stairs all right. We were in a hurry to go back to the pumps. That business could not wait. A bad leak is an inhuman thing.

'One would think that the sole purpose of that fiendish gale had been to make a lunatic of that poor devil of a mulatto. It eased before morning, and next day the sky cleared, and as the sea went down the leak took up. When it came to bending a fresh set of sails the crew demanded to put back – and really there was nothing else to do. Boats gone, decks swept clean, cabin gutted, men without a stitch but what they stood in, stores spoiled, ship strained. We put her head for home, and – would you believe it? The wind came east right in our teeth. It blew fresh, it blew continuously. We had to beat up every inch of the way, but she did not leak so badly, the water keeping comparatively smooth. Two hours' pumping in every four is no joke – but it kept her afloat as far as Falmouth.

'The good people there live on casualties of the sea, and no doubt were glad to see us. A hungry crowd of shipwrights sharpened their chisels at the sight of that carcass of a ship.

And, by Jove! they had pretty pickings off us before they were done. I fancy the owner was already in a tight place. There were delays. Then it was decided to take part of the cargo out and caulk her topsides. This was done, the repairs finished, cargo reshipped; a new crew came on board, and we went out – for Bankok. At the end of a week we were back again. The crew said they weren't going to Bankok – a hundred and fifty days' passage – in a something hooker that wanted pumping eight hours out of the twenty-four; and the nautical papers inserted again the little paragraph: "*Judea*. Barque. Tyne to Bankok; coals; put back to Falmouth leaky and with crew refusing duty."

'There were more delays – more tinkering. The owner came down for a day, and said she was as right as a little fiddle. Poor old Captain Beard looked like the ghost of a Geordie skipper – through the worry and humiliation of it. Remember he was sixty, and it was his first command. Mahon said it was a foolish business, and would end badly. I loved the ship more than ever, and wanted awfully to get to Bankok. To Bankok! Magic name, blessed name. Mesopotamia wasn't a patch on it. Remember I was twenty, and it was my first second-mate's billet, and the East was waiting for me.

'We went out and anchored in the outer roads with a fresh crew – the third. She leaked worse than ever. It was as if those confounded shipwrights had actually made a hole in her. This time we did not even go outside. The crew simply refused to man the windlass.

'They towed us back to the inner harbour, and we became a fixture, a feature, an institution of the place. People pointed us out to visitors as "That 'ere barque that's going to Bankok – has been here six months – put back three times." On holidays the small boys pulling about in boats would hail, "*Judea*, ahoy!" and if a head showed above the rail shouted, "Where you bound to? – Bankok?" and jeered. We were only three on board. The poor old skipper mooned in the cabin. Mahon undertook the cooking, and unexpectedly developed all a Frenchman's genius for preparing nice little messes. I looked languidly after the rigging. We became citizens of Falmouth. Every shopkeeper knew us. At the barber's or tobacconist's they asked familiarly, "Do you think you will ever get to Bankok?" Meantime the owner, the underwriters, and the charterers squabbled amongst themselves in London, and our pay went on. . . . Pass the bottle.

'It was horrid. Morally it was worse than pumping for life. It seemed as though we had been forgotten by the world, belonged to nobody, would get nowhere; it seemed that, as if bewitched, we would have to live for ever and ever in that inner harbour, a derision and a byword to generations of long-shore loafers and dishonest boatmen. I obtained three months' pay and a five days' leave, and made a rush for London. It took me a day to get there and pretty well another to come back – but three months' pay went all the same. I don't know what I did with it. I went to a music-hall, I believe, lunched, dined, and supped in a swell place in Regent Street, and was back to time, with nothing but a complete set of Byron's works and a new railway rug to show for three months' work. The boat-man who pulled me off to the ship said: "Hallo! I thought you had left the old thing. *She* will never get to Bankok." "That's all *you* know about it," I said, scornfully – but I didn't like that prophecy at all.

'Suddenly a man, some kind of agent to somebody, appeared with full powers. He had grog-blossoms all over his face, an indomitable energy, and was a jolly soul. We leaped into life again. A hulk came alongside, took our cargo, and then we went into dry dock to get our copper stripped. No wonder she leaked. The poor thing, strained beyond endurance by the gale, had, as if in disgust, spat out all the oakum of her lower seams. She was recaulked, new coppered, and made as tight as a bottle. We went back to the hulk and reshipped our cargo.

'Then, on a fine moonlight night, all the rats left the ship.

'We had been infested with them. They had destroyed our sails, consumed more stores than the crew, affably shared our beds and our dangers, and now, when the ship was made seaworthy, concluded to clear out. I called Mahon to enjoy the spectacle. Rat after rat appeared on our rail, took a last look over his shoulder, and leaped with a hollow thud into the empty hulk. We tried to count them, but soon lost the tale. Mahon said: 'Well, well! don't talk to me about the intelligence of rats. They ought to have left before, when we had that narrow squeak from foundering. There you have the proof how silly is the superstition about them. They leave a good ship for an old rotten hulk, where there is nothing to eat, too, the fools! . . . I don't believe they know what is safe or what is good for them, any more than you or I."

'And after some more talk we agreed that the wisdom of rats had been grossly overrated, being in fact no greater than that of men.

'The story of the ship was known, by this, all up the Channel from Land's End to the Forelands, and we could get no crew on the south coast. They sent us one all complete from Liverpool, and we left once more – for Bankok.

'We had fair breezes, smooth water right into the tropics, and the old *Judea* lumbered along in the sunshine. When she went eight knots everything cracked aloft, and we tied our caps to our heads; but mostly she strolled on at the rate of three miles an hour. What could you expect? She was tired – that old ship. Her youth was where mine is – where yours is – you fellows who listen to this yarn; and what friend would throw your years and your weariness in your face? We didn't grumble at her. To us aft, at least, it seemed as though we had been born in her, reared in her, had lived in her for ages, had never known any other ship. I would just as soon have abused the old village church at home for not being a cathedral.

'And for me there was also my youth to make me patient. There was all the East before me, and all life, and the thought that I had been tried in that ship and had come out pretty well. And I thought of men of old who, centuries ago, went that road in ships that sailed no better, to the land of palms, and spices, and yellow sands, and of brown nations ruled by kings more cruel than Nero the Roman, and more splendid than Solomon the Jew. The old bark lumbered on, heavy with her age and the burden of her cargo, while I lived the life of youth in ignorance and hope. She lumbered on through an interminable procession of days; and the fresh gilding flashed back at the setting sun, seemed to cry out over the darkening sea the words painted on her stern, "*Judea*, London. Do or Die."

'Then we entered the Indian Ocean and steered northerly for Java Head. The winds were light. Weeks slipped by. She crawled on, do or die, and people at home began to think of posting us as overdue.

'One Saturday evening, I being off duty, the men asked me to give them an extra bucket of water or so – for washing clothes. As I did not wish to screw on the fresh-water pump so late, I went forward whistling, and with a key in my hand to unlock the forepeak scuttle, intending to serve the water out of a spare tank we kept there.

'The smell down below was as unexpected as it was frightful. One would have thought hundreds of paraffin-lamps had been flaring and smoking in that hole for days. I was glad to get out. The man with me coughed and said, "Funny smell, sir." I answered negligently, "It's good for the health they say," and walked aft.

'The first thing I did was to put my head down the square of the midship ventilator. As I lifted the lid a visible breath, something like a thin fog, a puff of faint haze, rose from the opening. The ascending air was hot, and had a heavy, sooty, paraffiny smell. I gave one sniff, and put down the lid gently. It was no use choking myself. The cargo was on fire.

'Next day she began to smoke in earnest. You see it was to be expected, for though the coal was of a safe kind, that cargo had been so handled, so broken up with handling, that it looked more like smithy coal than anything else. Then it had been wetted – more than once. It rained all the time we were taking it back from the hulk, and now with this long passage it got heated, and there was another case of spontaneous combustion.

'The captain called us into the cabin. He had a chart spread on the table, and looked unhappy. He said, "The coast of West Australia is near, but I mean to proceed to our destination. It is the hurricane month, too; but we will just keep her head for Bankok, and fight the fire. No more putting back anywhere, if we all get roasted. We will try first to stifle this 'ere damned combustion by want of air."

'We tried. We battened down everything, and still she smoked. The smoke kept coming out through imperceptible crevices; it forced itself through bulkheads and covers; it oozed here and there and everywhere in slender threads, in an invisible film, in an incomprehensible manner. It made its way into the cabin, into the forecastle; it poisoned the sheltered places on the deck, it could be sniffed as high as the mainyard. It was clear that if the smoke came out the air came in. This was disheartening. This combustion refused to be stifled.

'We resolved to try water, and took the hatches off. Enormous volumes of smoke, whitish, yellowish, thick, greasy, misty, choking, ascended as high as the trucks. All hands cleared out aft. Then the poisonous cloud blew away, and we went back to work in a smoke that was no thicker now than that of an ordinary factory chimney.

'We rigged the force-pump, got the hose along, and by-and-by it burst. Well, it was as old as the ship – a prehistoric hose, and past repair. Then we pumped with the feeble head-pump, drew water with buckets, and in this way managed in time to pour lots of Indian Ocean into the main hatch. The bright stream flashed in sunshine, fell into a layer of white crawling smoke, and vanished on the black surface of coal. Steam ascended mingling with the smoke. We poured salt water as into a barrel without a bottom. It was our fate to pump in that ship, to pump out of her, to pump into her; and after keeping water out of her to save ourselves from being drowned, we frantically poured water into her to save ourselves from being burnt.

'And she crawled on, do or die, in the serene weather. The sky was a miracle of purity, a miracle of azure. The sea was polished, was blue, was pellucid, was sparkling like a precious stone, extending on all sides, all round to the horizon – as if the whole terrestrial globe had been one jewel, one colossal sapphire, a single gem fashioned into a planet. And on the lustre of the great calm waters the *Judea* glided imperceptibly, enveloped in languid and unclean vapours, in a lazy cloud that drifted to leeward, light and slow; a pestiferous cloud defiling the splendour of sea and sky.

'All this time of course we saw no fire. The cargo smouldered at the bottom somewhere. Once Mahon, as we were working side by side, said to me with a queer smile: "Now, if only she would spring a tidy leak – like that time when we first left the Channel – it would put a stopper on this fire. Wouldn't it?" I remarked irrelevantly, "Do you remember the rats?"

'We fought the fire and sailed the ship too as carefully as though nothing had been the matter. The steward cooked and attended on us. Of the other twelve men, eight worked while four rested. Everyone took his turn, captain included. There was equality, and if not exactly fraternity, then a deal of good feeling. Sometimes a man, as he dashed a bucketful of water down the hatchway, would yell out, "Hurrah for Bankok!" and the rest laughed. But generally we were taciturn and serious – and thirsty. Oh! how thirsty! And we had to be careful with the water. Strict allowance. The ship smoked, the sun blazed. . . . Pass the bottle.

'We tried everything. We even made an attempt to dig down to the fire. No good, of course. No man could remain more than a minute below. Mahon, who went first, fainted there, and the man who went to fetch him out did likewise. We lugged them out on deck. Then I leaped down to show how easily it could be done. They had learned wisdom by that time, and contented themselves by fishing for me with a chain-hook tied to a broom-handle, I believe. I did not offer to go and fetch up my shovel, which was left down below.

'Things began to look bad. We put the long-boat into the water. The second boat was ready to swing out. We had also another, a 14-foot thing, on davits aft, where it was quite safe.

'Then, behold, the smoke suddenly decreased. We redoubled our efforts to flood the bottom of the ship. In two days there was no smoke at all. Everybody was on the broad grin. This was on a Friday. On Saturday no work, but sailing the ship of course, was done. The men washed their clothes and their faces for the first time in a fortnight, and had a special dinner given them. They spoke of spontaneous combustion with contempt, and implied *they* were the boys to put out combustions. Somehow we all felt as though we each had inherited a large fortune. But a beastly smell of burning hung about the ship. Captain Beard had hollow eyes and sunken cheeks. I had never noticed so much before how twisted and bowed he was. He and Mahon prowled soberly about hatches and ventilators, sniffing. It struck me suddenly poor Mahon was a very, very old chap. As to me, I was as pleased and proud as though I had helped to win a great naval battle. O! Youth!

'The night was fine. In the morning a homeward-bound ship passed us hull down – the first we had seen for months; but we were nearing the land at last, Java Head being about 190 miles off, and nearly due north.

'Next day it was my watch on deck from eight to twelve. At breakfast the captain observed, "It's wonderful how that smell hangs about the cabin." About ten, the mate being on the poop, I stepped down on the main-deck for a moment. The carpenter's bench stood abaft the mainmast: I leaned against it sucking at my pipe, and the carpenter, a young chap, came to talk to me. He remarked, "I think we have done very well, haven't we?" and then I perceived with annoyance the fool was trying to tilt the bench. I said curtly, "Don't, Chips," and immediately became aware of a queer sensation, of an absurd delusion – I seemed somehow to be in the air. I heard all round me like a pent-up breath released – as if a thousand giants simultaneously had said Phoo! – and felt a dull concussion which made my ribs ache suddenly. No doubt about it – I was in the air, and my body was describing a short parabola. But short as it was, I had the time to think several thoughts in, as far as I can remember, the following order: "This can't be the carpenter – What is it? – Some accident – Submarine volcano? – Coals, gas! – By Jove! we are being blown up – Everybody's dead – I am falling into the after-hatch – I see fire in it."

'The coal-dust suspended in the air of the hold had glowed dull-red at the moment of the explosion. In the twinkling of an eye, in an infinitesimal fraction of a second since the first tilt of the bench, I was sprawling full length on the cargo. I picked myself up and scrambled out. It was quick like a rebound. The deck was a wilderness of smashed timber, lying crosswise like trees in a wood after a hurricane; an immense curtain of soiled rags waved gently before me – it was the main-sail blown to strips. I thought, The masts will be toppling over directly; and to get out of the way bolted on all-fours towards the poop-ladder. The first person I saw was Mahon, with eyes like saucers, his mouth open, and the long white hair standing straight on end round his head like a silver halo. He was just about to go down when the sight of the main-deck stirring, heaving up, and changing into splinters before his eyes, petrified him on the top step. I stared at him in unbelief, and he stared at me with a queer kind of shocked curiosity. I did not know that I had no hair, no eye-brows, no eyelashes, that my young moustache was burnt off, that my face was black, one cheek laid open, my nose cut, and my chin bleeding. I had lost my cap, one of my slippers, and my shirt was torn to rags. Of all this I was not aware. I was amazed to see the ship still afloat, the poop-deck whole – and, most of all, to see anybody alive. Also the peace of the sky and the serenity of the sea were distinctly surprising. I suppose I expected to see them convulsed with horror. . . . Pass the bottle.

'There was a voice hailing the ship from somewhere – in the air, in the sky – I couldn't tell. Presently I saw the captain – and he was mad. He asked me eagerly, "Where's the cabin-table?" and to hear such a question was a frightful shock. I had just been blown up, you understand, and vibrated with that experience, – I wasn't quite sure whether I was alive. Mahon began to stamp with both feet and yelled at him, "Good God! don't you see the deck's blown out of her?" I found my voice, and stammered out as if conscious of some gross neglect of duty, "I don't know where the cabin-table is." It was like an absurd dream.

'Do you know what he wanted next? Well, he wanted to trim the yards. Very placidly, and as if lost in thought, he insisted on having the foreyard squared. "I don't know if there's anybody alive," said Mahon, almost tearfully. "Surely," he said, gently, "there will be enough left to square the foreyard."

'The old chap, it seems, was in his own berth winding up the chronometers, when the shock sent him spinning. Immediately it occurred to him – as he said afterwards – that the ship had struck something, and he ran out into the cabin. There, he saw, the cabin-table had vanished somewhere. The deck being blown up, it had fallen down into the lazarette of course. Where we had our breakfast that morning he saw only a great hole in the floor. This appeared to him so awfully mysterious, and impressed him so immensely, that what he saw and heard after he got on deck were mere trifles in comparison. And, mark, he noticed directly the wheel deserted and his barque off her course – and his only thought was to get that miserable, stripped, undecked, smouldering shell of a ship back again with her head pointing at her port of destination. Bankok! That's what he was after. I tell you this quiet, bowed, bandy-legged, almost deformed little man was immense in the singleness of his idea and in his placid ignorance of our agitation. He motioned us forward with a commanding gesture, and went to take the wheel himself.

'Yes; that was the first thing we did – trim the yards of that wreck! No one was killed, or even disabled, but everyone was more or less hurt. You should have seen them! Some were in rags, with black faces, like coal-heavers, like sweeps, and had bullet heads that seemed closely cropped, but were in fact singed to the skin. Others, of the watch below, awakened by being shot out from their collapsing bunks, shivered incessantly, and kept on groaning even as we went about our work. But they all worked. That crew of Liverpool hard cases had in them the right stuff. It's my experience they always have. It is the sea that gives it – the vastness, the loneliness surrounding their dark stolid souls. Ah! Well! we stumbled, we crept, we fell, we barked our shins on the wreckage, we hauled. The masts stood, but we did not know how much they might be charred down below. It was nearly calm, but a long swell ran from the west and made her roll. They might go at any moment. We looked at them with apprehension. One could not forsee which way they would fall.

'Then we retreated aft and looked about us. The deck was a tangle of planks on edge, of planks on end, of splinters, of ruined woodwork. The masts rose from that chaos like big trees above a matted undergrowth. The interstices of that mass of wreckage were full of something whitish, sluggish, stirring – of something that was like a greasy fog. The smoke of the invisible fire was coming up again, was trailing, like a poisonous thick mist in some valley choked with dead wood. Already lazy wisps were beginning to curl upwards amongst the mass of splinters. Here and there a piece of timber, stuck upright, resembled a post. Half of a fife-rail had been shot through the foresail, and the sky made a patch of glorious blue in the ignobly soiled canvas. A portion of several boards holding together had fallen across the rail, and one end protruded overboard, like a gangway leading upon nothing, like a gangway leading over the deep sea, leading to death – as if inviting us to walk the plank at once and be done with our ridiculous troubles. And still the air, the sky – a ghost, something invisible was hailing the ship.

'Someone had the sense to look over, and there was the helmsman, who had impulsively jumped overboard, anxious to come back. He yelled and swam lustily like a merman, keeping up with the ship. We threw him a rope, and presently he stood amongst us streaming with water and very crestfallen. The captain had surrendered the wheel, and apart, elbow on rail and chin in hand, gazed at the sea wistfully. We asked ourselves, What next? I thought, Now, this is something like. This is great. I wonder what will happen. O youth!

'Suddenly Mahon sighted a steamer far astern. Captain Beard said, "We may do something with her yet." We hoisted two flags, which said in the international language of the sea, "On fire. Want immediate assistance." The steamer grew bigger rapidly, and by-and-by spoke with two flags on her foremast, "I am coming to your assistance."

'In half an hour she was abreast, to windward, within hail, and rolling slightly, with her engines stopped. We lost our composure, and yelled all together with excitement, "We've been blown up." A man in a white helmet, on the bridge, cried, "Yes! All right! All right!" and he nodded his head, and smiled, and made soothing motions with his hand as though at a lot of frightened children. One of the boats dropped in the water, and walked towards us upon the sea with her long oars. Four Calashes pulled a swinging stroke. This was my first sight of Malay seamen. I've known them since, but what struck me then was their unconcern: they came alongside, and even the bowman standing up and holding to our main-chains with the boathook did not deign to lift his head for a glance. I thought people who had been blown up deserved more attention.

'A little man, dry like a chip and agile like a monkey, clambered up. It was the mate of the steamer. He gave one look, and cried, "O boys – you had better quit."

'We were silent. He talked apart with the captain for a time, – seemed to argue with him. Then they went away together to the steamer.

'When our skipper came back we learned that the steamer was the *Somerville*, Captain Nash, from West Australia to

Singapore *via* Batavia with mails, and that the agreement was she should tow us to Anjer or Batavia, if possible, where we could extinguish the fire by scuttling, and then proceed on our voyage – to Bankok! The old man seemed excited. "We will do it yet," he said to Mahon, fiercely. He shook his fist at the sky. Nobody else said a word.

'At noon the steamer began to tow. She went ahead slim and high, and what was left of the *Judea* followed at the end of seventy fathom of tow rope – followed her swiftly like a cloud of smoke with mast-heads protruding above. We went aloft to furl the sails. We coughed on the yards, and were careful about the bunts. Do you see the lot of us there, putting a neat furl on the sails of that ship doomed to arrive nowhere? There was not a man who didn't think that at any moment the masts would topple over. From aloft we could not see the ship for smoke, and they worked carefully, passing the gaskets with even turns. "Harbour furl – aloft there!" cried Mahon from below.

'You understand this? I don't think one of those chaps expected to get down in the usual way. When we did I heard them saying to each other, "Well, I thought we would come down overboard, in a lump – sticks and all – blame me if I didn't." "That's what I was thinking to myself," would answer wearily another battered and bandaged scarecrow. And, mind, these were men without the drilled-in habit of obedience. To an onlooker they would be a lot of profane scallywags without a redeeming point. What made them do it – what made them obey me when I, thinking consciously how fine it was, made them drop the bunt of the foresail twice to try and do it better? What? They had no professional reputation – no examples, no praise. It wasn't a sense of duty; they all knew well enough how to shirk, and laze, and dodge – when they had a mind to it – and mostly they had. Was it the two pounds ten a month that sent them there? They didn't think their pay half good enough. No; it was something in them, something inborn and subtle and everlasting. I don't say positively that the crew of a French or German merchantman wouldn't have done it, but I doubt whether it would have been done in the same way. There was a completeness in it, something solid like a principle, and masterful like an instinct – a disclosure of something secret – of that hidden something, that gift of good or evil that makes racial difference, that shapes the fate of nations.

'It was that night at ten that, for the first time since we had been fighting it, we saw the fire. The speed of the towing had fanned the smouldering destruction. A blue gleam appeared forward, shining below the wreck of the deck. It wavered in patches, it seemed to stir and creep like the light of a glow-worm. I saw it first, and told Mahon. "Then the game's up," he said. "We had better stop this towing, or she will burst out suddenly fore and aft before we can clear out." We set up a yell; rang bells to attract their attention; they towed on. At last Mahon and I had to crawl forward and cut the rope with an axe. There was no time to cast off the lashings. Red tongues could be seen licking the wilderness of splinters under our feet as we made our way back to the poop.

'Of course they very soon found out in the steamer that the rope was gone. She gave a loud blast of her whistle, her lights were seen sweeping in a wide circle, she came up ranging close along-side, and stopped. We were in a tight group on the poop looking at her. Every man had saved a little bundle or a bag. Suddenly a conical flame with a twisted top shot up forward and threw upon the black sea a circle of light, with the two vessels side by side and heaving gently in its centre. Captain Beard had been sitting on the gratings still and mute for hours, but now he rose slowly and advanced in front of us, to the mizzen-shrouds. Captain Nash hailed: "Come along! Look sharp. I have mail-bags on board. I will take you and your boats to Singapore."

' "Thank you! No!" said our skipper. "We must see the last of the ship."

' "I can't stand by any longer," shouted the other. "Mails – you know."

' "Ay! ay! We are all right."

' "Very well! I'll report you in Singapore. . . . Goodbye!'

'He waved his hand. Our men dropped their bundles quietly. The steamer moved ahead, and passing out of the circle of light, vanished at once from our sight, dazzled by the fire which burned fiercely. And then I knew that I would see the East first as commander of a small boat. I thought it fine; and the fidelity to the old ship was fine. We should see the last of her. Oh, the glamour of youth! Oh, the fire of it, more dazzling than the flames of the burning ship, throwing a magic light on the wide earth, leaping audaciously to the sky, presently to be quenched by time, more cruel, more pitiless, more bitter than the sea – and like the flames of the burning ship surrounded by an impenetrable night.

*

'The old man warned us in his gentle and inflexible way that it was part of our duty to save for the underwriters as much as we could of the ship's gear. Accordingly we went to work aft, while she blazed forward to give us plenty of light. We lugged out a lot of rubbish. What didn't we save? An old barometer fixed with an absurd quantity of screws nearly cost me my life: a sudden rush of smoke came upon me, and I just got away in time. There were various stores, bolts of canvas, coils of rope; the poop looked like a marine bazaar, and the boats were lumbered to the gunwales. One would have thought the old man wanted to take as much as he could of his first command with him. He was very, very quiet, but off his balance evidently. Would you believe it? He wanted to take a length of old stream-cable and a kedge-anchor with him in the long-boat. We said, "Aye, aye, sir," deferentially, and on the quiet let the things slip overboard. The heavy medicine-chest went that way, two bags of green coffee, tins of paint – fancy, paint! – a whole lot of things. Then I was ordered with two hands into the boats to make a stowage and get them ready against the time it would be proper for us to leave the ship.

'We put everything straight, stepped the long-boat's mast for our skipper, who was to take charge of her, and I was not sorry to sit down for a moment. My face felt raw, every limb ached as if broken, I was aware of all my ribs, and would have sworn to a twist in the backbone. The boats, fast astern, lay in a deep shadow, and all around I could see the circle of the sea lighted by the fire. A gigantic flame arose forward straight and clear. It flared fierce, with noises like the whirr of wings, with rumbles as of thunder. There were cracks, detonations, and from the cone of flame the sparks flew upwards, as man is born to trouble, to leaky ships, and to ships that burn.

'What bothered me was that the ship, lying broadside to the

swell and to such wind as there was – a mere breath – the boats would not keep astern where they were safe, but persisted, in a pig-headed way boats have, in getting under the counter and then swinging alongside. They were knocking about dangerously and coming near the flame, while the ship rolled on them, and, of course, there was always the danger of the masts going over the side at any moment. I and my two boat-keepers kept them off as best as we could, with oars and boat-hooks; but to be constantly at it became exasperating, since there was no reason why we should not leave at once. We could not see those on board, nor could we imagine what caused the delay. The boat-keepers were swearing feebly, and I had not only my share of the work but also had to keep at it two men who showed a constant inclination to lay themselves down and let things slide.

'At last I hailed, "On deck there," and someone looked over. "We're ready here," I said. The head disappeared, and very soon popped up again. "The captain says, All right, sir, and to keep the boats well clear of the ship."

'Half an hour passed. Suddenly there was a frightful racket, rattle, clanking of chain, hiss of water, and millions of sparks flew up into the shivering column of smoke that stood leaning slightly above the ship. The cat-heads had burned away, and the two red-hot anchors had gone to the bottom, tearing out after them two hundred fathom of red-hot chain. The ship trembled, the mass of flame swayed as if ready to collapse, and the fore top-gallant-mast fell. It darted down like an arrow of fire, shot under, and instantly leaping up within an oar's-length of the boats, floated quietly, very black on the luminous sea. I hailed the deck again. After some time a man in an unexpectedly cheerful but also muffled tone, as though he had been trying to speak with his mouth shut, informed me, "Coming directly, sir," and vanished. For a long time I heard nothing but the whirr and roar of the fire. There were also whistling sounds. The boats jumped, tugged at the painters, ran at each other playfully, knocked their sides together, or, do what we would, swung in a bunch against the ship's side. I couldn't stand it any longer, and swarming up a rope, clambered aboard over the stern.

'It was as bright as day. Coming up like this, the sheet of fire facing me was a terrifying sight, and the heat seemed hardly bearable at first. On a settee cushion dragged out of the cabin Captain Beard, his legs drawn up and one arm under his head, slept with the light playing on him. Do you know what the rest were busy about? They were sitting on deck right aft, round an open case, eating bread and cheese and drinking bottled stout.

'On the background of flames twisting in fierce tongues above their heads they seemed at home like salamanders, and looked like a band of desperate pirates. The fire sparkled in the whites of their eyes, gleamed on patches of white skin seen through the torn shirts. Each had the marks as of a battle about him – bandaged heads, tied-up arms, a strip of dirty rag round a knee – and each man had a bottle between his legs and a chunk of cheese in his hand. Mahon got up. With his handsome and disreputable head, his hooked profile, his long white beard, and with an uncorked bottle in his hand, he resembled one of those reckless sea-robbers of old making merry amidst violence and disaster. "The last meal on board," he explained solemnly. "We had nothing to eat all day, and it was no use leaving all this." He flourished the bottle and indicated the sleeping skipper. "He said he couldn't swallow anything, so I got him to lie down," he went on; and as I stared, "I don't know whether you are aware, young fellow, the man had no sleep to speak of for days – and there will be dam' little sleep in the boats." "There will be no boats by-and-by if you fool about much longer," I said, indignantly. I walked up to the skipper and shook him by the shoulder. At last he opened his eyes, but did not move. "Time to leave her, sir," I said quietly.

'He got up painfully, looked at the flames, at the sea sparkling round the ship, and black, black as ink farther away; he looked at the stars shining dim through a thin veil of smoke in a sky black, black as Erebus.

' "Youngest first," he said.

'And the ordinary seamen, wiping his mouth with the back of his hand, got up, clambered over the taffrail, and vanished. Others followed. One, on the point of going over, stopped short to drain his bottle, and with a great swing of his arm flung it at the fire. "Take this!" he cried.

'The skipper lingered disconsolately, and we left him to commune alone for a while with his first command. Then I went up again and brought him away at last. It was time. The iron-work on the poop was hot to the touch.

'Then the painter of the long-boat was cut, and the three boats, tied together, drifted clear of the ship. It was just sixteen hours after the explosion when we abandoned her. Mahon had charge of the second boat, and I had the smallest – the 14-foot thing. The long-boat would have taken the lot of us; but the skipper said we must save as much property as we could – for the underwriters – and so I got my first command. I had two men with me, a bag of biscuits, a few tins of meat, and a breaker of water. I was ordered to keep close to the long-boat, that in case of bad weather we might be taken into her.

'And do you know what I thought? I thought I would part company as soon as I could. I wanted to have my first command all to myself. I wasn't going to sail in a squadron if there were a chance for independent cruising. I would make land by myself. I would beat the other boats. Youth! All youth! The silly, charming, beautiful youth.

'But we did not make a start at once. We must see the last of the ship. And so the boats drifted about that night, heaving and setting on the swell. The men dozed, waked, sighed, groaned. I looked at the burning ship.

'Between the darkness of earth and heaven she was burning fiercely upon a disc of purple sea shot by the blood-red play of gleams; upon a disc of water glittering and sinister. A high, clear flame, an immense and lonely flame, ascended from the ocean, and from its summit the black smoke poured continuously at the sky. She burned furiously; mournful and imposing like a funeral pile kindled in the night, surrounded by the sea, watched over by the stars. A magnificent death had come like a grace, like a gift, like a reward to that old ship at the end of her laborious days. The surrender of her weary ghost to the keeping of stars and sea was stirring like the sight of a glorious triumph. The masts fell just before daybreak, and for a moment there was a burst and turmoil of sparks that seemed to fill with flying fire the night patient and watchful, the vast night lying silent upon the sea. At daylight she was only a charred shell, floating still under a cloud of smoke and bearing a glowing mass of coal within.

'Then the oars were got out, and the boats forming in a line moved round her remains as if in procession – the long-boat leading. As we pulled across her stern a slim dart of fire shot out viciously at us, and suddenly she went down, head first, in a great hiss of steam. The unconsumed stern was the last to sink; but the paint had gone, had cracked, had peeled off, and there were no letters, there was no word, no stubborn device that was like her soul, to flash at the rising sun her creed and her name.

'We made our way north. A breeze sprang up, and about noon all the boats came together for the last time. I had no mast or sail in mine, but I made a mast out of a spare oar and hoisted a boat-awning for a sail, with a boat-hook for a yard. She was certainly over-masted, but I had the satisfaction of knowing that with the wind aft I could beat the other two. I had to wait for them. Then we all had a look at the captain's chart, and, after a sociable meal of hard bread and water, got our last instructions. These were simple: steer north, and keep together as much as possible. "Be careful with that jury-rig, Marlow," said the captain; and Mahon, as I sailed proudly past his boat, wrinkled his curved nose and hailed, "You will sail that ship of yours under water, if you don't look out, young fellow." He was a malicious old man – and may the deep sea where he sleeps now rock him gently, rock him tenderly to the end of time!

'Before sunset a thick rain-squall passed over the two boats, which were far astern, and that was the last I saw of them for a time. Next day I sat steering my cockle-shell – my first command – with nothing but water and sky around me. I did sight in the afternoon the upper sails of a ship far away, but said nothing, and my men did not notice her. You see I was afraid she might be homeward bound, and I had no mind to turn back from the portals of the East. I was steering for Java – another blessed name – like Bankok, you know. I steered many days.

'I need not tell you what it is to be knocking about in an open boat. I remember nights and days of calm, when we pulled, we pulled, and the boat seemed to stand still, as if bewitched within the circle of the sea horizon. I remember the heat, the deluge of rain-squalls that kept us baling for dear life (but filled our water-cask), and I remember sixteen hours on end with a mouth dry as a cinder and a steering-oar over the stern to keep my first command head on to a breaking sea. I did not know how a good man I was till then. I remember the drawn faces, the dejected figures of my two men, and I remember my youth and the feeling that will never come back any more – the feeling that I could last for ever, outlast the sea, the earth, and all men; the deceitful feeling that lures us on to joys, to perils, to love, to vain effort – to death; the triumphant conviction of strength, the heat of life in the handful of dust, the glow in the heart that with every year grows dim, grows cold, grows small, and expires – and expires, too soon, too soon – before life itself.

'And this is how I see the East. I have seen its secret places and have looked into its very soul; but now I see it always from a small boat, a high outline of mountains, blue and afar in the morning; like faint mist at noon; a jagged wall of purple at sunset. I have the feel of the oar in my hand, the vision of a scorching blue sea in my eyes. And I see a bay, a wide bay, smooth as glass and polished like ice, shimmering in the dark. A red light burns far off upon the gloom of the land, and the night is soft and warm. We drag at the oars with aching arms, and suddenly a puff of wind, a puff faint and tepid and laden with strange odours of blossoms, of aromatic wood, comes out of the still night – the first sigh of the East on my face. That I can never forget. It was impalpable and enslaving, like a charm, like a whispered promise of mysterious delight.

'We had been pulling this finishing spell for eleven hours. Two pulled, and he whose turn it was to rest sat at the tiller. We had made out the red light in that bay and steered for it, guessing it must mark some small coasting port. We passed two vessels, outlandish and high-sterned, sleeping at anchor, and, approaching the light, now very dim, ran the boat's nose against the end of a jutting wharf. We were blind with fatigue. My men dropped the oars and fell off the thwarts as if dead. I made fast to a pile. A current rippled softly. The scented obscurity of the shore was grouped into vast masses, a density of colossal clumps of vegetation, probably – mute and fantastic shapes. And at their foot the semicircle of a beach gleamed faintly, like an illusion. There was not a light, not a stir, not a sound. The mysterious

East faced me, perfumed like a flower, silent like death, dark like a grave.

'And I sat weary beyond expression, exulting like a conqueror, sleepless and entranced as if before a profound, a fateful enigma.

'A splashing of oars, a measured dip reverberating on the level of water, intensified by the silence of the shore into loud claps, made me jump up. A boat, a European boat, was coming in. I invoked the name of the dead: I hailed *Judea* ahoy! A thin shout answered.

'It was the captain. I had beaten the flagship by three hours, and I was glad to hear the old man's voice again, tremulous and tired. "Is it you, Marlow?" "Mind the end of that jetty, sir," I cried.

'He approached cautiously, and brought up with the deep-sea lead-line which we had saved – for the underwriters. I eased my painter and fell alongside. He sat, a broken figure at the stern, wet with dew, his hands clasped in his lap. His men were asleep already. "I had a terrible time of it," he murmured. "Mahon is behind – not very far." We conversed in whispers, in low whispers, as if afraid to wake up the land. Guns, thunder, earthquakes would not have awakened the men just then.

'Looking round as we talked, I saw away at sea a bright light travelling in the night. "There's a steamer passing the bay," I said. She was not passing, she was entering, and she even came close and anchored. "I wish," said the old man, "you would find out whether she is English. Perhaps they could give us a passage somewhere." He seemed nervously anxious. So by dint of punching and kicking I started one of my men into a state of somnambulism, and giving him an oar, took another and pulled towards the lights of the steamer.

'There was a murmur of voices in her, metallic hollow clangs of the engine-room, footsteps on the deck. Her ports shone, round like dilated eyes. Shapes moved about, and there was a shadowy man high up on the bridge. He heard my oars.

'And then, before I could open my lips, the East spoke to me, but it was a Western voice. A torrent of words was poured into the enigmatical, the fateful silence; outlandish, angry words, mixed with words and even whole sentences of good English, less strange but even more surprising. The voice swore and cursed violently; it riddled the solemn peace of the bay by a volley of abuse. It begun by calling me Pig, and from that went crescendo into unmentionable adjectives – in English. The man up there raged aloud in two languages, and with a sincerity in his fury that almost convinced me I had, in some way, sinned against the harmony of the universe. I could hardly see him, but began to think he would work himself into a fit.

'Suddenly he ceased, and I could hear him snorting and blowing like a porpoise. I said—

' "What steamer is this, pray?"

' "Eh? What's this? And who are you?"

' "Castaway crew of an English barque burnt at sea. We came here to-night. I am the second mate. The captain is in the longboat, and wishes to know if you would give us a passage somewhere.'

' "Oh, my goodness! I say. . . . This is the *Celestial* from Singapore on her return trip. I'll arrange with your captain in the morning, . . . and, . . . I say, . . . did you hear me just now?"

' "I should think the whole bay heard you."

' "I thought you were a shore-boat. Now, look here – this infernal lazy scoundrel of a caretaker has gone to sleep again – curse him. The light is out, and I nearly ran foul of the end of this damned jetty. This is the third time he plays me this trick. Now, I ask you, can anybody stand this kind of thing? It's enough to drive a man out of his mind. I'll report him. . . . I'll get the Assistant Resident to give him the sack, by . . . ! See – there's no light. It's out, isn't it? I take you to witness the light's out. There should be a light, you know. A red light on the—"

' "There was a light," I said, mildly.

' "But it's out, man! What's the use of talking like this? You can see for yourself it's out – don't you? If you had to take a valuable steamer along this Godforsaken coast you would want a light, too. I'll kick him from end to end of his miserable wharf. You'll see if I don't. I will—"

' "So I may tell my captain you'll take us?" I broke in.

' "Yes, I'll take you. Goodnight," he said, brusquely.

'I pulled back, made fast again to the jetty, and then went to sleep at last. I had faced the silence of the East. I had heard some of its language. But when I opened my eyes again the silence was as complete as though it had never been broken. I was lying in a flood of light, and the sky had never looked so far, so high, before. I opened my eyes and lay without moving.

'And then I saw the men of the East – they were looking at me. The whole length of the jetty was full of people. I saw brown, bronze, yellow faces, the black eyes, the glitter, the colour of an Eastern crowd. And all these beings stared without a murmur, without a sigh, without a movement. They stared down at the boats, at the sleeping men who at night had come to them from the sea. Nothing moved. The fronds of palms stood still against the sky. Not a branch stirred along the shore, and the brown roofs of hidden houses peeped through the green foliage, through the big leaves that hung shining and still like leaves forged of heavy metal. This was the East of the ancient navigators, so old, so mysterious, resplendent and sombre, living and unchanged, full of danger and promise. And these were the men. I sat up suddenly. A wave of movement passed through the crowd from end to end, passed along the heads, swayed the bodies, ran along the jetty like a ripple on the water, like a breath of wind on a field – and all was still again. I see it now – the wide sweep of the bay, the glittering sands, the wealth of green infinite and varied, the sea blue like the sea of a dream, the crowd of attentive faces, the blaze of vivid colour – the water reflecting it all, the curve of the shore, the jetty, the high-sterned outlandish craft floating still, and the three boats with the tired men from the West sleeping, unconscious of the land and the people and of the violence of sunshine. They slept thrown across the thwarts, curled on bottom-boards, in the careless attitudes of death. The head of the old skipper, leaning back in the stern of the long-boat, had fallen on his breast, and he looked as though he would never wake. Farther out old Mahon's face was upturned to the sky, with the long white beard spread out on his breast, as though he had been shot where he sat at the tiller; and a man, all in a heap in the bows of the boat, slept with both arms embracing the stem-head and with his cheek laid on the gunwale. The East looked at them without a sound.

'I have known its fascination since; I have seen the mysterious shores, the still water, the lands of brown nations, where a stealthy Nemesis lies in wait, pursues, overtakes so many of the conquering race, who are proud of their wisdom, of their knowledge, of their strength. But for me all the East is contained in that vision of my youth. It is all in that moment when I opened my young eyes on it. I came upon it from a tussle with the sea – and I was young – and I saw it looking at me. And this is all that is left of it! Only a moment; a moment of strength, of romance, of glamour – of youth! . . . A flick of sunshine, upon a strange shore, the time to remember, the time for a sigh, and – goodbye! – Night – Goodbye. . . !'

He drank.

'Ah! The good old time – the good old time. Youth and the sea. Glamour and the sea! The good, strong sea, the salt, bitter sea, that could whisper to you and roar at you and knock your breath out of you.'

He drank again.

'By all that's wonderful it is the sea, I believe, the sea itself – or is it youth alone? Who can tell? But you here – you all had something out of life: money, love – whatever one gets on shore – and, tell me, wasn't that the best time, that time when we were young at sea; young and had nothing, on the sea that gives nothing, except hard knocks – and sometimes a chance to feel your strength – that only – what you all regret?'

And we all nodded at him: the man of finance, the man of accounts, the man of law, we all nodded at him over the polished table that like a still sheet of brown water reflected our faces, lined, wrinkled; our faces marked by toil, by deceptions, by success, by love; our weary eyes looking still, looking always, looking anxiously for something out of life, that while it is expected is already gone – has passed unseen, in a sigh, in a flash – together with the youth, with the strength, with the romance of illusions.

The Works of Joseph Conrad

1895 *Almayer's Folly – A Story of an Eastern River*
1896 *An Outcast of the Islands*
1897 *The Nigger of the Narcissus – A Tale of the Sea* (First edition to include Preface, 1914)
1898 *Tales of Unrest* (Contents: 'Karain, a Memory', 'The Idiots', 'An Outpost of Progress', 'The Return', 'The Lagoon')
1900 *Lord Jim – A Tale*
1902 *Youth: A Narrative; and Two Other Stories* (Contents: 'Youth', 'Heart of Darkness', 'The End of the Tether')
1903 *Typhoon, and Other Stories* (Contents: 'Typhoon', 'Amy Foster', 'Falk', 'Tomorrow')
1903 *Romance – A Novel* (In collaboration with Ford Madox Hueffer)
1904 *Nostromo – A Tale of the Seaboard*
1906 *The Mirror of the Sea – Memories and Impressions*
1907 *The Secret Agent – A Simple Tale*
1908 *A Set of Six* (Contents: 'Gaspar Ruiz', 'The Informer', 'The Brute', 'An Anarchist', 'The Duel', 'Il Conde')
1911 *Under Western Eyes*
1912 *A Personal Record* (originally *Some Reminiscences*)
1912 *Twixt Land and Sea – Tales* (Contents: 'A Smile of Fortune', 'The Secret Sharer', 'Freya of the Seven Isles')
1913 *Chance – A Tale in Two Parts*
1915 *Victory – An Island Tale*
1915 *Within the Tides – Tales* (Contents: 'The Planter of Malata', 'The Partner', 'The Inn of the Two Witches', 'Because of the Dollars')
1917 *The Shadow-Line – A Confession*
1919 *The Arrow of Gold – A Story between Two Notes*
1920 *The Rescue – A Romance of the Shallows*
1921 *Notes on Life and Letters*
1923 *The Rover*
1925 *Suspense – A Napoleonic Novel*

1925 *Tales of Hearsay* (Contents: 'The Warrior's Soul', 'Prince Roman', 'The Tale', 'The Black Mate')
1926 *Last Essays*
1923– Uniform Edition of the Works of Joseph Conrad
1928 (Reissued as Collected Edition, 1946–54)

Acknowledgements

The publishers would like to thank the following for kind permission to reproduce copyright material: the Estate of Arnold Bennett and the Oxford University Press for the extract from a letter by Arnold Bennett; and Weidenfeld & Nicolson Ltd for extracts from *Joseph Conrad, A Critical Biography* by Jocelyn Baines.

Critical Supplement

Extract from a letter from Arnold Bennett to H. G. Wells, 8 December 1897

I owe you a good turn for pointing out Conrad to me. I remember I got his first book, *Almayer's Folly*, to review with a batch of others from Unwin, & feeling at the time rather bored (you know the feeling – I get through 50 or 60 novels a month for two papers) I simply didn't read it at all – wrote a vague & discreet par. & left it.

I have just read his new book *The Nigger of the Narcissus*, which has moved me to enthusiasm. Where did the man pick up that style, & that *synthetic* way of gathering up a general impression & flinging it at you? Not only his style, but his attitude, affected me deeply. He is so consciously an artist. Now Kipling isn't an artist a bit. Kipling doesn't know what art is – I mean the art of words; *il ne se préoccupe que de la chose racontée.* He is a great writer but not an artist.

Extract from an unsigned review in the *Spectator*, 25 December 1897

As a picture of rough seafaring life, frank yet never offensively realistic, and illustrating with singular force the collective instincts of a ship's crew, as well as the strange and unlikely alliances that spring up on shipboard, this book is of extraordinary merit. What is more, Mr Conrad has an abiding sense of the mystery of the immortal sea, and the happy gift of painting her changing moods in words that glow with true poetic fire. Lest this should seem exaggerated praise, let us quote the passage describing the view from the *Narcissus* as she entered the Channel:

[quotes Chapter 5: 'Below its steady glow ... in the open sea.']

Mr Conrad is a writer of genius; but his choice of themes, and the uncompromising nature of his methods, debar him from attaining a wide popularity. Illumined though it is by such shining moments as the passage just quoted, we own to having found *The Nigger of the Narcissus* at times almost unbearably depressing.

From *Joseph Conrad* by Jocelyn Baines (Weidenfeld & Nicolson, 1960)

The Nigger of the Narcissus is the culmination of Conrad's apprenticeship as a novelist; in it he showed not only that he had fully mastered the art which he had been learning from Flaubert and Maupassant but that he could accomplish something significantly unique, though according to their formal prescription. The author seldom intrudes himself into the action and comment is kept down to the minimum. He rarely goes inside the characters, but gains his effect through the minute recording of external impressions ... There is a shadowy, anonymous narrator, one of the crew who occasionally reveals himself through the use of 'we' or 'us', as at the start of *Madame Bovary*, and only emerges individually as 'I' or 'me' at the end, after the crew has been paid off; this device, by indicating that the account of the voyage comes from a member of the crew, adds a sense of authenticity and immediacy to the story, but leads Conrad into a number of solecisms, such as his account of the last scene between Donkin and Jimmy or of the mental processes of various characters which the narrator could not have reported.

The style of *The Nigger* is far more flexible and the imagery, for the most part, more visually precise than that of Conrad's previous work; there are some excellent scenes of violence and action – during the storm, Captain Allistoun's humiliation of Donkin, the burial of Jimmy – as well as some fine descriptive passages.

[. . .] Conrad's portrayal of the crew of the *Narcissus* has been compared to Flaubert's of the Carthaginian troops at the beginning of *Salammbô*, but in this case he excelled his master. He knew just what he needed for his purpose and there is no superfluous description. The major characters are presented with vivid detail. The others are hit off in a few picturesque phrases, down to the shadowy but effective Knowles and Davies.

[. . .] Then, once introduced, the characters are fully exploited to comment on and develop the action; for example, Singleton with his dotty theory about head winds (which is ironically and by coincidence borne out), Podmore with his raving about hell and wickedness:

> 'Look here, cook,' interrupted Mr Baker, 'the men are perishing with cold.' 'Cold!' said the cook, mournfully; 'they will be warm enough before long.' – 'What?' asked Mr Baker. . . . 'They are a wicked lot,' continued the cook solemnly, but in an unsteady voice, 'about as wicked as any ship's company in this sinful world! Now, I . . .'

And others who, with one remark, or in the case of Wamibo and the other two Norwegians with unintelligible noises, supply the spark to light up a scene.

[. . .] He [Conrad] told a friend that he had 'tried to get through the veil of details at the essence of life' and years later he defined the subject as the portrayal of 'the crew of a merchant ship, brought to the test of what I may venture to call the moral problem of conduct'.

In fact, *The Nigger of the Narcissus*, which was the first of Conrad's novels to have the seas as a setting, contains, more than anything else he wrote, the essence of his experience at sea and of his views on the practical conduct of life. To Conrad the sea was neither a god to be submitted to nor a devil to be overcome. The relationship of a sailor individually to the seas provided a test of character and skill; it resembled that of a lion-tamer to a lion or a bullfighter to a bull, offering exceptional opportunities for the exercise of prowess but leading to harsh, even fatal, consequences in the event of failure through loss of nerve or inefficiency. The sea also provided a test of those corporate ideals of human solidarity on which Conrad considered that society must be based in order to survive. The merchant navy, possibly more than any other sphere of life, has relied on a sense of human solidarity. Among landsmen this sense arises only in moments of crisis; in the regular services discipline deprives it of its spontaneity and therefore its virtue; but, 'discipline is not ceremonious in merchant ships, where the sense of hierarchy is weak, and where all feel themselves equal before the unconcerned immensity of the sea and the exciting appeal of the work.' Although life on a merchant ship provided an excellent setting for the test of human solidarity Conrad always emphasized the universal application of this theme and vehemently defended himself against the classification of a writer of sea-tales which dogged him throughout his life.

[. . .] Of all his books *The Nigger* seems to have been that which gave Conrad the most pleasure, or least agony, in writing and the most satisfaction when finished. He retained a special feeling for it throughout his life, calling it 'the story by which, as a creative artist, I stand or fall, and which, at any rate, no one else could have written. A landmark in literature, I can safely say, for nothing like it has ever been done before.' And although he was to go on to more ambitious and greater achievements, *The Nigger* holds a unique position in his work as a masterpiece of poetic realism.

[. . .] A few months after finishing *The Nigger*, Conrad wrote a preface to it in which he gave his conception of the aim of the artist and declared his own method. This preface is supremely important for the understanding of Conrad's intention as an artist; it is also, together with the preface to *A Personal Record*, the finest piece of non-fictional prose that he wrote, although it is slightly marred by repetitiveness.

In it Conrad achieves a subtle and satisfying fusion between the artist and the moralist. He begins by defining art as 'a single-minded attempt to render the highest kind of justice to the visible universe, by bringing to light the truth, manifold and one, underlying its every aspect'. He then goes on to expound the nature of artistic communication: 'All art . . . appeals primarily to the senses, and the artistic aim when expressing itself in written words must also make it appeal through the senses. . . . It must strenuously aspire to the plasticity of sculpture, to the colour of painting, and to the magic suggestiveness of music – which is the art of arts.' Therefore, 'My task . . . is by the power of the written word to make you hear, to make you feel – it is, before all, to make you *see*.' [. . .] The method is thus wholly sensuous, but the result achieved is also moral. If the artist succeeds in his aim he 'may perchance attain to such clearness of sincerity that at last the presented vision ... shall awaken in the hearts of the beholders that feeling of unavoidable solidarity; of the solidarity in mysterious origin, in toil, in joy, in hope, in uncertain fate, which binds men to each other and all mankind to the visible world'.

Extract from an unsigned review in the *Manchester Guardian*, 10 December 1903

'Youth' in this conception of Mr Conrad's, is not the time of freedom and delight, but 'the test, the trial of life'. No labour is too great, no danger is too close for this great adventure of the spirit. And through this come the precious moment, the exultation of endeavour, the joy in a strength to be broken on the wheel, the splendours of agony, a sense of the awfulness of life. The story is told with a surprising humour, and its details are perfectly devised. Closely relevant are the old captain, pathetically anxious to save his first command, dogged against all unhappy chances, and the indomitable crew, upborne in their enormous labours by 'something solid like a principle and masterful like an instinct – a disclosure of something secret, of that hidden something, that gift of good or evil that makes racial difference, that shapes the fate of nations'. The narrative does something to enlarge our conceptions of heroism; the sea-faring man is justified, he has found a friend in high places.

[...] Mr Conrad's style is his own – concentrated, tenacious, thoughtful, crammed with imaginative detail, breathless, yet missing nothing. Its grim earnestness bends to excursions of irony, to a casual humour, dry, subdued to its surroundings. Phrases strike the mind like lines of verse; we weary under a tension that is never slackened. He is one of the greatest sea-writers and the most subjective of them. His storms are not the picturesque descriptions of gigantic phenomena, we see them in the 'weary, serious faces', in the dreadful concentration of the actors. Mr Conrad is intensely human and, we may add with some pride of fellowship, intensely modern.

From *Joseph Conrad* by Jocelyn Baines
(Weidenfeld & Nicolson, 1960)

On the title-page Conrad described 'Youth' as 'a Narrative', and it is in fact a recreation of an episode of his life at sea. But it is also more than a narrative. Marlow describes the voyage of the *Judea* as one of 'those voyages that seem ordered for the illustration of life, that might stand for a symbol of existence', and 'Youth' is an evocation of a mood of exhilaration, in which experience is grasped for the sake of the pleasure that it gives; it is a rhapsody on the glamour of youth and of the East. The refrain of the joy of youth constantly recurs: 'O youth! The strength of it, the faith of it, the imagination of it!' 'Oh, the glamour of youth! Oh, the fire of it, more dazzling than the flames of the burning ship...' 'Youth! All youth! The silly, charming, beautiful youth.' And the East: 'Bankok! I thrilled.' 'To Bankok! Magic name, blessed name. Mesopotamia wasn't a patch on it.'

[...] Although it is Conrad's most consistently cheerful story, even 'Youth' has a taste of ashes: 'Oh, the glamour of youth! Oh, the fire of it, more dazzling than the flames of the burning ship, throwing a magic light on the wide earth, leaping audaciously to the sky, presently to be quenched by time, more cruel more pitiless, more bitter than the sea – and like the flames of the burning ship surrounded by an impenetrable night.' Not only is 'Youth' an evocation, it is a recollection of a mood, of an attitude that cannot be recaptured; thus the narrative ends on a note of nostalgia and melancholy:

> And we all nodded at him ... our weary eyes looking still, looking always, looking anxiously for something out of life, that while it is expected is already gone – has passed unseen, in a sign, in a flash – together with the youth, with the strength, with the romance of illusions.

Conrad's method is to collect together a group of people: 'We were sitting round a mahogany table that reflected the elbows. There was a director of companies, an accountant, a lawyer, Marlow, and myself.' Then: 'Marlow (at least I think that is how he spelt his name) told the story, or rather the chronicle, of a voyage.' This recalls a similar technique in Turgenev's *First Love* or Gobineau's *Les Pléiades*. The story is then set forth in Marlow's words by the narrator. It is given actuality by periodic references to the setting; there is the often repeated 'pass the bottle' – 'I never saw her again – Pass the bottle' – the chatty asides – 'What could you expect? She was tired – that old ship. Her youth was where mine is – where yours is – you fellows who listen to this yarn' – and the deliberately casual colloquial style of 'She belonged to a man Wilmer, Wilcox – some name like that.' And then at times Marlow will stand back and reflect on the action which he is describing: 'There was a completeness in it, something solid like a principle, and masterful like an instinct – a disclosure of something secret – of that hidden something, that gift of good or evil that makes racial difference, that shapes the fate of nations.'

This was the first time that Conrad used the device of Marlow and as 'Youth' was aiming at a straightforward effect, Marlow's role was simple: to give the tone of the narrative. But Conrad must have felt at ease with the style which the use of Marlow allowed him and must have realized the advantages of having a character who could both tell and comment upon the story because he again used Marlow in his next two stories, and gave him an increasingly complex role.

W. Somerset Maugham

Of Human Bondage 95p

In this, perhaps the most famous of Somerset Maugham's novels, we follow the story of Philip Carey, an orphaned cripple, in his quest for life and love. Turning from the bohemian life of a Parisian art student and the demands of the tragic Fanny, he studies medicine in London, where Mildred, superficial but irresistible, nearly brings about his ruin.

Cakes and Ale 60p

Cakes and Ale was the book by which Maugham most wanted to be remembered. As he traces the fortunes of a famous writer and his extraordinary wife, Maugham's superb ironic skill combines with a great lyrical warmth to make a uniquely unforgettable novel.

The Narrow Corner 65p

This tale of the sea came from a passage in *The Moon and Sixpence*, which Maugham had written twelve years earlier. The villainous Captain Nichols brings his passenger, Fred Blake, a fugitive from the law, to the remote island of Kanda after a violent storm – and what starts as a thrilling tale of sea adventure becomes a tragic tale of love as Fred and the beautiful young Louise bring sorrow on her island home . . .

The Razor's Edge 75p

The story of three of Maugham's most brilliant characters – Isabel, whose choice between passion and wealth has lifelong repercussions . . . Her uncle, Elliott Templeton, a classic American snob . . . And Larry Darrell, Isabel's ex-fiancé who leaves his stockbroking life in Chicago to seek spiritual peace in a Guru's *ashram* in Southern India.

Henry Fielding
Tom Jones 70p
abridged by Somerset Maugham

One of the world's great novels – the rollicking, bawdy story of a passionate young rogue . . .

Henry Fielding's zest for life, contempt of hypocrisy, abounding wit and keen sense of farce illuminate some of the greatest comic passages in English literature. The characters in this classic picaresque story of an adventurous young rogue in eighteenth-century England are drawn from the very stuff of life itself. We become involved in the joys and sorrows, triumphs and disasters of Tom and the friends he makes in his journeying through the English countryside and in London.

Joseph Andrews 70p

In *Joseph Andrews* Fielding demonstrates his theory of a new eighteenth-century genre: the comic romance. Neither totally romantic nor entirely burlesque, it is a perfect medium for serious comment. For the hilarious adventures of Parson Abraham Adams and Joseph Andrews are at once a crushing parody of Richardson's *Pamela*; a scathing satire on the affectations of society; and, in his portrait of the Quixotic parson, a brilliant use of the mock-heroic to define the author's ideals.

Moll Flanders 70p
Daniel Defoe

These 'true confessions' of a remarkable and passionate young woman are thought to have been based on the adventures of a real prisoner in Newgate, where Moll was born. Ostensibly written as a warning to wrongdoers, the moral of Defoe's candid and cautionary tale is often lost in the sheer vitality of Moll – one of the supreme characters of English comic fiction.

Her fortunes and misfortunes – 'twelve years a Whore, five times a Wife (once to her own brother), twelve years a Thief, eight years a transported Felon' – plunge the reader into the exciting world of eighteenth-century low life.